Idols and Underdogs

An Anthology of Latin American Football Fiction

First published in 2016

Freight Books
49–53 Virginia Street
Glasgow, G1 1TS
www.freightbooks.co.uk

English edition of *Por amor a la pelota: Once cracks de la ficción futbolera* (Editorial Cuarto Propio, 2014)

A CIP catalogue reference for this book is available from the British Library.

ISBN 978-1-910449-84-4
eISBN 978-1-910449-85-1

Typeset by Freight in Plantin
Printed and bound by Bell and Bain, Glasgow

the publisher acknowledges investment from
Creative Scotland toward the publication of this book

Idols and Underdogs

An Anthology of Latin American Football Fiction

Edited by Shawn Stein and Nicolás Campisi
Translated by George Shivers, Shawn Stein
and Richard McGehee

FREIGHT BOOKS

Shawn Stein is from the state of Colorado in the United States, and earned his PhD from the Department of Hispanic Studies at the University of California, Riverside. He is currently an associate professor of Spanish and Portuguese at Dickinson College in Pennsylvania, USA, where he teaches Latin American letters with a focus on literary and cultural studies. Stein's scholarship includes work on narrative satire, film and football fiction. He is the founder of a community engagement organisation called the *Día de Fútbol* (Day of Football). Although he does not have a pledged allegiance to any particular team, he is an ardent fan of the game.

Nicolás Campisi was born in Santa Rosa, La Pampa, Argentina. He holds a B.A. in Hispanic Studies and Art History from Washington College in Maryland, USA. His academic interests include 20th and 21st Century Southern Cone narratives, avant-garde poetics, travel literature, trauma and memory studies, and world literature. He is a fan of Club Atlético River Plate in Argentina. Currently, he is a doctoral candidate in the Department of Hispanic Studies at Brown University in Rhode Island, USA.

Table of contents

Foreword

Football fans consume vast amounts of non-fiction. Every day there's a new twist to the ongoing drama of the game – in fact, in this age of minute-by-minute reports and the ever-ready 'refresh' button, the idea of daily team news seems quaintly old-fashioned. To take one example: in the few hours after Manchester United's Champions League match finished last night, my phone flashed up six newspaper articles, all written during and/or after the game, all edited, checked and online before I went to bed. There was: 1) a straight match report detailing the bald facts of who did what, when; 2) a more nuanced report focusing on the contribution of one star player; 3) another focusing on a recently side-lined squad player now getting his chance; 4) a piece on tactics; 5) a broader view segueing into a thought piece on how the 'journey' of the manager at the club is playing out; and then 6) a humour article making fun of it all. (I fell asleep reading number six.) The appetite for football-related writing is massive. It's worldwide. And it demands commentary instantly. This we know.

But there's now evidence that fans are also increasingly open to fiction about football. That makes sense. After all, what is a transfer rumour if not speculation, and what is speculation if not making things up? Though it's gone largely unnoticed, fiction has been, for many years, a crucial part of the media's football soap opera. Imagination has been central to telling the story, whatever the story is that day. This has usually been labelled 'journalism', though it doesn't always need to be, and I feel strongly that fiction can make a contribution that the on-demand world can't. It can tell us something more meaningful than straightforward stats. That's why I'm interested in it – because football is a reflection. Which means it's a different game in Ecuador, in Uruguay, in

Peru. When this book was sent to me by Adrian at Freight, with the email header 'Your kind of thing?', he already knew it was.

In the UK, football fiction is relatively new, but there are examples of the form which have blown apart the idea that somehow sport is sacred, and writers are not allowed to fictionalise it. Arguably, the leader for this has been David Peace, the first literary writer I came across who was brave enough to break apart the conventional historical story in order to get to a kind of deeper truth. This book was *The Damned United* (2006), a novel which was nothing less than a revelation for me, a weaving together of two stories involving Brian Clough during his successful spell managing Derby County in the 1970s, and disastrous one managing Leeds. Peace inhabited Clough's voice. He imagined himself into dressing rooms during key events, but more than that, did all those things that literary fiction does at its best – revealing a world readers wouldn't usually have access to, and doing it with character, detail, charm, subtlety. Much of which is absent in the hectic now-now-now of contemporary football reporting, especially within the sanitised environs of clubs preoccupied with 'developing our brand'.

Though on one level *The Damned United* was a novel about Brian Clough's 44-day period leading a team he despised, it fascinated me even though I have no interest in Leeds United. How? Because it was written with the rhythms and tics of Clough's DNA. And because, like all good football fiction, it wasn't really about football at all. It was about male relationships, about a fast-disappearing England, about a man cursed and blessed. Which is deeper, broader, more intriguing, than the bald facts. I thought of Peace when reading Selva Almada's "Team Spirit", a story which examines the impact the game has on Argentinian women whose men are obsessed by sport. This is the contribution well-written fiction makes. To look off the field as well as on it.

The Damned United was the direct inspiration for my own football fiction, *Bring Me the Head of Ryan Giggs*. I saw what Peace had done and felt liberated. So I invented the least successful player ever for Manchester United (based on half a dozen real ones), and made him fall in love with United's most successful. By stretching and remoulding history we are able to show the world we truly live in. And I wanted to write about the tension between what modern commercial cash-rich clubs think they are for (money) and what the communities that follow those clubs think they are for (identity). The more I looked around, the more I noticed – as Shawn and his team have done – that I was just one of many people using football in fiction. While I was writing my book, Peace was penning *Red or Dead* (2013), a stunning fictional portrait of Bill Shankly's Liverpool. Soon after I discovered the writing of Roberto Bolaño, to whom nothing, not even football, was off limits. There was a whole tradition here.

Freight was publishing football fiction even before it existed. Freight Books began proper in 2013, but many years before that was doing one-off projects as part of Freight Design, its sister company. The first of these was *The Hope that Kills Us* (2003), an anthology of Scottish football fiction which was an unexpected cult success, and which encouraged Adrian at Freight to experiment further. (And now here we are.) Part of what made that book impressive was that, along with the fiction, it contained plenty of truth in it too, hinted at by that memorable title which sums up the attitude of many Scottish football fans over the years who have endured their teams specialise in glorious failure. So again we see that good football fiction reflects the societies it presents. Which brings me to *Idols and Underdogs*.

Literary fiction is a niche of the vast world of fiction publishing. Football fiction is a niche of literary fiction. And Latin American football fiction is a niche of a niche of a niche. So why should an independent like Freight publish this book? Simple: because it's great writing that makes a contribution to our understanding of Latin American cultures. Also, for those of us in Europe used to a sporting narrative that has, this summer alone, seen a 20-year-old move from Liverpool to Manchester City for an eye-watering £49 million pounds – not even the most expensive signing of the transfer window which exchanges millionaires like slaves – this book shows a world where the audience is within spitting distance of the players. Yes, the Premier League, La Liga et al are full of South Americans: Messi (Argentina), Neymar (Brazil), Falcao (Colombia), Rondon (Venezuela). But by the time they get to cash-rich Europe, their pasts in these countries are so far behind them it's almost as if they never existed. Falcao may have been born in Santa Marta, and have the handsome, distinctive indigenous look of the area, but is it possible for El Tigre to relate to people at home when being paid a staggering £140,000 a week in England? (That's a big cut – at Man United, it was more like £265,000.) Does Rondon's new life in Birmingham have anything in common with that of Miguel Hidalgo Prince in Venezuela? This book takes us back to those streets where footballers are born, and vividly shows us that glorious continent where football is sometimes still part of the community, rather than looking down on the community, charging fortunes. Yes, it has many imperfections. It's often chaotic, unpredictable, corrupt, infuriating. But to me it's somehow more real. These stories feature amateur and semi-professional football, as well as professional teams where the players are living anything but the star lifestyle. The characters here may be idols, but they're not superheroes, they're underdogs, and as any good literary writer will tell you, that's far more interesting to read about.

In 2013 and 2014, my wife and I lived in Chile, Argentina and Bolivia – we followed all the games of the Chilean national team during World Cup qualifying, one of my favourite experiences of our time there. Watching these matches within the nations of Latin America, often huddled around a TV with half the town in attendance or watching a dodgy screen in a rowdy street bar, we got a tiny glimpse into what football means to people there. In Bolivia, we paid the equivalent of cinco Bolivianos (about five pence) for polystyrene floats to sit on, as there were no seats, only concrete, with thousands of supporters packed in tight for the Cochabamba derby, with yet more supporters still piling in from the markets outside. The atmosphere was amazing, the bands played from first minute to last, and the crowd partied like I've never seen in the reserved family stand at Old Trafford where nervous silence is the norm, despite decades of success. Few outside Bolivia cared about that game we attended, but it didn't matter. What matters is authentic experience, and the stories in this book strike me as authentic. Each one contains the flavour and the passion I remember from my time watching football in Latin America. And each one sets me off idly dreaming about a return.

I won't go through each story here, as Shawn and Nicolás do that very well in their own piece, and soon you'll read the stories for yourself – but I do want to say it's exciting not only to have stories here from writers I already know and love, like Juan Villoro or Roberto Fuentes, but also a host who were new to me before reading this book, and will be to most UK readers. Too little Latin American writing is translated into English, and it's a pleasure to be a small part of bringing the likes of Ricardo Silva Romero, Sergio Galarza and Carlos Abin to the attention of English-speaking readers. This project is truly exciting for us. Firstly, because we believe this anthology to be something genuinely new and different. Secondly, because the interviews included here with each writer give an insight into the writers' processes and their home countries in a way rarely glimpsed before. And thirdly, because – forget the context – they're simply great stories. Thank you to the authors. Thank you to those who valued the stories enough to publish them in their original language, those who translated them with such skill, and especially to those who brought them to us. And thanks to you too, for keeping football fiction alive.

Rodge Glass
Fiction Editor, Freight Books

Prologue in the form of a literary challenge

This anthology is the result of professional serendipity. Despite being a professor of Latin American literature and my lifetime love of football (Latin American "fútbol", "futbol" and "futebol" or North American "soccer"), I only became aware of football fiction a few years ago. While browsing the contemporary literature section of a bookstore in Santa Teresa, Río de Janeiro, a collection of Brazilian short stories focused on football caught my attention. I am not a typical gringo. Although my parents wanted me to become a lawyer or an engineer, I grew up wanting to be Diego Maradona. During my undergraduate studies, I came to terms with the fact that my fascination with playing football greatly exceeded my ability on the pitch. Instead of following a career path that would please my parents, I chose the impractical field of literature, but I never stopped playing football. I have had the privilege of being able to play longer than any reasonable lifetime should allow. I confess that before the tragic murder of Andrés Escobar after the 1994 World Cup hosted here in the United States, I was completely unaware of the social impact of football in most countries around the world. A few years after that World Cup, I began to coach football youth teams in the USA, a country where the game is growing but still suffers from underdevelopment and from a lack of public interest.

Back then Major League Soccer (MLS) was just beginning, and football games in Europe or Latin America were rarely broadcast. However, World Cup games were, and this is how I gradually became a fan of the game without supporting any particular club. Unlike the majority of my North American compatriots, I began to follow the World Cup with an obsession that rivalled the intensity of the other billions of football fanatics on the planet. I now cherish every opportunity I have to go to a stadium, to revel in the stands and join in the choruses of club chants and songs, wherever I happen to be in the world. When I discovered football fiction as an emerging corpus in Latin America, the topic first aroused my academic curiosity and then ignited a quixotic search for the stories that best illustrated this fascinating new genre.

This anthology is also the result of professional indignation. There are no extensive bibliographies in existence and surprisingly few critical studies of Latin American football fiction. In recent years, this topic has become a primary research interest. Whenever I make professional trips to Latin America I devote days and weeks to scouring the collections of national libraries and bookstores. Once I added football fiction to the list of books I was searching for, I encountered dozens of librarians and bookstore clerks who would respond to my questions about where I might find fictional football stories with perplexity written on their faces. The inevitable, often irritated, reply was: "We don't have anything like that here." Sometimes I would leave a single bookstore that supposedly didn't keep anything like "that" on its shelves with half a dozen novels, short story collections and anthologies – often great works of literature – related to this astoundingly popular sport. Astonishingly, football fiction is a subgenre that has been marginalised from the stigma of being "lowbrow" and is still unknown to many of the "guardians" of literature, even though excellent short stories and novels focused on football abound in the catalogues of national public libraries. It is odd and also unexpected that football fiction is so disregarded and dismissed in the "football" countries of Latin America where its potential as a lens for the struggles and pleasures of the region is so great.

This anthology is also the result of an unexpected collaboration. The idea arose in 2013 when I was directing an independent study of Latin American football fiction for my young collaborator from Argentina, Nicolás Campisi. It made for a strange paradox that a young Argentine writer and football fan could not name at least two or three representative authors of football fiction in his own country. Together, we gradually discovered the geography and the characteristics of this new literary territory. We first identified those countries with strong traditions of football fiction, such as World Cup champions Argentina, Brazil and Uruguay. But we also learned of the virtual lack of any such tradition in many neighbouring Latin American countries. We discovered that much of the fault lay with a tension created by Jorge Luis Borges, Adolfo Bioy Casares, Ezequiel Martínez Estrada, Graciliano Ramos and Lima Barreto, among other Latin American intellectuals, who never managed to see beyond the rigid dichotomy dividing intellectuality and mass culture, the interpretation of football as the opium of the people or a catalyst for brutish behaviour. For example, according to popular mythology, Borges stated – among other public provocations – that "football is popular because stupidity is popular" and "football is a game of imbeciles".

In spite of the imposing weight of anti-football intellectuals' dogmatic criticism, a diverse body of literature has been produced. Without a doubt, we uncovered many works that were stereotypically uninspired, but also many jewels that stood out for their aesthetic originality and their authentic representation of the football imaginary. This project partly arose as an attempt to tear down the aforementioned stereotypes that classify sports literature as an irrelevant or inferior subgenre. Fruitlessly reviewing the incomplete canon of football fiction, we began to dream of a kind of literary Copa America which would unite the several national expressions devoted to the sport that dominates the South American continent; hence the choice of eleven authors representing the ten nations (Argentina, Bolivia, Brazil, Chile, Colombia, Ecuador, Paraguay, Peru, Uruguay and Venezuela) of the South American Football Confederation (CONMEBOL), plus Mexico as a special invitee from the Confederation of North, Central American and Caribbean Association Football (CONCACAF), as has been the tradition at the Copa America for the past twenty years.

Finally, this book is the result of an arduous process. In order to locate and assemble the selected stories, we have thoroughly mined the catalogues of libraries from Washington, D.C. to Montevideo, eventually arriving at the conclusion that these particular pieces represent the best of contemporary football fiction in Latin America. We might well have put together a very different team. In the case of those countries with the strongest traditions, there is an ample list of talent. In Argentina, for example, Roberto Fontanarrosa and Osvaldo Soriano contributed to the dissemination of the genre throughout the continent with an excellent body of work, but we chose to avoid hierarchies. Rodrigo Fresán, Ariel Magnus, Eduardo Sacheri, Inés Fernández Moreno, Rubem Fonseca, Antonio Skármeta, Hernán Rivera Letelier and Patricio Jara are among many talented authors whose works we might have chosen. And although there is no doubt that women have not contributed extensively to football fiction and that little has been written about the often tense relationship of women to this traditionally male-dominated game, we learned that several female writers have contributed very important stories to the genre. Hence, the inclusion of Selva Almada in our collection as the representative of Argentina, the country where the presence of football in fiction has perhaps the deepest roots. Since our idea was to include the current views of the authors themselves, we needed to invite those who have not yet left the "game". Thus, classic authors such as Mario Benedetti or Roberto Bolaño, were not considered. At times the process of making contact with some of the authors made us feel a bit like talent scouts wandering from pitch to pitch in search of the next great discovery.

Eventually we recruited our wise colleague George Shivers to help us navigate publishing procedures and to weigh in during the final selection. We are very grateful for the considerate guidance and assistance that George and many other friends and colleagues around the world gave us throughout the process. Of course, this book would never have been possible without the generous collaboration of the authors and publishers. The authors' answers to our interview questions provide excellent material for examining cultural difference and the intersections between football, politics and literature, as well as the individual impacts that football has in different regions of the continent. A comparison of their responses provide us with a rich, yet complex, image of the role of football in Latin American societies, such as the unbridled passion of fans contrasted with deep seeded disinterest of others, or the benefits versus the social costs of mega events like the 2014 World Cup in Brazil organised by multinational conglomerates such as FIFA.

Football's social and economic impact across the globe is undeniable. Simply put, we hope that this anthology helps to promote this emerging genre. Football fiction presents a unique means of achieving a deeper understanding of the football imaginary in Latin America. The selection of stories that comprise this anthology took into account a diverse reading public. No doubt erudite football fans will devour these pages, but we also challenge curious readers who know nothing about football culture to explore these extraordinary spaces of sports drama and delve into the rich cultural differences found across large portions of the geopolitical space known as Latin America.

Besides featuring treasures of this undeservedly ignored literary genre, our anthology provides a close look at the different ways in which football is articulated, lived and imagined in the eleven societies that are represented (Argentina, Bolivia, Brazil, Chile, Colombia, Ecuador, Mexico, Paraguay, Peru, Uruguay and Venezuela). Football fiction visibly reflects how sports affect us emotionally, physically, psychologically and financially. Among many different categories that we might have used to present these stories, we opted for a simple division based on the level at which the game is played: amateur, semi-professional, and professional.

The stories that take place at an amateur level attempt to preserve the innocent joy of the game, employing plots that reveal the profound impact football has during childhood and adolescence. Sergio Galarza (Peru) underscores the problematic impact of rigid social hierarchies that are reproduced in the game, as he narrates the frustrated expectations of a high school student who wants to have a more significant role on his team. In addition to glossing the tense relationship between football, academic life and the pursuit of sports glory, Carlos Abin (Uruguay) illustrates the way in which football played during adolescence can create emotional ties that unite people for the rest of their lives. Abin uses football to show how humanity can, in the end, overcome the violent inhumanity of totalitarianism. Miguel Hidalgo Prince (Venezuela) offers us a mind-blowing account of adolescent "futbolito" (or "futsal"), which stresses the tensions between friendship and competition in sports. Roberto Fuentes (Chile) constructs an anatomy of the neighbourhood football game that questions the parameters of politically correct behaviour. Ricardo Silva Romero (Colombia) offers us a story that narrates the decisive game in the career of a high school coach whose team has to win so he won't be fired. The unexpected connections between the coach, the referee, the players and the fans accentuate the ethical and ideological divisions in an educational environment.

The stories that deal with semi-professional leagues portray the frustrations and difficulties that characterise the experiences and perceptions of football on the margins of sports hegemony. Selva Almada (Argentina) presents provincial football in a supremely authentic manner. Despite employing a light yet acid humour and declaring herself an Argentine woman who hates football, Almada manages to profoundly humanise the little-known world of organised female fan groups. Edmundo Paz Soldán (Bolivia) captures the uncontainable potential of football-related passion as he reconstructs the scene of a murder that takes place on the pitch itself, employing the voices of an extensive number of witnesses.

The stories that deal with professional football critique the mercenary forces that threaten to corrupt the fabric of the football imaginary. Sérgio Sant'Anna (Brazil) portrays a coach's final days on the job. In spite of having achieved enormous success, he is now coaching a struggling, small team with a long history that has fallen victim to the logic of the marketplace, which turns everything it touches into merchandise. The high level of self-awareness regarding his precarious professional situation offers a privileged reading of the sports psyche. José Hidalgo Pallares (Ecuador) depicts the revenge of a goalie on the fans who have "crucified" him throughout his career. Juan Villoro (Mexico) gives us a magnificent articulation of the forces of corruption in professional football as well as of the difficulties that arise during the transition from professional player to coach. Javier Viveros (Paraguay) uses the perspectives of various individuals associated with a commercially successful club to satirise – without reservation – the powerful influence of the corporate model in professional football.

More than anything else, this book is a labour of love. In our humble critical opinion, these stories are representations of the best of Latin American football fiction as they show the human side of the sport, raise existential concerns and draw connections between sport and ego, question the myth of fair play by deconstructing the mechanisms of the mediated spectacle, and fictionalise masterfully the simple game as it is played in streets, fields and stadiums around the world. We believe that the stories and interviews in this anthology contribute to a better understanding of human existence by delving into irreverent attitudes toward football and lifting the game of football up as a cohesive and communal experience.

Shawn Stein and Nicolás Campisi

Argentina
SELVA ALMADA

Selva Almada was born in Entre Ríos, Argentina, in 1973. She is the author of two volumes of short stories, *Niños* (Edulp, 2005) and *Una chica de provincia* (Gárgola, 2007); of a collection of poems, *Mal de muñecas* (Carne Argentina, 2003); and of the novels *El viento que arrasa* (Mardulce, 2012) and *Ladrilleros* (Mardulce, 2013), which have received unanimous praise from critics. She also authored the nonfiction work *Chicas muertas* (Random House, 2014). Her stories are also found in several anthologies, *Una terraza propia* (Norma, 2006), *Narradores del siglo XXI* (Programa Opción Libros del GCBA, 2006), *De puntín* (Mondadori, 2008), *Timbre 2 Velada Gallarda* (Pulpa, 2010) and *Die Nacht des Kometen* (Edition 8, 2010). Recipient of a fellowship from the Fondo Nacional de las Artes (2010), Almada is one of the directors of the reading series *Carne Argentina*. Her blog is "Una chica de provincia: unachicadeprovincia.blogspot.com". "Team Spirit" (La camaraderia del deporte) first appeared in Spanish in the anthology *De puntín* (Mondadori, 2008).

Team Spirit

As she left the house Laura saw that light and intermittent clouds were beginning to cover the sky, and the wind was picking up, so she went back in and grabbed a jacket. She quickly covered the two dark blocks that lay between her and the main avenue. The neighbourhood brats never left a single streetlight intact.

"Motherfuckers, damned shitheads," she thought to herself, and immediately smiled remembering how she and her friends, as children, had done the same thing and how much fun it had been. There was more light along the avenue. There wasn't a soul in sight. She glanced at her watch: 2:35am. She hoped the Red Line hadn't come by yet. She lit a cigarette and looked across the street to see if Mariana was coming. Nothing.

"Did that idiot oversleep?" she wondered, yawning and exhaling smoke, both at the same time. It would be now when they were being stricter than ever about being on time. Ever since they made him supervisor, that queer Sosa had forgotten that until a month ago he was gutting chickens like the rest of them.

She saw the front of the Red bus appear three or four blocks away and hurried to finish her cigarette. She heard a noise behind her, turned her head and saw Mariana running and waving her arms. A minute later she was beside her. Mariana grabbed Laura's shoulder with one hand and hugged herself with the other.

"I didn't think I was going to make it," she said, panting.

"You're a disaster, you idiot," Laura blurted out, holding out her arm to stop the bus, even though the drivers knew them by now and would stop anyway.

The door opened with a wheezing sound and they got on.

"The melons are expensive these days," stated Raúl, the driver on rotation, staring at Mariana through the lens of the Raybans that he never took off.

"Stuff it, Raúl, I'm tired."

"Nights were made for sleeping."

"So you want to tell me what the hell we're doing up at this hour," replied Mariana and they both laughed.

"The week should start on Tuesday," stated Raúl putting the bus into gear and moving out onto the asphalt.

"I second that motion," said Mariana moving to the back of the bus to sit down beside Laura on one of the last double seats remaining.

Laura was next to the window, staring outside. Beside the two of them there was a young guy sleeping and a forty-something woman in a nurse's uniform.

"What happened? Did you go to sleep?"

"No, I stayed out."

"Get yourself together, nutcase. You know Sosa's not going to let you get away with anything."

"What an asshole! It turns out we were better off with Cabrera. He was a pain in the ass, but at least he was consistent. Poor guy. Have you heard anything about him?"

"The last I heard on Friday is that he's the same. The worst part is that when he gets out of the hospital, they'll have to take him home."

"But he's just a vegetable."

"What do they care at Social Services? Either they take him home or they unplug him. They made it real clear to his wife. Poor girl. The best thing would be for them to unplug him and that's that."

"Shut up, Lauri. Don't say that."

"Well, girl. In the shape he's in that's no life for him or his family. How was the game?"

"Don't even ask me. Messed up."

"I wanted to get it on the radio. But ever since their youngest started playing basketball, my aunt's idiot husband doesn't listen to anything else. They think the brat is going to save them all."

"Which one?"

"Gerardo. One of the youngest. I don't know if you've met him."

"Well, the game wasn't worth shit. I don't know what was going on with those slackers. Our guys were completely out of sync. And the Bovril team players, poor guys, are useless. But even at that we couldn't get one goal past them, not even on a rebound."

"I was going to call you last night to see if you guys were doing anything. But I was so bored after that dull party, I wasn't up to it."

"What did you tell me they were celebrating?"

"My grandparents' fiftieth anniversary. Damned if you'd find me spending fifty years with the same guy."

"Seriously, how boring. But anyway, they must love each other, right? Wait! I didn't tell you what happened."

"Ring the bell, Mariana, Raúl must be sleeping."

"And he reprimands me, the jackass."

They went through the front gate and up the cement esplanade that led to the low, square building, illuminated by white lights, like a morgue. A sign painted on the wall announced Cresta Dorada Chickens. Some twenty bicycles were lined up on one side of the entrance to the administrative offices. They said hello to a few co-workers who, already wearing white uniforms and rubber boots, were finishing their cigarettes at the door. Sosa was standing in the hallway, beside the time clock, smiling under the fluorescent light that accentuated the blue of his recently shaved beard.

"How are your tits hanging?" He commented trying to be funny.

Mariana and Laura answered him with a dry "what's up, Sosa"; they found their time cards and pushed them into the slot in the machine.

"A minute later and you would've been late," said Sosa, glancing at his watch. "That's the way I like it. We wouldn't want you to mess up your work record."

Without looking at him the girls returned the cards to their places and walked up the corridor toward the dressing rooms.

"That guy's such a jerk-off," said Mariana. "I'd like to kick his ass."

"Let it go. Don't pay attention to him. What bothers those guys the most is when you ignore them."

In the dressing room they undressed and put on the white uniforms. They hung their street clothes in their respective lockers along with their shoes. Then they sat down on a long bench to put on rubber boots, also white. Finally they adjusted their hairnets, making sure that every lock of hair was covered.

"Do we have time to smoke half a cigarette?" asked Mariana.

Laura looked at her watch.

"No, we'd better go. Our shift is already starting."

"Shit."

"Listen, so why did you stay out?" asked Mariana. "Wasn't Nestor going to Mendoza on Friday?"

"Uh huh."

"So did he go?"

"Yep."

"What then?"

"It's time to cut up chickens, *mami*. I'll tell you later."

The shift in the plant is from 3:00 am until 12 noon. At 8:00 am the employees have a half hour for coffee and to eat something. Laura and Mariana went out onto the cement esplanade with steaming paper cups in their hands. The day was still cloudy and windy.

They sat on a long, low wall where other employees were also drinking coffee or *mate* and smoking.

"So, who were you with last night, slut?"

"I was out drinking with Chilo."

"With Chilo? What about his girlfriend? That redhead doesn't let him out of her sight..."

"It seems like they took some time off. I don't know... Hey, stop it. Be quiet, here come the Triplets."

The Triplets work in the plucking area, where the process gets underway: the chickens come to them without heads and covered with feathers, still warm. The girls are not sisters and don't look alike, but since they're always together they called them the Triplets. One of them, the one with the singsong voice, is very tall. The other two, shorties, always go around flanking the tall girl, one on each side.

"That was quite a fuss yesterday, wasn't it?" said the tall Triplet.

"What do you mean? What happened?" asked Laura.

"You idiot, I was just about to tell you," said Mariana.

"A fucking mess," stated the tall Triplet. "I thought we'd end up in jail."

The short Triplets laughed.

"Tell me already, dude. What happened?" insisted Laura.

"You tell her, because whenever I think about it I almost pee my pants laughing," said Mariana.

The Triplets laughed too.

"Hurry up, you nitwits, we're going to have to go back inside any minute."

"There was a big scuffle with the "Defen" girls from Bovril."

"No. The Rusitas?"

"Yeah. It turns out that those crazy *gringas* came in all dressed alike, short shorts and tight tee-shirts, like the Diablitas, you know, but sixty extra pounds on each one. Dressed all in green. They had made up little songs and everything. We messed our pants laughing."

"And they got onto the field?"

"No. They tried before the game started, but the ref ran them off. They raised a ruckus from the sidelines, with their ridiculous chants that sounded awful. The game started out strange and kept on that way. A disaster. And those nitwits with their chants, waving their arms, shaking their asses and all that nonsense. The thing is we were out front. The three of us, Mariana, Anita, the Negra that fell in with two other slackers who are always hanging out with the directors; I don't know what they were doing there, they were coming from a barbecue or something like that, I didn't really understand. The thing is they were with our fans. There they were, all cheering, saying this and that, cheering them on. After twenty minutes we had had it. We couldn't even talk trash. It was like the return of the living dead. At least the guys on the other team were just as bad, because if they had managed to score a goal at that point I would have gone in myself to kick their fucking asses. The thing is we all bummed out. And there in front those nitwits with 'Give me a D, I give you an E, and I ask for an F' and to hell with it."

The tall Triplet stopped her story to laugh in chorus with Mariana and the shorties and to light a cigarette.

A gust of wind blew several paper cups by.

"I think it's gonna rain at any minute," said Mariana glancing at the sky.

"On the radio they said noon," said Sosa, who was prowling among the groups of employees trying to get into a conversation. "Don't tell me you're afraid of a little downpour."

No one answered him.

"So, how are you getting ready for Wednesday?"

"Wednesday? What's happening on Wednesday?" asked the tall Triplet.

"What do you mean what's happening? We play against the Sagemuller team."

"Huh?" burst out the shorties in sync.

"Who're the "we" that are playing?" asked the tall Triplet sarcastically.

"What d'ya mean who? Us. Cresta Dorada against Molinos Sagemuller."

"Oh, hum..." puffed Laura.

"I imagine you're going to come and give us your support."

"So, what do we have to do with it?"

"What do you mean what do you have to do with it? Aren't you running around everywhere behind the Union team?"

"The Union is our beloved team, sweetie," uttered the tall Triplet, forgetting that Sosa was now her superior.

"And we're the team for the freezing plant. And as far as I know you still work here. Right?" responded Sosa, a little pissed off.

"Since when does the chicken plant have a team?" asked Mariana.

"Since I became supervisor," replied Sosa. "It's to promote team spirit among the employees."

"And where did they teach you that? At the Walmart?" slipped in Laura, her voice tinged with irony.

Before going to work at Cresta Dorada, Sosa had worked in the supermarket and whenever he could, he would bring into the conversation the marketing and personnel training techniques of the Yankee multinationals, always exaggerating them.

"As long as they don't make us women play volleyball," said the tall Triplet stomping out her cigarette butt. "The first jump and I'm out."

"You'd have to cut back on the smoking," said Sosa.

The tall Triplet glared at him as if she could eat him alive, but didn't say anything.

"O.K., dolls. Get inside. The break's over," the supervisor ordered.

"Hold on, Sosa. She was telling me something," Laura complained.

"Leave the gossip for when you get together for *mate*, girls. You're here to work. I'm the one who gets the flak later."

"Just a little more time, Sosa. If you hadn't come along and interrupted we would already have wrapped it up."

"I didn't come over to interrupt. I came to bring you up to date. If it wasn't for me, you'd miss the game. You're part of the team. Talk with the girls in the business office later. They're preparing something for Wednesday."

The five girls looked at each other; they couldn't stand the women who worked in the offices.

"Yeah, yeah," said Laura. "Don't worry. But give us a little more time."

"All right," sighed Sosa. "We'll say that my watch is five minutes slow. Just this once. So later you don't go around talking behind my back and saying I'm a snitch. So you can see that even though they promoted me, I'm still just one of you."

Sosa marched off to hurry another group along, and the tall Triplet finished her story.

The Rusitas are the wives, girlfriends and sisters of the

Defensores de Bovril, a team in the Rural League that shortly would face the Unión de Paraná team, the one the girls support.

There's no rivalry between the teams, but there is between their female fans who have been itching for a fight for a long time. The Defensores' fans feel put down by the Union fans, scorned for being from the country and Protestants, and they're terrified that one of their guys will hook up with one of the Paraná girls, so they accompany them everywhere they go and are always on the defensive.

That Sunday, as the tall Triplet told it, they came prepared with their green outfits – the team colour – knee socks, chants and choreography. Ready to show off. If it had been allowed, they would have gone onto the pitch to spur on their beloved Defensores before the game and that way make it real clear to the Paraná team that the Bovril boots have someone to polish them. After their first offensive attack was stymied, they didn't give up. If their guys gave it their all on the field, they would give it their all on the sidelines. The premise was not to stop cheering them on for even a minute. Maybe some of them were overweight, as the tall Triplet said, but they were all used to working hard in the country and had the stamina to keep it up.

The Union girls were in a bad mood because of the way the game was going and besides that they were facing the sun in the stands, on a hot afternoon. But if Shakira hadn't turned up, things would surely not have gone beyond a barrage of insults from the local fans directed at the visiting team and maybe a shove in the women's restroom.

Shakira is a well-known transvestite from Ramírez Avenue, near the bus terminal. But before she became "Shakira", she played for the second team of the Union and she carries their blue and white colours on her chest. She always says that her love of football began on the pitch and continued in the locker rooms.

In the club everybody loves her. The gossips say that from time to time the fun with Shakira livens up the players' parties, but if anybody dares mention it, Shaki gets furious: "What do you think, that the Union guys are a bunch of homos?" and that's the mildest response that a comment like that merits from her.

The thing is that on this Sunday Shaki comes in crunching the bleacher boards with her stiletto heels. She wasn't having a good day. She was in love with a doctor from the Medical Centre and the man had her all messed up, making her head spin with false promises. Early that morning they had ended the affair with mutual insults. And Shaki came to the pitch to unload.

She asked how the game was going. Badly, they told her, and on top of that we have to put up with these crazy bitches acting like cheerleaders. Shaki's eyes, impenetrable behind her dark glasses, quickly found their target.

"What happened? Are the woods burning and driving out all the magpies?" she said. "I'll show these bitches what's what, coming here and making out like the Diablitas."

Half-time had hardly begun, she stood up, adjusted her jean skirt which had bunched up, and put her hands on her hips.

"Follow me, bad girls," she said and turned, crunching the bleacher boards again, stepping down without looking where she was walking like the showgirls in the cabarets.

The other girls looked at each other. They had no idea what Shaki had in mind, but were ready to follow her to the end.

They walked behind the goal and covertly placed themselves on the visiting team's side. The Rusitas kept up their routine, singing and dancing, determined not to stop, whatever happened. Two or three had stepped out of the line and were drinking water from canteens and stretching getting ready to go back in whenever the choreography would allow.

The second period began. Shaki, without prior notice, jumped like a cat onto the fence behind the goal, stuck the tips of her shoes and her fingers with their long red nails in the fence and climbed up. Rubbing her corpulent body against the wire she pulled herself up until her tits were in the air. Holding on to the metal, she began to move herself backward and forward and with a shout worthy of the goal that never was to be in that game, howled: "Boooooovriiiiiil, make me a baaaby."

For a few seconds everything seemed to freeze. The cheerleaders kept on singing and dancing, trying not to lose their rhythm, but they all looked with alarm toward Shaki, who kept up her movements from above them. Hers was a war cry. Once the moment of surprise had passed, the rest of the Union girls hurled themselves at the net and started to climb, and the chorus "Bovril, make me a baby" grew in volume, violent like a wave, overpowering the rhythms of Ricky Martin and the Colombian Shakira that the Rusitas were singing at the top of their voices, no longer attempting to keep in tune, vainly trying to shut out that other, obscene, diabolical message, being directed at their husbands, boyfriends and brothers.

When they saw that they were getting nowhere with their songs, they dropped their signs and pom poms and headed for the Union girls pulling them off the fence by the hair. It ended up with all of them tussling on the ground: Anita, the Triplets, the Negra and their friends from the Board of Directors, all of them against the Rusitas. Except for Mariana who was in the restroom and got there when the battle had already started. And Shakira, whose rule was never to hit a woman and who got down from the fence and went over to the stands to have a smoke and watch the spectacle along with the guys who didn't bother to separate them.

Laura and the tall Triplet split up, laughing hysterically in the hallway and each returning to her work; they still had a half-shift to finish.

Mariana and Laura work in the evisceration section, one of the last steps in the production process: the chicken glides along the belt, plucked and with a vertical cut along the breast, they stick in their hand, pull out the guts, throw out what's no good, sort out what's usable, put it in little bags and then back into the chicken. Women are more efficient for this job because their small hands fit quickly into the opening. Although they wear gloves, the warm softness of the guts penetrates the fine latex and even though they've been doing the same thing for years, they can't help but draw back with disgust every morning when they stick their hand in for the first time. Later they get used to it and with the third or fourth chicken the tips of their fingers lose all feeling and they act like mechanical hooks.

Laura spent the rest of the shift laughing to herself about the tall Triplet's story.

At noon they went back to the locker room, showered and rubbed a whole tube of deodorant all over their bodies. However much they scrubbed and applied scent, the odour of chicken followed them like a dog.

Again they put on their "human clothes," as Laura called them; they clocked out and left.

"I'm dead tired, loser," said Mariana.

At the bus stop they lit cigarettes. The day was still clouded over, humid and windy, a typical spring day in Paraná.

"So you went to have a drink with Chilo."

"Yeah. It looks like he's leaving."

"Chilo? Where to?"

"Buenos Aires. There's an opportunity for him to try out for a club out in the suburbs. With Lanús."

"Look at you. So he's just leaving?"

"Yeah... he has to take advantage of it; he doesn't have much time left. He's got relatives there. An uncle who has a laundromat. He's going to work with him at the beginning. That's why he had a fight with la Colorada."

"Know what I never understood, Mariana?"

"What?"

"Chilo and you. You've been seeing each other on and off since you were twelve. You've had other boyfriends and he other girlfriends, but you're always seeing each other. Nestor's a great guy, but..."

"But what? I love Nestor."

"But you were always in love with Chilo."

"Well, O.K., Lauri, sometimes that's the way it goes and you have to take things as they are. What do you want me to say?"

"How come you never told each other how you feel?"

Mariana inhaled one more time and threw the butt away. Her eyes sparkled.

"Here it comes, Lauri."

"The bus stopped and they got on. It was full. They held onto the dangling handles in silence. All at once Mariana said:

"Bovril, make me a baby. That Shakira's crazy."

They both laughed.

Interview with Selva Almada

What role did football play in your youth?

When he was young, my father was a player and he was always a football fan. When he stopped playing, he kept going as coach for a children's team and as a trainer for the bigger leagues. So every weekend and even on weekdays my father had some activity related to football. Activities that took him away from home and family, from his children's birthday parties (that were always on Sundays), from school programs and meetings. So I don't have good memories of football: throughout my childhood that's what robbed me of my father. Although, thinking back, I have some brighter memories like going to watch the games at night in the summer, with my aunts and my mother, the football field illuminated, and around it the empty lots, dark, with the sky blanketed with stars.

What was the atmosphere like for female fans when you would go to the stadium to see games in the summer with your aunts and mother?

That was in the 80s, in a provincial town where everything was laidback, even football. It was a family atmosphere; lots of women went (wives or mothers of the players); it wasn't at all dangerous for us kids to wander around. It was far removed from what a stadium is like nowadays. Even in my hometown, I don't believe that the atmosphere is the same as it was back then; I don't think many women go to the pitch to watch games today.

Do you support a particular team?

No. Sometimes I say the Rosario Central team, but the truth is that I have no idea who plays for them.

What motivates you to write fiction that takes place within a provincial context?

I'm a country girl. The universe I know best is the interior of the country: its landscapes, way of speaking, characters, for me all that is more powerful for narrative than the city.

How do football and politics intersect in Argentina?

I'm not up on that. But if we go back a little in history, we can't forget that a World Cup took place in this country to put a positive spin on a brutal dictatorship and that we all ignored the reality back then.

What is the place of football fiction in the literature of your country?

There are some good writers like Eduardo Sacheri, Osvaldo Soriano and Roberto Fontanarrosa in whose works football occupies an important place. Especially Fontanarrosa, his influence is so great that most football stories that I have read try to imitate him and fail, of course.

"Team Spirit" speaks to the challenges that women face, both in football and throughout patriarchal society. Could you comment on the influence of these social problems on your experience as a woman and as a female author in Argentina?

These themes always appear in my stories because they're part of that universe which I choose to narrate, generally interior geographies of the country, rather marginalised, where the law is governed by patriarchy, where women live in the shadow of men. The female characters in "Team Spirit" are working-class women and with them football works a little like it does with men who are football fans: like an escape valve, a release from everyday problems.

What is your opinion on the underdevelopment of female football in a country like Argentina where the male national team is a two-time World Cup champion (1976 and 1986) and three-time runner-up (1930, 1990 and 2014)?

The truth is that I don't like football, am not a fan of any club, and don't even watch the World Cup games! So I have no idea how women's football works. In any case, living in a misogynous society like Argentina's, it doesn't surprise me that female football is underdeveloped.

Your writing is decidedly constructed around oral registers, from the interior provinces and from urban Buenos Aires. However, on many occasions, and contrary to what some critics suggest, you have stated that your literature does not pertain to a hyperrealist vein. To which literary traditions and practices do you turn as a basis for constructing your literary universe that uses orality as a point of departure?

I have always been interested in oral registers. I think perhaps that I'm not such a good observer, but I have a really good ear for capturing the tones, the special features of the spoken language, the idioms. There's music there, and I like to recapture that rhythm and incorporate it into my writing. But it's not just a matter of cutting and pasting. That's why I say that it's not a hyperrealist language; it's a construction, a fiction, a hybrid that I invent based on different kinds of jargon, not only from different geographical spaces, but also from different historical times. That's the job of a writer: to operate on language and transform it, bring it to life.

Bolivia
EDMUNDO PAZ SOLDÁN

Edmundo Paz Soldán was born in Cochabamba, Bolivia, in 1967. He is the author of nine novels, among which are *Río Fugitivo* (Alfaguara, 1998), *La materia del deseo* (Alfaguara, 2001), *Sueños digitales* (Alfaguara, 2001), *El delirio de Turing* (Santillana, 2004), *Palacio Quemado* (Alfaguara, 2006), *Los vivos y los muertos* (Alfaguara, 2009), *Norte* (Mondadori, 2011) and *Iris* (Alfaguara, 2014). He is also the author of several volumes of short stories, including *Las máscaras de la nada* (Los amigos del libro, 1990), *Desapariciones* (Ediciones Centro Simón I. Patiño, 1994), *Amores imperfectos* (Santillana, 1998), *Simulacros* (Santillana, 1999) and *Billie Ruth* (Páginas de Espuma, 2013). He recently published a collection of articles *Sam no es mi tío: Veinticuatro crónicas migrantes y un sueño americano* (Alfaguara, 2012). He is co-editor of *Se habla español* (Alfaguara, 2000) and *Bolaño salvaje* (Candaya, 2008). His works have been translated into eight languages, and he has received a number of literary prizes, including the Juan Rulfo Prize for the short story (1997) and Nacional de Novela in Bolivia (2002). He is currently professor of Latin American literature at Cornell University in the United States. He is a fan of Wilster in Bolivia, Boca in Argentina, Juventus in Italy and Real Madrid in Spain. "Just Like Life" (Como la vida misma) first appeared in Spanish in the collection *Billie Ruth* (Páginas de Espuma, 2013).

Just Like Life

I know that you, like every other journalist, want to know exactly what happened. Reconstruct the facts and see if that turns up some truth. There are plenty of witnesses, so it won't be hard to put together a coherent story. The problem, I guess, will be to make the facts speak for themselves. Because even though in principle all this is easy to explain, or maybe has more than one explanation, you'll see that ultimately there's something that can't be explained, can't be subjected to reason. Just like life, by the way.

I take care of the fields in the stadium. They don't pay me much, and they keep me on the run all the time; over here, Elizardo, over there, Elizardo, but I inherited this job from my granddad, may he rest in peace, so it's here I'll stay till I die. Every day, early in the morning, I get a schedule with the list of the guys who'll be using the auxiliary fields. There's all kinds of championship games, inter-school leagues, factory tournaments, inter-bank games, non-amateurs A league, first team practices, second team practices, and a lot more... Do you smoke?

The Saturday game is an old tradition, you see... I don't know when it started. You want another beer? We'll stop drinking later... It's open to all the ex-professional players. I've been coming for three years now... Like many others, with my family. My wife, the kids. It's like a gathering of comrades. Somebody brings roast pork *chola* sandwiches, somebody else soft drinks... The kebab vendors show up, the ice cream and candy guys, and lots of spectators, an atmosphere that's like a real game. We make bets for cash and sometimes for the food bill after the game.

Elizardo. Elizardo Pérez. Did I already tell you? So many games and so many fields that at times things get confused. So I don't just take care of the fields; I have to straighten out confusions, send some guys to the pitch over there, others to the one over this way. Sometimes guys try to sneak in without reserving a field, just to play a pick-up game, and I have to throw them out. At times they ignore me. Well, I'm by myself, I don't have any help from the police, so what can I do? I watch a game every once in a while, but just for a few minutes, always on the move, you know.

Some guys who played on the national team come, like Cordero, famous for that goal he scored against Brazil in the Maracanã... He shows up in his BMW, he's made it big, hung it all up and opened a football school. Now he's got like six athletic clothes stores all over the country. He's one of the few success stories, most of them just go on struggling, up to their necks in debt, problems... The Croat, for example, a womaniser and a drunk, anytime now they'll auction off his house. Now he was a great goalie, a spider. Did you see him saving goals when he was with Wilster? Sure you did. So tell me, have you ever seen anything more pathetic than an ex-football player? You must be about thirty-five, I'd guess. Thirty-four maybe. And you're just beginning to be known... We, on the other hand, at that age we're retiring. And we still have half a lifetime ahead of us to live off of memories. Sometimes I surprise myself moving my head in the air like I'm in the middle of a game. Other times I can't sleep at night because I'm reliving some bad play that resulted in a penalty, so I try to create a parallel history, one where my late pass to another defender actually gets to where it's supposed to. It's hard. Ice cold beer, just the way I like it, keeps the digestion moving, all right, let's get on with it... Of course, none of this justifies what happened Saturday. So don't get confused and think I'm trying to make excuses for Portales.

One game I never miss is the one the Mutual League plays on Saturdays. They play on the best pitch we have, the turf's well cared for, the lines marked. Now in this case, they might be calling me because somebody got into a fight on the other side, but I don't budge, not for anything. Such a treat, to see the old glories of our national football team in action. They're a little long in the tooth now and don't run much, huge bellies that you wouldn't believe, but so what, the ones who know, know, and that's that. The way they handle the ball, real elegance. They're euphoric, take their football real seriously, anybody would say they're playing the final game in a professional championship. The thing is, football is a magnificent passion. But however that may be, I would never have thought that I would witness what I saw last Saturday. I get chills just remembering it.

We know Gerardo Portales as Gery. A great striker, you know, a big guy, you look at him and you say he's a real tank, nevertheless he's one of those guys with a crazy dribble and a resourcefulness that not even Tucho could match. I played with him for three years. A great guy too, always ready with a joke, a smile, a prank in the locker room. Hey, there was the time he hid the boots of all the defenders right before an important game against Bolívar. He kept that shit going as long as he could; they almost had to cancel the game. A shame that he tore ligaments in his right knee at his peak. He managed to play again, but he was never the same after that. His step was off, knee injuries are the worst. Besides the psychological damage, he was afraid to strike the ball with power. Just a shadow of his former self. A real shame. He retired from professional football before he was thirty.

He became a star again in the Mutual, top scorer every year, always in good physical shape and smelling like Bengay.

Naturally, with everybody playing in slow motion, his setbacks weren't so noticeable. We said things to him that were really in bad taste, like we'd yell at him, saying, "Been, gay, been, gay," and he never let it get to him. He's one of the guys that just can't wait for those Saturday games. He always shows up with his wife and two kids. The kids are seven and five, and I think it bothered him that they'd never seen him play in his moments of glory. So the Saturday games are a kind of consolation prize.

Gery arrived with his wife and kids. The children look a lot alike, black, curly hair, like their dad. Big smiles, wide-open eyes. That's what hurts me the most. That they saw the whole thing. And not just them, Aldunate's kid too. He's a little older, about eleven, and he understands what happened. They all ran to see what was going on. Like everybody else, of course. If they hadn't been there, maybe I could have accepted a little more what happened. Why fuck up the lives of kids that way?

I just sell shish kebabs. I didn't see anything.

Some people say he's a fine fellow. I don't buy it. Real proud, thinks he's God or something. According to him, if it hadn't been for the injury, he would have made it to the national team, and, who knows, maybe ended up playing abroad. In my opinion the injury just let him create a myth of someone destined for greater things until fate played a dirty trick on him. Something out of a B movie. Really, though, I think he's a spoiled kid from a good family who's never lacked for anything, and just doesn't have the mettle it takes. He didn't play with heart. The true greats have been able to come back from worse injuries. He gave up. But since we're all so classist, nobody spoke the truth. And now it turns out that the news media feel sorry for him, and are trying to justify what he did. Aldunate's family is poor, so there won't be many who'll defend him. Except for the simple facts.

Ah, Aldunate. Never shut up. I liked him, he would stop and

talk with me, give me a tip. Seeing him so small and, at that, a central defender, people tended to underestimate him. But he had impressive reflexes, he would confront even the biggest guys, and I don't know how he did it, at the last second he'd stretch out his leg and end up with the ball. The forwards hated him. If I hadn't been a groundskeeper, I'd have played professionally and been a central defender like Aldunate. It looks like the smoke is bothering you. My wife's always complaining about that, these cigarettes do smell pretty bad, I guess.

Gery hated playing against Aldunate; his mood turned sour as soon as he saw him arrive. Aldunate wasn't one of the players who showed up every Saturday. He had a workshop where he made dental plates and other devices. Sometimes there was so much work on the weekend he couldn't get away. The truth is Gery couldn't get the ball past Aldunate, and that bothered the poor guy. Gery once told me that Aldunate played dirty, stuck him with pins in the corners, used mind games, saying he was a spoiled brat who made up his injury because the game was too much for him, things like that. Look, it doesn't make any sense to me. Of course that's normal with football players; a lot of us can't stand each other on the pitch but after the final whistle we go eat barbecue together in one of the restaurants near the stadium.

My dad's not a criminal. My dad's not a criminal. My dad's not a criminal. Sure, he killed somebody, but in self-defence.

I'm sorry, I can't talk about it. My Gery... my Gery. Saturday morning we went to the supermarket. People who do things like that don't go to the supermarket. I'm really sorry, I won't say another word. He did that, and yet he went to the supermarket with me, so there's just something here that I don't understand.

Being a referee is not a vocation. It's a destiny. I was studying philosophy at the university in La Paz, when I realised there was something else for me. Somebody had to dress in black and be God for those Sunday crowds. A God who controls the course of events on the basis of good and bad calls, somebody who's loved, insulted, cursed, and so on. I never got to referee a game in the first division, but that's another story, I'll tell you about it if you really want to know. I feel honoured to referee the Mutual games. What happened... what happened. My words can't possibly do justice to the facts. Unfortunately for you, and for me, language just can't make sense of the reality of it all. That's why I prefer to keep my mouth shut on the pitch and let my whistle do the talking, and my cards.

A very quiet week, nothing to complain about, nothing at all, Gery's one of those guys who never raises his voice, accepts things as they are, great character. He never mentioned to me that he couldn't stand... sorry, I just can't utter his name. His poor family. His wife, his son. Will it be cold at night? They let me take him a couple blankets, but he says the Hilakata took them away from him.

All I want is justice. That what happened to my husband not be in vain. I want that son of a bitch to rot in jail.

My brother lives by and for football. It's been like that since he was a kid. He has videos of all the World Cup games. Videos with the best of Maradona, Pelé. CDs with the anthems of Barcelona, Boca, Flamengo. Posters with team photos of the clubs Wilsterman, Oriente, The Strongest. Shirts they gave him at the end of the game, one from Borja, stained with blood, another from Gastón Taborga, a guy he identifies with, because, he says, if it hadn't been for all his injuries, Taborga would easily have been the best player in the history of national football. Balls from historic games, one signed by Jairzinho. Autographs on napkins, on handkerchiefs, some signed at stadium doors, one of Erwin Romero, of Baldivieso, of El Diablo. Tons of editions of *El Gráfico*. I ask myself if somebody capable of collecting all that, of having that kind of devotion to football, could be the same one who did what he did. And I just don't believe it. I wasn't there, I didn't see what happened, so I just won't believe it. It's true, a lot of people say it happened, no way around that. Maybe it's a case of collective hallucination. Maybe my brother, the joker, pretended to hit Aldunate with the pipe, and Aldunate dropped to the ground, and that's the way he hit his head.

Lots of green. Green, with white lines, red and yellow shirts, black and blue shorts, red and white stockings, and black shoes, old and dirty, red banners, and splotches of brown in the background, beyond the green and white, and a really pale blue, and black spots over our heads, and the smell of kebabs, and the dust, and beyond the edges of the white lines, heads above clothes, shirts and pants, and the grey cement of the hut. A lot of green.

Alfonso Aldunate's team was winning one to nothing at the end of the first period, a goal by Alvarengo, a free kick to the corner where even the spiders are asleep. A couple shoves between Portales and Aldunate, ruled by the referee in favour of Portales, and the game goes on, the ball comes and goes, who would have thought that blood would wind up in the river. In the second period Aldunate crashes into Portales, they exchange insults, the referee separates them and shows Portales the yellow card. Two to nothing, a spectacular cross by Cordero to Cholo Marzana, gets past his defender and into the box, stares down the Croat and blasts the ball into the back of the net. Spectacular. They may be old-timers, but the professionals should come here to learn. Twenty minutes left in the game. A great play by Portales, nutmegs Aldunate and he's off, he's about to get into the box when Aldunate knocks him to the ground. The last man, for me it should be red, no doubt. The referee is walking more than running, the poor guy's kind of fat. All at once Portales gets up and starts to kick Aldunate. We all try to separate them. The ref throws Portales out of the game and gives Aldunate a yellow card. A mistake. He should've thrown them both out.

So I'm not his family doctor, but I have seen Mr Portales' medical records. I operated on his knee. Anterior cruciate ligament rupture, a common operation. Early signs of arthritis, the bones and cartilage were in really bad condition. It should be noted that he had been injured a while back, probably in high school, but they didn't operate, and he believed it wasn't a big deal and went on playing. After the surgery I prescribed some pills to control the inflammation in his knee. A few months ago I gave him sleeping pills, but nothing strong. He was suffering from insomnia, but he didn't tell me why, and, to be honest, I didn't ask. I've read his case history, nothing out of the ordinary, if you ask me. I know about the theory that criminals are born, and the other theory that they're made, that it's the environment, a bump on the head as a child, blah blah blah. But there's nothing like that in Mr Portales' medical history. At least as far as I know. Maybe his neighbours, his family members, can tell you more than I can. Probably.

Gery left the pitch by the rival team's goal... Nothing would have happened, but he turned around and saw Aldunate's smile. A smile that said, I screwed you again. And maybe nothing would have happened if it hadn't been for that metal pipe lying on the ground by the goal... The groundskeeper is an old guy; he takes good care of the fields but the space all around the fields is a mess, a real junkyard. As far as I'm concerned, it was the groundskeeper's fault. Another beer? Gery saw the pipe and lost control... I don't believe he even had time to think about it.

He picked up the pipe, ran onto the pitch behind Aldunate, whose back was to him. We all reacted too late. Even those of us who saw what was about to happen; we just couldn't believe it... I think the first blow was all it took, straight to the back of the neck; if it didn't kill him, at the very least it would have left him paralysed. Aldunate fell to the ground and before anyone could stop Gery he had already hit him six or seven more times... There was blood everywhere.

My son had a great childhood. Anything he wanted. He was raised in a healthy home. His father and I never fought. But then, of course, the miserable devil left me all of a sudden, but by then Gery had already grown up and was playing in the first division. Friends from the best families, a good boy, not the best student, but O.K. A fight in school once in a while, you know how kids are. Are you insinuating...? I'm sorry, I'm not saying another word to you. How dare you?

Alfonso had framed photographs of his football career in his house. Not too many, he used to say that he wanted to avoid the traps of nostalgia. He idolised Beckenbauer, Passarella, those courageous defenders, capable of carrying a whole team on their shoulders. Sometimes he wished he was a little taller, but then he always said that if Maradona had gotten so far, as short as he was, there was no need to talk about it anymore. He didn't often read the sports supplements in the newspapers, nor the sports magazines either and he didn't even like to watch sports shows on TV. He used to say that they glorified the forwards and ignored the goalies and the defenders. "The world seems to belong to the attackers," I heard him say more than once, and "the rest of us are good for nothing." The last few years he had got interested in tennis, and practised every morning from seven till eight. He didn't want his son to be a football player. He wanted him to be a dentist.

I'll be a football player. I'll also be a dentist.

It all happened just fifteen feet from where I was. I'd be lying if I told you I realised what happened. I looked down for a second, lost my concentration, the sun was in my eyes like it always is at that time of the afternoon in Cochabamba, real nice and warm, a clear sky. It was like I had blinked, and when I looked up some guy I didn't know was beating the shit out of another guy I didn't know. I don't think I'll ever have another opportunity like that to see up close how a human being kills and another dies. And I missed it. Pathetic, right?

Lots of green. And then red, a lot of red.

Ingrates. Look how I've taken care of their fields, watered them, had the grass cut, filled in the holes, painted the goal frames and gotten new flags for the corner markers, and then they have the nerve to say that I was partly to blame, just because I had left that pipe behind the goal. Tell me, is the guy who leaves a revolver on a table at fault or the one who uses the revolver? We're talking about civilised men, guys that have been in the newspapers, given a thousand interviews and signed a ton of autographs, guys with families who come out to have fun for a few hours on Saturday afternoons. Does bloodshed make any sense in that setting? So just keep me out of it.

Don't insist. I already told you, language, reality. My whistle, the cards.

Listen, Portales was out of his head. Such a strong guy, it took three of us to hold him down. Somebody called the police using his cell phone. There were a lot of spectators, and the news soon spread to the other fields. It wasn't long before the pitch was full of curiosity seekers. I wonder if we'll be able to play on Saturdays again? Not right there anyway.

Sure, it's an extreme case, but who knows, maybe it'll help people understand a little better what we have to deal with... The moment of glory, the worship of the masses, being on the cover of a sports supplement, idolised by both young and old, and then the messy reversal of fortune, sinking slowly into oblivion, the lingering agony... Now, of course, I'm not suggesting that this would not have happened in a championship game in the inter-bank league. But, O.K., it happened here, so we've gotta try to understand it here.

Portales hasn't made a statement. He hasn't explained what went through his head in those seconds before he exploded. The week before the explosion. The years before. The frustrations, hatred, rancour that gradually accumulated in him, without his even realising it. Or maybe he did realise it and thought it was no big deal, not big enough to even talk to his wife or to his friends about it. He tore a picture to shreds and left us to try to put it together again. Maybe he knows how to do it, but probably not.

Everybody ran onto the field. I saw it all from a distance, figured it was too late to do anything, and I was the only one who ran over to where Gery's wife and kids were. Marina asked me what had happened. "The worst," I said. "It looks like Dad killed somebody," his oldest son, Gery Jr. said, "I wonder if they'll go on with the game?" asked Edwardito, the youngest. Aldunate's wife and son were nearby. His wife burst out crying. She started running toward the scene of the crime. The kid didn't move, maybe he was in shock from what he'd just seen. I think his thoughts were all locked up inside. I guess. He's a strange kid. Observes everything and never gets involved.

My dad's dead. I saw the whole thing. Don't ask me to tell you about it. What I saw, it wasn't me that saw it, it was somebody inside me, who knows me well but would rather stay hidden. I'll keep on living, next week I'll go back to school, and I'll play with my friends again and dream of being a professional football player. That person will remember me for everything that happened and some day will try to take revenge. He still doesn't know how. But he'll figure it out.

I can understand everything, except doing something like that in front of the children. Portales should have said to himself, my kids and his kid are here. I'd better wait till we're alone. That's unforgivable. I dream about them, watching from the edge of the pitch what their fathers are doing. I mean, what one of them is doing, what the other is having done to him.

Did you reach any conclusion?

Interview with Edmundo Paz Soldán

What role did football play in your youth?
It was really important. I played a lot, both in school and in the lower divisions of several Cochabamba teams. Unfortunately I never had the discipline, the rigour necessary to practise every day, and as the years went by other things distracted me. In any case, thanks to a full football scholarship from the University of Alabama in Huntsville, I got to the United States and received my B.A. in Political Science. I played three years for the University of Alabama.

Do you support a particular team?
Many. In Bolivia, it's Wilster. In Argentina, Boca. In Italy, Juventus. In Spain, Real Madrid.

How do football and politics intersect in Bolivia?
Evo Morales, the president, is a big fan of football. He has tried to intervene in the way football is managed in Bolivia, influencing the naming of Azkagorta as the coach of the national team, although I think his influence could be more important if he decided that the state should invest in the training of players.

How would you describe the impact in Latin America of Brazil having hosted the World Cup in 2014?
Mixed. When Brazil was chosen to host the World Cup there was a lot of enthusiasm. But as the years went by, the economic crisis showed that Brazil hosting the Cup was not as great an idea as it seemed at first. I lived in Rio last year in the months before the Cup, and I was surprised to see such

a subdued atmosphere. I went to a couple of demonstrations where protesters chanted "Não vai ter Copa! (The Cup is not going to happen!)" I think it was healthy to see that in such a football-crazy country many people didn't lose perspective and saw that football may be great to lift the spirits of the people, but it is even greater if, instead of building new stadiums, the government can invest in education, health, etc.

What is your opinion about the recent developments in the scandal surrounding corruption in FIFA?
It is a shame, and an embarrassment to all of us who love the sport. But it is everybody's fault. We, the fans, are so caught up in the game itself that we have turned a blind eye to the exploits of the FIFA executives. As long as we have the circus, we let FIFA get away with murder. If we want our sport cleaned up, sponsors and fans should ask for an independent committee to study and recommend changes or else refuse to sponsor FIFA by watching pay-per-view games, buying shirts, etc.

Do you see any connection between the creative process and the way in which someone plays football or behaves as a fan?
In my opinion football is art. A combination of strength and aesthetic precision. In that sense it comes closer to certain novels than to the short story.

Did any writer of football fiction influence this story?
No one specifically, but I have stolen fragments from interviews with ex-players. I've always believed that being an ex-player is a great drama that merits more literature. I don't know what I would do if they told me at age 35 I had to stop practising what I love the most. You still have your whole life ahead of you

to drown in memories. It seems to me that there's something tragic there.

What is the place of football fiction in Bolivian literature?
It's less important than it ought to be. We need a Fontanarrosa. There are anthologies of stories devoted to particular teams, like The Strongest, who can count on faithful fans, but that doesn't translate into great narrative.

Do you see any lingering reluctance to incorporating football or sport as a dominant theme or plot driver among your generation of authors?
Yes, and it is mystifying to me. Football is so important in Latin American culture, and there is so much drama surrounding it, that I wonder why we don't have a great football novel yet. As somebody told me, maybe it is because the epic of football is written every week in the sports sections of the newspapers, and in songs and in TV shows, so literature is not so needed. But that is just a partial answer. We have great essays about football, and some excellent short stories, so I still hope we can get more poetry, more novels about football.

How is football culture treated by Bolivian and/or North American academia?
An Argentine friend of mine who teaches literature at Harvard told me that his most popular course is one about the semiotics of football. Another friend who teaches at Princeton has studied the constructions of Mexican football stadiums as part of building a modern Mexico. I think North American academia has treated it as a key component of Latin American cultural studies. In Bolivia one of our most respected intellectuals, Luis "Cachín" Antezana, has a book devoted to Garrincha and is a

highly respected football analyst.

Is there a particular identity or style associated with football in Bolivia?
We're more quick-passing than brute strength. In the 90s we were associated with the success of Tahuichi, a football academy in Santa Cruz that won lots of international championships and created the generation of '94 that carried us into our last World Cup.

What is your evaluation of the Bolivian national team's performance in the 2015 Copa América?
Better than expected. We didn't think we would advance to the second round, since the team is poorly ranked and the games leading up to the Copa América were a disaster. But we beat Ecuador and then we got our hopes high for the quarterfinals game against Peru. And then reality bit back.

What does the Bolivian team need in order to have World Cup hopes in the future?
Miracles don't happen overnight. We need to train players from the ground up, invest in the lower divisions. Our players tend to be very fragile from the physical and the psychological point of view: we need to work in both areas. Talent is worthless without physical and mental strength.

Brazil
SÉRGIO SANT'ANNA

Sérgio Sant'Anna was born in Rio de Janeiro, Brazil, in 1941. He began his career as a writer with the volume of short stories *O sobrevivente* (Estória, 1969), a book which resulted in his participation in the International Writing Program at the University of Iowa. Besides *O sobrevivente*, he is the author of the following short story collections: *Notas de Manfredo Rangel, repórter (a respeito de Kramer)* (Civilização Brasileira, 1973), *Concerto de João Gilberto no Rio de Janeiro* (Ática, 1982), *A senhorita Simpson* (Companhia das Letras, 1989), *Breve história do espíritu* (Companhia das Letras, 1991), *O monstro* (Companhia das Letras, 1994), *O voo da madrugada* (Companhia das Letras, 2003), *O livro de Praga – Narrativas de amor e arte* (Companhia das Letras, 2011, recipient of the Prêmio Clarice Lispector of the Fundação Biblioteca Nacional), *Páginas sem glória* (Companhia das Letras, 2012) and *O homem-mulher* (Companhia das Letras, 2014). He is also the author of the novels *Confissões de Ralfo: uma autobiografia imaginária* (Civilização Brasileira, 1975), *Simulacros* (Civilização Brazileira, 1977, *A tragédia brasileira* (Guanabara, 1987), *Amazona* (Nova Fronteira, 1986, recipient of the Prêmio Jabuti), and *Um crime delicado* (Companhia das Letras, 1997, recipient of the Prêmio Jabuti). Sant'Anna has also written for the theatre, *Um romance de geração* (Civilização Brasileira, 1981), as well as poetry, *Circo* (Quilombo, 1980), and *Junk-Box* (Ánima, 1984). He is a fan of the Fluminense team. "In the Mouth of the Tunnel" (Na boca do túnel) appeared first in Portuguese in *Concerto de João Gilberto no Rio de Janeiro* (Ática, 1982).

In the Mouth of the Tunnel

The sentence that I had asked my assistant to write was there on the locker room blackboard: "The weak man derives his strength from the knowledge of his own weakness."

To disguise their nervousness – they're going to play against the league-leading team in the Maracanã Stadium – they come in joking around and pay no attention to what's on the board. If I had written "Push the ball forward, guys," maybe they would've paid more attention.

The thing is I just need to start my speech:

"A great team, when it plays against us, takes the pitch relaxed. They put the ball on the ground, pass it back, to the side, warm up, think. If we kick off..."

I'm interrupted by a loud noise. Somebody kicked a ball hard against a locker and broke the lock. There's a moment of silence in front of my stare. No one has signed the starting lineup, so there's still time for a substitution. "On a team like this, playing with one player or another makes no difference," I'm about to say. But I don't say it. It would be *anti-psychological*.

"If we kick off" – I begin again – "remember what we said repeatedly during tactical training. Pass the ball to Jair, he knows what he has to do."

Maybe because I'd said his name, they remembered. I hear a yell from over on the massage table. Somebody threw an ice cube at Jair, and he is muttering to himself, pissed off. He's seen better days and better clubs. So have I.

The best response is just to pretend I'm not even there.

"Jair's going to send the ball into an empty space; one of the wingers will come in from the side."

I pause and try to carry my thoughts a bit further.

"Everyone's trying to send the ball to the wingers from midfield. It's an old Brazilian vice, ever since Zagallo was the left-winger and later the coach of our national team. Even if now, given the quality and creativity of Zico and Sócrates, the players near the box have been advancing more to get in scoring position, freeing up the wingers offensively. But only the really good players join the revolution at the beginning. The wingers will be our offensive weapon, moving out fast to drive the other team's defence crazy. And one of the weapons of the weak is surprise, an ambush. If we're lucky and land a goal with a setplay, we can fall back and calmly let time pass. But with or without our goal, this will be our tactic: the team will fall back except for the wingers. Jair takes the ball and sends a long pass to the wingers. Does everybody understand?"

I've never known a football player who doesn't shake his head affirmatively when the coach asks if he understands. Then they all go out there and do everything a different way. You have to insist and insist again. Tactical training, pre-game lectures, until it all becomes instinctive for them.

Our striker, for example, listened to me without saying a word. But it was as if I could sense that inside him there was a sarcastic smile that just didn't show up on his face. And later, when I looked him in the eye, there was a moment when he started to open his mouth to say something.

"This business of the weapon of the *weak*" – he might have said, asking for an explanation. He's a really strong black guy, and the only reason I didn't scratch him from the team is because he's the striker: he scores some goals against the small clubs but does nothing against the big ones. But he's the team striker. If he were scratched, the members would raise hell in the club. So, since I didn't want him out front, jamming up the box and attracting their defenders back there, I just moved him over to the right wing. But I preferred a faster player there, and even then the guy didn't like it. He's like a tank, he uses his size, goes into the box crashing into everybody. Any good back wipes him out no problem, no problem.

You feel like saying: "Look at elephants, kid. Go to the circus and watch the tricks the trainers have them do." But I don't say it. It would be *anti-psychological.*

"You boys who are on the first team for the first time have a big responsibility," I said. "I scratched guys who had been in the club for a long time in order to put you guys on. Why? Speed, audacity! Your weapon is enthusiasm, youth."

My hope is on the young left-winger, a guy who distinguished himself in the lower divisions, to the extent a player can stand out among the young guys on our team. And if I go on talking, it's more for him; as far as the veterans go, with the privileges of seniority, they're first in line to sign up. The Manager doesn't like delay: "Fines are for big teams."

So I take advantage of the shyness of the kid there at the end of the line and conclude:

"Confidence alone sometimes makes the difference, the exact line between doing something or not doing it, success or failure."

That's the way a coach is: he has to feign enthusiasm and confidence that he no longer has. I feel just like a ball on the penalty spot just before some crazy player runs up to kick it with the toe of his shoe. It goes too high, over the crossbar, over the wall and out onto the street. And all it takes is for me to lose one more game and the President will come and kick me out the same way. A man who bankrolls the underground lottery has to protect his name.

I pat Jair on the back as he climbs the steps that lead to the field.

"Play it more to the left-winger than to the big guy."

It wasn't necessary. Jair nods his head. He already knew.

Our centre-half, Jair, is one of those ace players (the word should be a redundancy for centre-midfielder) who knows everything about football and several times was about to be chosen for the national team. A lot of guys like him existed and still exist – Roberto Pinto, Afonsinho, Zé Carlos do Cruzeiro, Dirceu Lopes, Edu do América, Bráulio – but a set of circumstances ended up denying them that more glorious destiny. So they stayed out there, offering up regional championships and victories to mediocre teams. Perhaps because they've lived in a period of great professionals in the position – like Gérson, Rivelino, Clodoaldo – or, who knows, maybe for some deeper reason, like the lack of *that desire to win*. Or because for them football isn't everything, as in the case of Afonsinho, who was always going out at night, mixing with artists, and ended up being in a Gilberto Gil song, "Centre- midfielder," the position that requires a mixture of athlete and artist, playing with the legs and the brain, almost with the soul, you could say.

And the greatest of them all, in fact, without a doubt was Ademir da Guia, predestined from his name and his surname and one of the greatest of all time in the position, but who never started for the Brazilian national team. He treated the ball as if it were part of his own body, and João Cabral de Melo Neto even devoted a poem to him, and that's more permanent than a statue in a public square, since a top-notch poem never tarnishes and pigeons don't shit on it. A poem remains there, invisible, like a goal recorded on videotape, just waiting for someone to pick it up and play it. Only it's made of words, an almost immaterial substance, almost like air, and that's why it can last more than a thousand years, passing down from generation to generation. All that someone has to do is go to the shelf, pick up the book and read it.

Words, fuck; I should be an announcer or a journalist, because I'm getting lost in words, getting lost, almost losing myself. Jair. You might say that Jair was practically born here in São Cristóvão and returned to São Cristóvão like someone who comes back home resigned to die there.

The neighbourhood has several of those guys, the ones who stopped playing. They sit in the bars, wearing clogs, toothpicks in their mouths, talking about the past. Whoever played football never adjusts to any other profession. After it's all over, they hang out with a face like a child who doesn't understand what happened.

Jair, for example. Before he became a player, he was nobody, just one of those skinny kids, typical of poor neighbourhoods in Brazil. With one difference: he knew how to kick a ball, a long way, with precision. And that, in our country, can make a big difference in someone's destiny. One day they practically dragged him by the arm here to Figueira de Melo, where he grew up so fast that after a brief time in Bangu and Portuguesa de Desportos he came to Santos. However it was a time when Santos was already living on past glories, they had started to lose against everybody and had to blame somebody, right? And it wasn't going to be Pelé, even though Pelé was already developing a spare tyre around the middle, becoming a little fat, a businessman, a publicity boy and even an actor. And Jair was travelling around there, from club to club, all over Brazil. He became one of those regional idols who local fans always consider the best in the country in his position but who never show up on the lists of those called up for the national team. One of those players who have already dined with the state governor, been a lover of famous whores, grown accustomed to drinking something here, something there and then marry a girl from the interior of the country. And they end up with that resigned air, like saying "that's the way life is, a moment that passes – and glory, an illusion." And they stay on the minor teams. Quiet, useful, good: "It's all about sending the ball to the winger, right?" So he sends it and just right. Now, if the winger doesn't know how to make the most of it, that's another problem. And Jair developed a way of just shrugging his shoulders when a play was lost. I think he even gets scared when one of those balls that he kicks ends up in the back of the net, taken advantage of by another player. Maybe he's one of those calm guys, too wise to desire immortality. Or maybe he started to play at a time when they still didn't understand the importance of videotape, which freezes a play in time. It won't be long before the top players will be collecting royalties. With videotape, football entered into the History of Art. And the goals and the passes became museum pieces. That mathematical pass by Gérson to Pelé, for example, in Brazil's second goal in the World Cup in '70. It was as if that ball was never going to come down. As if its trajectory was eternal, that's what I mean to say. But it has to be a goal or a pass in an important game. In today's game the greatest play of all time could happen, but if it's our team nobody's going to archive it at the TV stations. The same stations that never tire of repeating Pelé's immortal plays during that World Cup, and even the ones that didn't become goals, like the shot he made from the centre of the pitch against Czechoslovakia or the chest dribble around the goalie Marzukiewsky, from Uruguay, when Pelé later did the hardest thing: placed it off-target.

The play that almost resulted in our goal came from a pass by Jair. They won the coin toss, chose the side of the pitch away from the sun. The kickoff was ours. As planned, the centre forward passed to the false nine, who passed way back to Jair. He held the ball only a couple of seconds, while the wingers took off quickly for the opponents' side of the field, arriving down the centre, diagonally. Jair has eyes like a lynx; some of his plays remind you of Didi or Gerson. And he saw that the best space was opened up by the right-winger, who penetrated through an opening, there between the fourth defender and the left-back, who were still practically just warming up for the game.

The pass was perfect, the ball landed in front of Jorge, the big striker, who didn't even need to control it, which is something he doesn't know how to do anyway. He's like a hurricane, devastating. As soon as the ball arrives, he shoots. And that's exactly what he did: he ran between the two defenders and took the shot.

The surprise and the speed of the play were such that their goalie didn't budge. But the ball rose up too much, that's one of the defects of players who are built like tanks. They don't look ahead of them; they just look at the ball, at the ground. Only the top players have the ball where they want it and don't need to see it and they look precisely at the space, the future point, they're always just a little ahead of the others. That applies to the top performer in any profession: domination of the space where things are going to happen.

The ball climbed, hit the crossbar and ended up in the stands. You could hear a slight "oh" travelling around the stadium, coming from their fans.

"Whoever doesn't score goals, watches them being scored," according to the wisdom of the fan. The logic of football is nothing more than the application of the Theory of Probability. A great team in a balanced game gets more or less from four to six chances to score a goal. If they waste some of them, it probably won't be long before their opponent, if they don't fall into the same bad luck, will score their own goal.

That maxim – "Whoever doesn't score goals, watches them being scored" – is even more applicable to a lesser team against a great team. The weaker team can generally count on only two or three good chances to score, while the other, thanks to its superior technical skill, if everything proceeds normally, will have at least ten.

My strategy, I realise, implied a risk: waking up the lion. Their coach squirmed on the bench and from over here I can guess the message he sent onto the field, in a mailing that goes from the masseur to the winger and from him to the stopper, who sends it on to the whole defence: "Tighten up the marking."

A great team is like a business, it must not fail. And "Whoever loses a point to a mediocre team doesn't win a championship" is another saying born out of the fans' experience. They stick to our wingers, since they already figured out the play. And they take off towards us with the authority of men who are used to winning. Our team, as is natural and was already planned, retreats en masse in the expectation of a new opportunity to repeat our counter-attack when they relax again. For the time being we have to strengthen our defence. And when they least expect it, with the defence moving forward in their desire to win the game, Jair receives another ball and passes it to one of the wingers, who's going to take off running and...

The straight line is not always the best path between two points. Against a tight defence like ours, it's best to open it up on the flanks, always less congested. Because down the middle there's no space to control and even our centre-forward has to drop back to help the defence. My "theory of the wingers arriving diagonally" applies only to a team playing in counter-attack. Not them. Intelligently, they begin to use the classic game through their wingers. If their wingers are mediocre, they're raining balls into the box, in the well-known suffocation game. Well, generally, the fullbacks in the goal area are tall and I've seen many shitty central defenders make their name that way: spending a whole game cutting down high balls over the box.

The suffocation game can yield an illusory gain, a false sense of control and, all at once, the opposing team comes on in a counter-attack and scores. And they end up winning the game, because the one who makes the best effort is not always the winner. That's what could happen today.

But their wingers are good: they don't grapple in the midfield, their dribbles are short, they get to the backline and send strong and low crosses. The ball hits everybody's legs, both attackers and defenders run into each other in the confusion, the goal could come from any one of them. Among many others, the great Mané Garrincha made his name that way.

Our defence panicked, kicking the ball in every which way. There's a succession of corner kicks, throw-ins, and Jair, as if I were on the pitch myself, approaches the central defender and signals: "Calm down, calm down."

Our central defender phoned his girlfriend this morning early and I overheard when he whispered to her, to avoid being teased by his fellow players, that today he was going "to play in the Maracanã Stadium." This kid is so green that he's still capable of thinking about his girlfriend during the game, just a small dot in the crowd. When anyone with more experience knows that, on the field, a player has to even forget his mother dying of cancer in the hospital who is saying that her final wish is to see her son.

Our goalie is one of those guys who has long hair, frequents discotheques in the suburbs and makes great saves with spectacular leaps where he shows an incredible flexibility. They're guys who, in one moment of life, in a city in the interior of the country, may have vacillated between being the lover of a farmer's wife, a circus trapeze artist or a goalie. Because they have the aptitude for everything that's difficult and risky. Meanwhile, with regard to dominion over simple things, like control over their own body within their small space, at times they're fragile and ingenuous and, all at once, they can get scored on like this:

Their left-winger got to the end line, crossed it on the ground with power, the ball bounced off their striker and right to our central defender. He could have controlled it, looked around, to find space to get out of the situation. But, flustered, he tried to kick the ball anywhere. The ball hit the fourth defender and the ball rolled between the goalie's legs and into the net.

Machista, insecure, a Brazilian, in general, considers it the epitome of humiliation to have a ball kicked "between his legs" in a football game. The players avoid making that kind of play against each other, considering it a lack of respect for the opponent, which can even lead to a fight. That didn't turn out to be the classic goal between the legs, since the ball wasn't deliberately kicked by anyone. It was an own goal, the result of the chaos in the box. Having incurred, at most, in a slight mistake or lack of reflection, our goalie could have recovered, continued playing as usual, as happens with top goalies after errors a lot more humiliating than that one, sometimes even in decisive games. There are even some people who turn their mistakes and the criticisms into a trampoline that launches them toward victory, toward successes. Unfortunately, our goalie is not one of those. He put his hands on his head, and then, fell down there and pounded the ground with his fists. And then he began to stare at his teammates, looking for someone *to blame* for the goal.

Our goalie is going to end his life without a fuckin' dime in his wallet, a prostitute's lover, maybe a masseur or locker room supervisor for a football team, that is if he doesn't end up on the street.

Our goalie and our fullback in the goal area don't have the control of their nerves that leads to emotional balance. When the ball was returned to the centreline, they started to argue, accusing each other with gestures and cursing. The other team quickly took the ball back after we kicked off and then came up to our box in complete control and, that time, after an amazing play, they were about to score when our central defender took down their centre-forward. A clear foul and nothing to discuss. Our centre-forward argued and was thrown out. I don't waste time giving reprimands to guys who aren't going to benefit from them. Silence, at times, is an attitude that makes a bigger impression on a man, makes him reflect.

Our centre-forward, already in the tunnel, must have heard the unmistakable sound of fans – theirs – celebrating a goal.

The destruction of our tactical plan which, at the very least, could have taken us to an honourable defeat, happened because, after that second goal, our team, at the initiative of some of the players, tried to stay on an equal footing with the other team and thereby to push forward, but we were far outranked. And for a top-ranked team to play counter-attack against a mediocre team is cowardly, because the better team's athletes even eat better. On our team, all the bench players get into the game, and only really favourable circumstances, including tactical discipline, could carry us to victory instead of this chaos.

As for them, they didn't let up on us. Their defence blocked our disorganised attacks and then, with three or four passes, they got to our box. Their centre-forward, who could be on the national team, doesn't complicate an easy play, chooses the corner, kicks the ball lightly and it's the third goal.

Socrates, the one who played for Corinthians and on the national team, if instead of studying medicine had opted, like his Greek namesake, for philosophy, including aesthetics, perhaps could have said that a style is often a synonym for avoiding complication. And his, Socrates' football, like that of the Dutch player Cruyff, consists of simplicity as much as ability.

Socrates' restraint impresses us even in the way he celebrates a goal, since, in an area where almost all players, for publicity reasons, celebrate their goals with actions that are more and more outlandish, that kind of restraint becomes an individual trait, a distinctive characteristic.

Perhaps something new – for better or worse – has begun to appear in Brazilian football since Reinaldo boarded the airplane that carried the national team to the World Cup competition in Argentina, reading *Hurricane over Cuba* by Jean-Paul Sartre. And since Socrates himself – following the example of another physician-player, Afonsinho – started to give interviews in which, among other things, he talked about politics and theatre.

A theory of Brazilian *ginga* (rhythm), however, could be extracted from the fact that, not possessing large green parks like the Europeans, Brazilian kids learned to play football – sometimes even with a ball made of socks – in the alleys, vacant lots, the slopes of *favelas*, street corners, giving birth to a new conception of and domination of space, more or less like this:

A kid, on a steeply sloping street, waits for a car to pass with his foot on the ball, makes a give-and-go pass with a wall while running uphill, avoids two opponents and bends a shot over a parked car, such that it hits a post, a beautiful improvisation, and ends up in the corner of the goal at the exact moment when a pedestrian passes by on the sidewalk blocking the view of the goalie.

This adaptability to unfavourable circumstances – or the much celebrated capacity of the Brazilian people for improvisation – can be seen in Socrates himself, in his characteristic back heel, the result of a balance problem due to the disproportionate size of his feet relative to his body. A play, however, which is being incorporated into the repertoire of other players who don't share that particular physical trait and becoming, therefore, a style not belonging to those individuals.

The fusion of players with short dribbles and a swaying style, generally of the black race, with others, usually white, with more sober and objective qualities, like Tostão, resulted in almost invincible Brazilian teams.

Can it be that in that kind of fusion – which in music resulted in samba and modern jazz – we find a pathway to an entire philosophy of our race?

Football is a spectacle and their left midfield player, a tall mulatto, when he received a long pass, swinging his body extravagantly, and barely touching the ball, took advantage of the moment to pass our striker, who fell back – and even passed Jair. That is to say, with his chest dribble, our team were the ones passing him while the ball continued its straight and smooth trajectory.

Then, lightly touching the ball, he slowed down, moved to the left, followed closely by our new sweeper, put in after our other defender was expelled. And from right there the midfielder could have fired a left-footed rocket, but no. Already near the end line and chased down by the right back, he stepped on the ball and let our defenders, out of breath, fly past, and when they tried to stop, they fell down out of bounds.

Our goalie did what he had to do. He came out of the goal and dove at the feet of the attacker, who, although the angle was slight, could have lifted a soft shot arching over the sprawled goalie for an easy shot. However, he didn't do that; he moved the ball slightly to the right, jumped over the goalie's arms and found a wide-open goal in front of him. And with the total calm of a game already won, he stopped for a fraction of a second, as if he were looking around the stadium and the landscape. And only then, when several defenders were approaching, did he tap the ball gently into the net.

The landscape surrounding a stadium is rarely appreciated, because people are concentrating on the game. But it's a fact experienced by many that, at the moment of an emotional shock or of great frustration, you can suffer a kind of disconnect from the focus of the tragedy, which protects us from the brutal reality. And, all at once, you find yourself paying attention, although perhaps diluted, to a lot of secondary details. For example, it's like being still in the middle of the wreckage of an accident that happened at night on the highway and you start to observe the blinking of the fireflies and to listen to the din made by the crickets in the grass, which did happen to me once.

And that's how it happens that, right now, I'm observing a patch of sunlight striking the grass obliquely; a drop of sweat running down our left-winger's face, as, panting, he's running close to the edge of the field, next to the tunnel. I also see the mountain peaks above the city of Rio de Janeiro, and a small house there on top, and power transmission towers. And finally an enormous blimp that is just now passing, above the arches of the stadium. I can even describe its painted allegory, a Venus in blue and white, completely nude, the lines of her breasts nicely delineated, her pubis and even her navel. It must have required weeks of careful work by a team of artisans in the suburbs.

In the middle of that, I'm still thinking how beautiful this city is, how it resists all that is done against it. But I don't stop thinking how dazzlingly beautiful the Rio de Janeiro region had to have been before the Europeans discovered it and fucked everything up. And much later they introduced a game called football.

A reflection on football at a depressing moment, when your team is losing four to nil almost at the end of the first half and you're there, at the mouth of the tunnel, on a bench anchored in cement, with a view of the pitch which consists mainly of legs running from one side to the other in search of a small leather sphere, in the midst of fierce roars from the stands, all of which can drive you to ask yourself, in a sudden angst about giving it up or surrendering to fate, old age, death, if any of this makes sense: men and women of all ages shouting with hysterical passion for something that's no more than a ball going into this net or that net? Shit, for a sensible person, what difference can that make?

Meanwhile, our fans possess something peculiar, since they are no more than two or three hundred people, if that many, accompanying a team that's playing in a tournament, certain that it doesn't have the least possibility of winning it. The most it can hope for is to win a few games against mediocre teams, manage another draw or win against a great team and not be eliminated from the next season.

So why keep on? Why? Maybe just to feed a tradition, because in some other traditional neighbourhood in this city a group of self-sacrificing people resolved one day to found a club and, with the passing of the years, perhaps they all became accustomed to its existence and believed it to be heresy to put it to rest. A tradition exists to be continued.

And there are fans, absolutely, why not? They are a handful of residents who meet with their banners in front of the clubhouse, after having spent Sunday morning getting drunk in the neighbourhood bars. And maybe there's a kind of dark humour in this, Mexican-like, of the person who observes his own wound and laughs at it, bearing it like a banner. It reminds me of the fans of a certain English club, second division, characterised by causing a big commotion at the games in which their team is almost invariably defeated. They're guys who've worked with great discipline all week in their offices, shops and factories – repeating "Yes, sir" to all the boss's orders – and on Saturdays go out to raise hell and fight in the stadiums for an absolutely mediocre team.

Defeat can almost come to have its own mystique, like Christian suffering. And there was a time when even a great club like Corinthians lived on that. But supporting a mediocre team offers the fans individuality, like that of members of minority political parties. There's something sophisticated in that, like bad taste or punk, raised to the level of art. And you can't deny a certain dose of sensibility and intelligence in that kind of attitude, even turned toward the dark side, which mostly affects they themselves anyway, and can all of a sudden become anti-social. The German Nazi party in its origins, for example.

O.K. Enough musings. The referee is blowing the whistle for the end of the first half and those very fans declare war on us by throwing radio batteries, oranges, paper cups, amid a tremendous booing. However a booing mixed with bursts of laughter and self-flagellation, since they don't take us or even themselves seriously, unlike the fans of good clubs, who can reach extremes like acts of aggression, and if they let them, maybe even murder.

Buffoons is what I'd call them, if I was still referring to England. But since we're not there, I'll say that our fans are just childish.

The silence in the locker room during the beginning of half-time is broken only by heavy breathing that takes time to get back to normal. What can a coach who's already defeated say at half-time? Desperately order them to attack, like a general who meets with the tatters of his soldiers for the decisive phase of a battle when he can't surrender? Like a bull riddled with *banderillas* that fights to the death?

No, that would only add more frustration to our defeat.

"You guys didn't follow my instructions," I said, coldly, maintaining the same calm that created a myth around my persona. "We're going to act now as though it were another game and the score were still nil to nil. We're going to at least use that in our favour: the calmness of those who have nothing to lose."

Jair, for example, is there quietly sucking an orange. He's either indifferent or a stoic, or whatever. If it depended on him alone, it would even be possible to turn a game like this around. O.K. Let's not exaggerate; it wouldn't be impossible to at least reduce the difference in the score.

"We're going to keep on going... Or better yet, we're going to start doing what I have been demanding since the beginning. Use the wingers coming in diagonally, and not allowing the goals to pile up any more, and at least not lose our dignity."

That's what I said, in the middle of a deadly silence, but I couldn't prevent a drop of sweat from dripping from my face onto my white jacket. Now I'm no longer the same, I think, pulling a blue handkerchief out of my pocket.

Me! What can be said about me in a few words? That even on summer afternoons I wear an immaculate suit? That I don't sweat (and that would be enough for anyone who's in the know)? That I'm a football mummy who refuses to die (and that life, for me, was always football)?

Me – this bundle of many and contradictory sensations who, until the end, is going to hope for peace and unity, like a championship won, that was the last of all championships? Aspirations that more and more are becoming memories, as time runs out?

Memories that can mingle vague banners waving in a stadium; a heavy rain, I don't know when or where, and me, there, a raincoat over my suit, shouting for the wingers to get moving? That they can still suddenly bring off a goal in the last minute of a game so decisive that it will forever be, here, for me, the mark of what *could have been (and wasn't)* if that ball had gone into the net? Or the memory, still, of a certain afternoon when you were carried in from the stadium to the clubhouse, but aware that you should enjoy that moment of glory to the maximum, because the ephemeral is a constant in the life of a coach? And for that very reason this memory is associated with another, the image of a woman's face waving for the last time from the window of yet another airport, when I was leaving forever and she was staying?

Me – a theorist, a scholar, as they say, because I was one of the first coaches to receive a degree? And who in his trips to Europe became known because, during his free afternoons and nights, instead of going to cabarets, he went to museums and theatres?

However they forget that I practically grew up inside stadium walls and fences and that the only reason I was never on the pitch was because of a crippled leg. And if they let me try, just one more time, the tactic of the wingers coming on diagonally, but with a great team, where the backs don't need to play so stuck on defence and could take over the space of the wingers who could get free, maybe in that situation, yes, maybe...

But isn't that really what we're always wanting, insatiably? One more love, a last story (like this one), a final championship? Until death breaks in on us in the middle, always in the middle, as if I were ending a narrative here, at this moment, and let myself lose, lying down on the locker room bench and shutting my eyes. But no, not yet... I have to endure everything all the way to the end.

I, who even coached an Arab team, in an emirate. Calling every player by his number (and even then pointing at him with my fingers), corresponding to a face and a position, instead of an unpronounceable name. And showing on the blackboard how those numbers should position themselves, at what moment the wingers should run, a fraction of a second after the midfielder passed the ball to them, so they wouldn't get caught offside.

And we were champions. Easy! "In the land of the blind..." you might argue...

Anyhow I became a national hero and the only reason I left was that I enjoyed having a beer once in a while and, on the other hand, I never enjoyed watching executions in the public square as a spectacle.

Me – rootless and without family, picking up the pieces in a poor, neighbourhood football club, halfway between the city centre and the suburbs? Me – an organiser, a brain, who even lectured on football and its tactics at the Military College. And always with my Theory of the Wingers, like an obsession. The wingers like guerrillas infiltrating the enemy's flank. "Gil, do you know Gil? Tell me: why did Gil only play well when he was with the Rivelino team?"

But I denied it. I denied to those gentlemen in uniform that, beyond winning the championship, my tactics had anything to do with the victorious popular revolution in that Muslim emirate. That's not what happened, I told them, that's just one more of the myths created around this humble person. And, in the end, was it a lecture or an interrogation?

This person – me! – a world that organises itself, here, in words that move around in my head like flies and that, spoken by my mouth to the athletes on my team, should serve, out there on the field, to turn an adverse reality around?

I, a speech that is articulated and claims to be honest and real both for myself and for others? But isn't this just a convention, an artifice that at any moment can shatter, this "I" delivering such a speech, text (imaginary?) for myself and for others? This "I" that becomes *other* to the extent to which I speak *of him*?

But it's as if not even in this way, with this speech, do *I* become a living being, does the illusion materialise, the chaos come together to form a reality beyond hallucination. As if that were the only way I could sit down on the bench again next to the pitch and understand myself within a role, that of coach of a defeated team. Knowing, stoically, that there has to be someone to play that role, just as there have to be humble linesmen (who sometimes want to trick you), ball boys, spectators, stadium workers, all of them having faith in us – or pretending to have faith – in the game.

Me! Putting on this mask again now, almost impassive like the ones worn by Japanese actors, but convincing me so completely of this, my role, that I now give little pats of encouragement on the backs of my players as they climb the stairs that lead to the pitch – and I manage to tell them, contradicting my usual style, "Go get 'em, boys!"

The fifth goal happened at a point in the game when, perhaps because of disinterest on their part, for the first time we had a slight territorial and tactical advantage. Jair had managed to advance the ball out of our box a short distance, which allowed our wingers and midfielders, who were able to stop retreating so much, to advance a bit as well. Their fifth goal arose from the technical superiority of a player who, all by himself, earns more than our whole team. Their fifth goal arose from one of those plays which by themselves are worth the spectacle and the fan goes home with it lodged in his memory and watches it replayed on TV, pointing it out to his wife, who has little interest in football.

Their fifth goal arose from a shot from outside the box, but not one of those bullets that strikes almost at random when no one is in a position to collect a pass. Their fifth goal arose when their player number ten, receiving a ball with his back to the goal in our midfield, chipped it over the defender who was coming up to mark him. And, spun around to face the goal but still a long way off.

With that sense of space that makes a great player, he immediately perceived that the goalie was slightly forward. And shot with the side of his foot and so effectively that the ball, besides the impulse to climb, spun on its own axis and was coming down and down while our goalie, typical of his style, stretched out backward and toward the corner of the goal, with great flexibility but not enough to reach the ball, which was gently coming to rest in the net, as if it was going to hang there weightless forever.

What more is there to say except just to bring what is already finished to an end? That their team, taking the ball, are now saving themselves for the next game? That some fans are already standing up to leave the stadium early? That our athletes also bureaucratically barely keep a commitment, being satisfied to not exhaust themselves unnecessarily? And that, for that very reason, they conceded yet another goal that they wouldn't have conceded if they had just kept fighting? One of those routine goals when someone instead of attempting a shot on goal from a free kick himself, passes it on to a teammate who is open due to our undisciplined defence and finishes with a first-time shot, a goal that added nothing to the game, just to our humiliation in numbers?

Monotony, routine, and tranquillity are feared by many, because they can't stand themselves, their solitude. That's the reason they come to the stadiums: the anxious need to fill, emotionally, the empty places inside themselves. And you can hear the booing from every corner of the Maracanã. As far as our fans are concerned, you don't need to explain why. As for theirs, since they're insatiable, they can't stand a single minute of monotony, even with the score at six to nil.

As for me, I'm fine now. I relax in the face of the inevitable, light a cigarette, enjoy that good feeling of being tired. I'm enjoying that vague moment when you aren't thinking about anything, not even the next game, because for me there won't be a next game.

But someone who is patient can also enjoy these moments of calm, always alert like a guerrilla or a bodyguard in an ambush. Someone like Jair. He's playing the same as always, playing the way he knows how. Perhaps with his mindset, the score no longer affects him emotionally. He's a professional.

A ball landed at his feet, didn't it? Almost at the penalty arc outside of our box. The young left-winger quickly ran for the middle and made an opening, as if only now did he grasp the full meaning of our tactic.

Jair kicks the ball 160 feet – that's right, 160 feet – and it's going to come down between their centre defender and their right defender. One of those tricky balls that a defender leaves for somebody else, thinking the other guy is on his way.

The kid in jersey number eleven shows up, steps into the box with the ball now under control and, perhaps because of the tranquillity that comes from such a lopsided score, has the calm to wait for the goalie to come out and then lightly shoots to the corner of the goal.

In tactical terms it was the best play of the day, but who's going to remember that consolation goal of a team that was massacred?

Nobody even bothered to hug player number eleven. And if our fans celebrate, it's as a joke. This ordinary goal will give them a reason to go down the ramp from the stands in a state of pandemonium, walk to the Praça da Bandeira, where they'll stop in a bar and then continue to the São Cristóvão neighbourhood, Figueira de Melo Street, to down this Sunday's final beers. Go home later and drop into bed, in a kind of stupor that will last until Monday morning.

The kid in jersey number eleven knows all about these things and doesn't turn to his teammates for hugs and not to the fans either. He jogs back to his position, for the next play. Now he's walking a little further, gets near the tunnel and with his right hand gives me a thumbs-up sign. He understood. And he's grateful.

I cough slightly, more like a frog in my throat, and the masseur looks over at me. We've worked together now in several clubs, so he knows me well. And who would think it, me, almost emotional, over one of those lousy little goals? And maybe it's about time...

We'll still endure a seventh goal, but the kid in jersey number eleven will leave here in a thoughtful mood, something happened inside him. Nobody is going to speak of that goal: it and the kid will be a tiny number in the season's statistics in the newspaper. There, at the end of the list, his name: "Evilásio – São Cristóvão – 1 goal."

However, in the midst of the general dejection of our side, in the locker room and later arriving at a small house in the suburbs there will be a young left-winger who played in the Maracanã for the first time and scored a goal. A goal that arose from a shot that was well planned and executed and he, the kid, will have learned something more about football.

Football is one of those things where you're either born to be good or not. But as to improving, you can improve. Sometime down the road that kid will play on some halfway decent team. The América team for example. He's going to be a winger with skills, able to be the third man at midfield or to play in an advanced position, scoring goals like the one today. The important thing is talent, intelligence, and it looks like he has both. With a little luck some coach in trouble will be able to hire him to be useful in a moment of crisis at Fluminense or Botafogo. And who knows, one day, a reserve spot on the national team?

Nobody surpasses his potential, but a man who knows himself well will attain the apex within that potential. Which reminds me of Dirceu, a less-than-good winger, but intelligent, who rose to the occasion at critical moments for the Brazilian national team. Today he's a wealthy man, playing for a foreign team.

Hell, can it be that I'm becoming a dreamer at my age?

"We all respect your past and your competence," said our Manager, now in the locker room, with his hand on my shoulder. "But you understand, the associates want results and seven to one against us is too much. São Cristóvão is a traditional community and our club, a real institution. It looks bad for the President."

"The man who bankrolls the underground lottery has to protect his name," I think, but don't say it. I pat the Director on the back, as if he, in his embarrassment, were the one in need of consolation. And what I do say is just this: "I'll drop by the club tomorrow to settle accounts and pick up my things."

Yes, São Cristóvão is a traditional neighbourhood and the club that bears the same name a true institution. Without the São Cristóvão team the *carioca* championship wouldn't be the same. In the end it serves to give the good teams big wins, which makes their mass of fans happy. It's true that, like all small teams, once in a while they come and pull off a surprise. And that once, although not many people know it, the team was even champion. But, if I'm not mistaken, that was back when a centre-forward striker named Caxambu was on the team. Later the team and the club started to go down hill, down to the point where they are today. However the biggest humiliation in their history wasn't due to a defeat, but when the magazine *Realidade* published an article on the decline of the club, with photographs of goats grazing on the turf in Figueira de Melo.

★

Figueira de Melo, in spite of the fact that nobody knows who this illustrious citizen was, is the name of one of the most traditional streets in this traditional neighbourhood. But not even the street is the same since they built a viaduct over it. And a viaduct, everybody knows, is good only for those who cross over it. That is, those who drive over it. Underneath it true desolation reigns: darkness, soot and sadness. Those who go under the viaduct always look like they'd like to hide.

And I'm passing under there now, wearing the same suit as always; limping a little as always and carrying a bag with all my stuff; but also with my head held high as always, like the creative midfielder that I could have been, except for the physical handicap. With a notion of the space all around me, without having to look hard in any direction. Just like Jair.

Behind me are the clubhouse and the club's field, where the great teams like Flamengo, Fluminense and Vasco no longer come to play. The stadium won't hold their fans who, the last few times they filled the stands, would rail chants at the Club Associates: "It's a chicken house, it's a chicken house."

At heart, all football fans, whether the club is big or small, are mostly poor. And there's no teasing more cruel than that directed by the poor against the poor. And by now I've seen a lot of blacks in the stands call another black man on the pitch *monkey*.

But the only teams that play here currently are Madureira, Serrano, Olaria, and Volta Redonda. And, as up there on top of the viaduct you have a reasonably good view of the field, on game days it's full of the kind of people who will attend any spectacle as long as it's free.

When you've lived in a neighbourhood for some time, you become impregnated with it, you know it inside out, even if you're blind or hardly ever leave the house, like my mother. This neighbourhood is São Cristóvão, with its grey tonality, its small industries, mechanics' garages, and auto parts shops, the Northeasterners' Fair, the Exhibition Hall. And last but not least, the Barracks, which for a long time caused the sports announcers, with their trite expressions, to call the team's players, with their neverchanging white kits *cadets*.

Every neighbourhood, however, has its secrets and, turning to the right on a street here, and another street on the left there, all at once you've walked back in time and are in old Rio with its vintage customs, women and old men at the windows of the houses, some chairs out on the sidewalk, children playing in the street, courting couples on balconies and street corners, bars with little marble-top tables, where sometimes you'll come upon an improvised session of choro or samba.

And I'm going to sit down in one of those bars right now. My leg is aching a little, as always, but I've never complained. And with a *cachaça* and a beer it's always easier to take. I no longer have to be an example for the athletes; that's the next coach's problem. The Portuguese barman at the counter doesn't ask me anything, just what I'm going to drink. By now he must know from the radio the news of my dismissal. And even if it wasn't considered newsworthy of the radio, the facts get around very quickly by word of mouth out here.

Over there in the back near the road it's cooler and I can observe a small stretch of the street, which is gradually growing darker. I can also see right away who's entering the bar and decide if it's worthwhile to make a friendly gesture and invite him to sit with me. If he's a former player, I invite him over even if he's falling-down drunk and sharing his sorrows about the past and about football.

But what I enjoy most is just watching and listening when the conversation is taking place near me. Mechanics, factory workers, loading dockworkers, retired office workers, petty delinquents. Talking about work, the city, life and football.

When you don't have any immediate commitments, you pay attention even to the chirping of the sparrows at the hour when they are roosting in the trees. I enjoy the singing of the crickets even more, when it's summer, and after dark the sounds of the street, people returning from work, and the schoolgirls returning home.

It's time for me to go too. Still upright in spite of the two shots and the beer.

Now walking past a window where a trustful little boy lets himself be held by his grandfather by the windowsill. A little further along a schoolgirl in her uniform is embracing a boy next to a pole, looking to both sides, as if she were hiding her love from her family. Still further on, there's a policeman ignoring a drunk collapsed on the sidewalk.

And, over everything else, the sound of voices from a TV soap opera and the scent of a reheated dinner. My mother is there too, reheating the beans, a little worried by my late arrival, unusual on a Monday, never a practice day at the club. I'm going to eat, take a bath, put on my pyjamas, watch TV. I have a little money saved up from all those years of football. With or without employment by the club, maybe I'll keep on living around here. I liked it. Sometimes there were ugly arguments in the bar, hassles on game days, nocturnal assaults, but no worse than in other neighbourhoods of the city.

A son living alone with his mother may be fifty years old, but he's still treated like a child. And a child with a physical handicap, you know how it is: the mother is even more protective, especially if the father died early.

I get home, the dishes and flatware are already on the table, I kiss my mother, sit down and a little later the beef, salad, rice and beans appear.

Why didn't I get married? In order to not leave the old woman alone? How then can I explain that I got mixed up with football trips, games, training camps? So is it possible that what is sometimes whispered about me can be true? That gossip, you never pay attention to or that nobody tells you about, but you feel it in the air. But what does it really matter what they say about you? It's much more their problem than yours.

And do they know what it's like to go to a party or a cabaret and be ashamed to dance? Do they know what it's like to hide behind a window and watch through the grill the other kids playing football? The most important thing in the world, at that moment, is to be one of them. Then you begin to achieve with your mind what others can do with their bodies and their feet. That's a way for you to be there, to score your goals using their feet.

O.K. That can be an explanation. A person acts in a certain way in his life and you can give a pile of explanations, but maybe one is as useless as another. What is truth? Logical and convincing words in the mouth of someone or on a piece of paper?

A room with blank walls, scantily furnished with an iron bed, a night table and a small wardrobe is ideal for a man to sleep in alone. You don't linger, you go right to sleep and sleep well. Maybe it's a habit, acquired from years and years of strict football schedules. Back in the day I used to put some trophies on top of the wardrobe, photographs of important games on the wall, that kind of thing. Later I started throwing it all away until the room remained as it is now.

Around 11:00 at night, when the last soap opera is ending, my mother warms a cup of milk for me. Ever since I was a child, that was always a signal that it was time for me to go to sleep, which never takes long.

Sometimes, however, very early in the morning, you're awakened by some conversation going on in the street, latecomers from nightlife or people already going to work on some faraway construction job. Or sometimes it's a really gentle harmony that is slowly enveloping everything, produced by a guitar or a flute, or faraway voices singing, or the almost inaudible striking of matches, so that you then recognise, as never before, that it's such and such a person on a night like this in a neighbourhood that could only be in Rio de Janeiro.

Yet on other nights it's a sudden, short and constant sound that pulls you from your sleep without your knowing where it's coming from or what it was that produced it. Since when you woke up you could no longer hear it, that sound that transports you back to one of those fleeting moments when a man doesn't know where he is or when it is. And feeling his way into himself, through an association that is not really with words, but rather a mixture, for example, of the imagined sound and movement of the sea with the smell of fish and the feel of a brisk wind and you intuit the far-off whistle of a ship enveloped in fog, and you, who have travelled so much, still didn't know, in that bare room, whether the place where you woke up is your house in São Cristóvão – with the port not far away – or some hotel in Fortaleza or Natal or in a city as far away and as improbable as Marseilles or Tenerife and, even, what team your club is going to play against and why. Whether it's just a friendly game or an important national or international cup competition.

If you wake up and have a job, a present to live in, your mind will conclude something like this: "Today is Tuesday and I have practice at nine o'clock."

But if all that is finished, you need to look for thoughts and words to organise a past, the only way you're going to feel like a real person.

And then there are other nights, nights of total darkness, not violated by a single sound or movement and during which someone awakens without the warmth of another person at his side or even a recent dream as a reference point. And that man, if you can call him that at this moment – this instantaneous infinite – not only doesn't know who he is, where he is and why, but also, more vaguely, it takes him a tiny, amazed fraction of time to know if he is even alive.

Interview with Sérgio Sant'Anna

What role did football play in your youth?
Football was very important in my childhood and youth. My father took me to the Fluminense games (my team) from the time I was five years old. I also played football during my childhood, adolescence and the beginning of young adulthood, in the street, in schools and on the beach. I became a reasonably good defender.

Do you support a particular team?
I support (I'm even a fan of) Fluminense, in Rio de Janeiro.

How do football and politics intersect in Brazil?
During the military dictatorship, the government of the generals exploited the World Cup won by Brazil in 1970 a lot. And it was the worst phase of the dictatorship, the government of General Emílio Garrastazu Médici. The players came from Mexico to Brasília and went directly to the government palace. Nowadays, fortunately, football isn't mixed up with politics.

How would you describe the impact in Brazil of having hosted the World Cup in 2014?
I think that the political and social impact of the 2014 World Cup was negative. Not only because disorganisation reigned but also because the various improvements promised for the country did not happen, except for the stadiums, which in some cases were in places where there is no public to see games. Then, the 1-7 loss to Germany was an embarrassment to everyone and it's still being talked about today. And consider this, that Germany stopped attacking so as not to further humiliate the

Brazilian team. The national team does not get anyone excited. Everybody – including myself – is more interested in the clubs that we support, which in my case is Fluminense.

As for the Olympics, I don't see any enthusiasm here in Rio de Janeiro because the country is in a serious economic crisis, caused largely by corruption. Happily there's a judge in Paraná, Sérgio Moro, who is conducting a serious investigation into cases of corruption and putting some important people in jail.

What is your opinion about the recent developments in the scandal surrounding corruption in FIFA?

My opinion on the corruption scandal in FIFA could only be anger and the desire that the guilty be punished in an exemplary fashion, beginning with the Brazilians. Even without being a fortune-teller, I knew about the corruption in FIFA and the CBF. But proving that is really important in order to cleanse football of these criminals.

What more can be said about the response from Brazilian society and Brazilian football to the 1-7 loss to Germany in the semifinal of the 2014 World Cup?

The reaction of Brazilian fans to the 7-1 score was, as I mentioned above, one of shame. When the team scores goals, like it did in the Copa América, no one cheers or sets off flares like they used to. In comparison, when it's your team that scores a goal and wins, the celebrations are still huge. A journalist for *O Globo*, Nelson Motta, said it well: the national team lost their former nobility.

Do you see any connection between the creative process and the way in which someone plays football or behaves as a fan?

I see a connection between my way of writing and the way a lot of top football players, past and present, play. I could cite, for example, Tostão and Ademir Da Guia, as football stylists.

Is there a particular identity or style associated with football in Brazil?
The style associated with Brazilian football is the dribble, swinging the body, but everybody writes in his own way, with his own style.

Do you see any lingering reluctance to incorporating football or sports as a dominant theme or plot driver among your generation of authors?
No, I don't think there are any qualms about incorporating football and sports as a dominant theme in literary works. One book, *O drible*, by an author who is part of the generation that are about fifty years old, won an important prize with that novel. The Portugal Telecom Prize. And, at least in my case, football has always been part of my books, sometimes as the only theme of a story, sometimes just referred to in passing. You may not be familiar with my most complex story about football, the title of which is *Páginas sem glória*. It's in the book with the same title, published by the Companhia das Letras, back in 2011, I think. But there aren't so many fiction writers who write about football, because you need to have a profound knowledge of the topic. Still, we have excellent sports writers in the newspapers, starting with Tostão, a *crack* world champion in 1970.

Chile
ROBERTO FUENTES

Roberto Fuentes was born in Santiago, Chile in March of 1973. He first earned a degree in engineering in land surveying technology and then in civil engineering. He is the author of more than ten books, among which are the short story collections *Está mala la cosa afuera* (Editorial Cuarto Propio, 2002) and *No te acerques al Menotti y otros cuentos* (Alfaguara, 2003). He won a competition sponsored by the magazine Paula for the latter story. He is also the author of the novels *Puro hueso* (Editorial Cuarto Propio, 2007) and *La mano pequeña* (Uqbar Editores, 2009). He published his first nonfiction book in 2012, *Síndrome de Down: Historia de un superhijo* (Aguilar, 2011). Currently he is working as a construction manager. He is also a dedicated marathon runner, having completed thirteen marathons. He is a fan of the Colo Colo team and resides in Santiago. "Just Another Dude" (Un huevón más) appeared first in Spanish in the anthology *Uno en quinientos* (Alfaguara, 2004).

Just Another Dude

Even though it was winter, I was sitting on the sidewalk under the walnut tree. It was also Sunday, so Dad and Mom had gone out together to the Amengual market. The only thing that's not clear to me is why I was alone, since at that hour at least one of my friends should have been passing by the street. Nevertheless, I was alone and sad. It had been two months since a girlfriend that I really loved had left for the United States and she still hadn't written me. Besides, the night before I had twisted my right ankle playing football. I stuck my head between my legs and felt a shy touch on my shoulder. Hi, someone said. I looked up, squinting. It wasn't one of my friends, it was Pato, a kid with Down's Syndrome who my friends and I called "the little Mongol of La Palma", the neighbouring *barrio*.

I didn't answer him right away, due to the strangeness of the situation. Pato had never shown up on my street before. He was about twenty, but looked like he was fourteen. He was short, fat, his neck was almost invisible, his mouth always hung open and he seemed to be happy. Even when he was mad he looked happy, as if anger or sadness for him were just performances, like a game. Hi, I said. He took my hand and helped me stand up. My ankle hurt and I frowned.

"You're sad," he said, and smiled.

From any other person the smile accompanied by that comment would have struck me as a joke.

"No, I'm not, it's just that my foot hurts a little."

I noticed that he was wearing a jacket. It wasn't that cold even though it was the end of June. I was only wearing a tee-shirt.

"My brother says that when you're sad you have to think about something nice and it goes away."

Pato worked with his brother in the market. They sold watermelons and cantaloupes in the summer and potatoes and onions in the winter.

"How come you're not at the market?"

"I go one Sunday and he goes the next."

I remembered that some Sundays, when I went with my mother to the market, I had seen him working by himself in his stand. People said that Pato was very good at counting. He never made a mistake giving change.

"Think about something nice," he suggested.

I shut my eyes and remembered the night in the square with Ingrid, my travelling friend. I smiled.

"What are you doing here?" I asked.

Pato started to sway from side to side. That's what he did whenever he was happy or nervous.

"It worked! My brother was right."

"Yeah, your brother was right, I feel better, but what are you doing here?"

There was no sharpness in my voice. I was just curious.

"We challenge you to a game."

Pato swayed even faster. I showed him my swollen ankle and gradually he stopped moving.

"Wow!" he exclaimed, raising his hands to his head in an exaggerated way.

"I can't play, but my friends can."

Pato smiled and told me:

"Tonight, at the park."

A couple months earlier they had installed lights there.

"I don't know."

I remembered that in the last championship game we almost came to blows with the La Palma team, and that it would be hard for my friends and me to raise our share of the fee. It was only at night, because of the lights, that they charged to use the field.

"It's just a friendly; we'll pay for the light," said Pato as if he had guessed what I was thinking.

"O.K.," I shrugged.

"Let's go rent the field," Pato proposed with so much enthusiasm that I couldn't turn him down.

We had never exchanged that many words. I had always seen him at a distance. Those guys, the ones from La Palma, were always laughing around him. They made fun of him, true, but that was a privilege limited to them. If somebody who didn't belong to their group bothered Pato, they defended him to the death. Pato was the one in charge of the club. He organised the games, got the players together and carried the bag with the jerseys. He washed the jerseys too. He lived with his brother, who'd sold at a stall in the market for years, and a sister who was rarely seen on the street. She kept house for them and was even fatter than Pato. Their parents had died in a traffic accident when Pato was small. They said that the bus that was carrying the parents and the sister on a trip south, had collided head-on with a truck. A lot of people died and it was in all the newspapers. The sister survived miraculously after being in a coma for a long time.

I felt strange walking beside him. I admit I felt embarrassed. Besides, I was limping a little and since when Pato walked he would swing his arms a lot, I thought we looked ridiculous. My friends weren't on the street and, in general, there were few people out. A kid, maybe three years old and looking scared, stood staring at us. Pato waved at him and the kid ran into his house.

We got to Don Lito's house, located in front of the entrance to the football complex made up of several pitches, and knocked hard on the door. Pato scratched his head and giggled from time to time. I rubbed my arms. It had gotten cloudy and a cool breeze had stirred up.

Don Lito came to the door, his hair a mess and rubbing his eyes.

"What the hell do you want?"

"To rent the field, Don Lito," Pato replied with a smile.

"What time?"

"From nine to ten," I said.

Pato nodded his head in agreement. His constant swaying had unnerved me a little, so I concentrated on Don Lito's sleep-deprived face.

"It'll cost you 500."

Pato took out a few coins, handed five of them to Don Lito and put the rest back.

"See you at nine, then," stammered Don Lito, and turned around.

"Wait, Don Lito," shouted Pato. The old man fumed and glared at us. "Can you lend me a ball to take some shots?"

I wasn't getting it at all. Don Lito finally went into the house and slammed the door. Pato covered his head with his hands and laughed. I was about to leave when a shadow made me duck my head. The ball came down next to me.

"Thanks, Don Lito."

Pato took the ball and ran onto the field. I stayed there watching him. He kicked the ball and followed it, kicked it again and chased after it again. Before the fourth kick he stopped suddenly and looked in my direction. He made wild gestures for me to come onto the field.

It wasn't hard for me to convince him to play goalie first. We agreed to change roles after the first goal. I kicked the ball slowly in his direction. The ball was made of leather and small, like the ones they used in kid's football. The idea was to score a nice goal on him, without having to kick it very hard. That way I avoided the pain in my ankle and also delayed the time I'd have to be the goalie. At the fifth try the ball went into a corner of the net. "Goal," shouted Pato.

"No good, no good," I said, and waved my hands in the negative.

"No good?"

"Yeah, I committed a foul before I took the shot."

"O.K.," Pato said, satisfied. "I'm a great goalie."

"A first-class goalie."

Five minutes later I put another shot into the net. Pato shouted the same as before.

"The referee overturns the goal because of the offside position of the forward," I said, imitating the tone of the radio announcers.

Pato thought my performance was funny and laughed so hard that it gave him hiccups. It wasn't long before he choked and I had to pound him hard on the back.

"We need a referee for tonight," he said as soon as he had recovered.

"Each team can act as referee for half the game."

Pato looked at me blankly. I was going to explain it to him, but he spoke up first:

"Menotti will ref for free."

I tried to tell him that I didn't think that was a very good idea, but he started walking away fast. He left the pitch and tossed the ball over the wall that surrounded Don Lito's house. I didn't like the idea of following him, I admit, but I was beginning to feel responsible for him. I couldn't let him go off alone to Menotti's house, a guy known by the whole town to be a fag who paid any teenager who would agree to let him perform oral sex.

"Do you know where Menotti lives?" I asked him when I caught up with him.

"No."

We reached the corner, I took his arm and made him turn to the left. We passed by my street and Perrito saw us pass. I pretended not to see him. Perrito ran up beside us.

"You make a cute couple," commented my friend in a mocking tone.

"Thanks," said Pato, and smiled.

Perrito looked at me, pointed to Pato and laughed.

"Stop the bullshit and get lost."

"The street belongs to everybody."

"We're on our way to your 'boyfriend's' house," I said, and Pato burst out laughing. I don't know if he was laughing just to laugh or because he had understood the irony.

Perrito, on the other hand, became real serious. Two nights earlier I had seen him with Menotti on the way to the trash heap, an open space used as the municipal dump, and up to then I had kept my mouth shut.

"I wonder if he's at home or at the dump?" I asked glancing up at the sky.

"If you snitch on me, I'll tell my brother to beat you up," threatened Perrito.

We came to a halt. I noticed that Pato seemed worried. Perrito's brother was called Mean Coquito and was my friend too.

"If Coquito finds out what I saw, you'll be the one he beats up."

"Why are you going to see Menotti now and with this guy?"

"None of your business. Just move along." Perrito didn't move a muscle. "Tell the guys there's a game tonight."

Perrito spit on the ground and walked away, while Pato

smiled with relief. He patted me on the shoulder. Let's go, I told him. Take this, he told me, and handed me a stone he took out of his pants pocket.

"It's for good luck," he added. "Kiss it three times in a row and you're all set."

"Where'd you get this?"

"My pants."

"I meant... Forget it, let's get going."

We knocked on Menotti's door. Pato was swaying like crazy.

"I hope he says yes."

"He never says no."

"What do you want?" asked Menotti, leaning out a second-story window.

We looked up and were both blinded by the sun.

"We want you to ref, Don Menotti," Pato said.

"We're playing tonight at nine," I said.

"Fine. I'll be there."

Pato jumped with joy. I felt uncomfortable. I lowered my eyes and even though I heard Menotti laughing, I promised myself I wouldn't look up.

"Come in and have a soda," invited Menotti.

Pato gave another jump and said:

"I love soda."

"We can't, we've got to go," I said quickly, grabbed Pato by the arm and we cut out.

"I want a soda," Pato repeated as he saw how I was pulling him along.

"There's some at home."

"But it has to be Fanta, Coca-Cola makes me burp like a pig."

I smiled and let go of his arm.

We got to the front door of my house and I stood a moment thinking. I couldn't let him go in. What would I tell my parents?

How would they react? Pato seemed less and less strange to me, but my family didn't know him, had only seen him around town and for them he was still "the little Mongoloid of La Palma". I think my mom was even a little afraid of him.

"Stay here. I'll bring you a drink."

Pato nodded yes and sat down on the sidewalk. Before going into the house I saw how he was entertaining himself watching some ants. I climbed the steps quickly. I had barely gotten into the dining room when I heard Aunt Nena calling me from the living room. I went in and endured her long kisses on each cheek, as well as her questions about my life, as best I could. I answered her in monosyllables and at the first silence escaped into the kitchen. Mom was concentrating on peeling some tomatoes. The drinks were on the cabinet top. As if it were the most natural thing in the world I picked up a bottle and filled a glass. It was neither Fanta nor Coca-Cola; it was Bilz, but in this case it was all the same. I went into the dining room and my grandmother Chela trapped me and told me that she had prepared lunch and that's why I should eat it all. Sure, I told her, and tried to get away. Besides, there's a surprise, she told me, as I stepped to one side. I stopped and looked at her.

"I bought chocolate ice cream, the kind you like best."

I smiled at her and left. I didn't have time to think about how rude I had been to her. I went out to the street and was bitterly surprised to see that Pato was no longer there. I poured the drink out next to a tree, stomped the ground, stirring up the pain in my ankle, kept myself from yelling, and went into the house.

I went to the fields with my friends, each of us carrying a red jersey in our hands, me too, even though I was just going to coach. We turned up Araucana Street and I saw the rival team walking about a hundred feet ahead of us. Pato was the last, and as always when there was a game, he had the bag of jerseys on his shoulder. As soon as I can I'll explain about the soda, I thought. We got to the pitch and I saw the lights on. Menotti and Don Lito were waiting for us in the middle of the field. I wanted to play real bad and felt bummed that I couldn't. The teams suited up and I gave my team the starting line-up.

"Coquito in the goal. Nino and Juanito in the back. Willi and Álvaro up front."

"What about me?" asked Perrito.

"When we make a substitution."

My friend didn't argue.

Menotti called for the captains. I looked at Pato. He was swaying back and forth as he always did before his team's games. Sometimes he clapped his hands and encouraged his players. We're going to win, he said. I hoped he was wrong. In the last championship, when the lights had been inaugurated, we had lost to La Palma five to four. Now was the perfect chance to take our revenge. Us, the Cayul bunch, never mix with the kids from the nearby *barrios*. To us they were trashy. Our neighbours always wanted to beat us for the same reason. They called us posers.

Five minutes into the game we were losing two to nil. Perrito was circling around me and Pato was jumping up and down with joy. On one of the many times I glanced at him I saw him take a stone out of his pants pocket, kiss it three times and put it back. Perrito saw it too.

"Look at that fucking dude," he said.

I didn't pay it any mind. I hoped he was looking somewhere else as I took out *my* lucky stone and performed the ritual three kisses. Less than a minute later Nino was calling for half-time. Fine, I said, and waved at Pato. He smiled at me, then looked toward the pitch and covered his goalie in expletives. Nobody from the La Palma team said anything. Before the game started up again, I took Álvaro out and sent in Perrito. That turned out to be a masterstroke. Juanito stole the ball, passed it to Perrito, who dodged a rival player and shot for the goal from three feet outside the box. The ball wasn't cleared before shooting, so the goal shouldn't have counted, and only Coquito, who because of his position couldn't see exactly what happened, celebrated it. To everyone's surprise, Menotti counted the goal. The rival team immediately attacked the referee. Pato was boiling with rage and stamping the ground. Perrito was laughing with my friends and hugging them. He was never able to look at me. Menotti was pampering him. Both of us knew it.

The La Palma players kept on complaining and surrounded Menotti. Pato joined the conference and he was the one who shouted the most expletives. Nino approached hoping to be a peacemaker, and was pushed out of the way. Nino grabbed the guy responsible for the shove and with one punch knocked him to the ground. That's when all hell broke out. Miserable coward that I am, all I did was cover my eyes. It was also an act of resignation. Menotti left the field, and the players kept on fighting, although, I should be perfectly clear, the blows were pretty sporadic, more shows of bravado than anything else. What caught my attention more than anything else was that Pato was shoving all my friends and not one of them turned on him. They ignored him and kept on acting tough with the other dudes on the La Palma team. Pato was making a fool of himself and I felt bad for him. I approached and tried to talk to him. I got a punch on the ear for my effort. I had no time to think (if I had I wouldn't have done what I did) and I sank my foot into his rear end. There was a long silence. I had kicked him with my bad leg and my ankle was killing me. Pato, looking scared, rubbed his ass and stared at me. Richard, the captain of the rival team, was the first one to jump on me. I fell to the ground under a torrent of punches. My friends tried to defend me, but the other team was enraged.

"Dude, you're a faggot," one of them yelled at me.

"Can't you see that Pato is sick," another one shouted at me.

I was thinking about that word "sick". For me now Pato was as healthy as anybody. Yeah, he was different, but not "sick". A kick in the ribs finally put an end to my musings.

Fortunately Don Lito showed up and everything calmed down. If a team didn't follow his orders, they'd never be able to play on that pitch again. It was the golden rule and everybody respected it. Don Lito opened the gate and let us leave first. I was limping and insults and some spit was raining down on me from the fence. I saw Pato who was laughing and waving at Don Lito, so I felt better.

"You fucked up, Betto," Nino told me.

"He's just another dude," I said out loud, and my friends looked at me like I had said something crazy.

That night I couldn't go to sleep. I kept reliving the scene where I had kicked Pato. I wasn't even thinking, I told myself. Besides if Pato gets himself into a fight, he has to accept the consequences. Several parts of my body were aching, but I swore I wouldn't tell my parents anything. I was convinced that I had reached the age when you have to look out for yourself. I finally fell asleep and a little while later, or so it seemed, I woke up for school still in pain and really sleepy.

I don't remember that morning in school at all. After school I walked home completely bummed out. I couldn't stop thinking about what happened with Pato. I promised myself that I'd apologise to him and warn him to keep far away from fights. I was convinced he would understand me. I hadn't been around him much, but in the little time we had shared, I had realised he wasn't as stupid as I had thought, just different, I insisted, and it even seemed to me that he was happier than any of us, the "normal guys".

Two blocks from home I saw Pato and his brother walking toward me. I'm really fucked, I thought, and my stomach tightened. Lucho, the brother, was smoking and about thirty feet from me he threw the butt on the ground. He was really tall, muscular and about twenty-five years old. As soon as Pato saw me he ran up. He gave me a big hug that completely disarmed me. Lucho stopped about fifteen feet from us and looked up at the tops of the trees, like he didn't really care that much what his brother was doing.

"Last night we tied," Pato said. "We have to play the return match."

"Yeah, sure, maybe so." Out of the corner of my eye I was carefully watching for any movements from his brother. "Did you tell your brother what happened last night?"

"About what happened last night? I don't think so. Have you used the lucky stone?"

I put my hand in my pocket and showed it to him.

"Not much. Listen, it'd be better if you didn't..."

"Kiss it three times."

I looked at Lucho and he was waving at a neighbour who was walking by on the sidewalk. I quickly kissed the stone three times and stuck it in my pocket again.

"It would be better if you didn't..."

"You're my friend," Pato said, and even his eyes were smiling.

"Yes, I am," I told him and took his hand. We gave each other a tight handshake. "I want to talk with you longer."

"I'll come see you."

"I have to go."

We said goodbye with another handshake, and Lucho and I greeted each other with a slight raising of our eyebrows.

"That's my friend, I just met him..." I managed to hear Pato tell his brother.

I walked faster.

I got to my room, threw my backpack on the bed, and the sound it made was different than usual. I looked carefully and saw that an envelope was showing under the backpack. I pulled it out quickly and my heart was beating a thousand miles an hour. It was Ingrid who was writing to me from New York. The envelope had a red and blue border all around it, like the ones for airmail, and on the stamp I could see the silhouette of two identical buildings. It took me a while to recover from the initial impact. I didn't dare look at the content of the letter. What would she tell me? Did she still love me? Will she come back soon? Once I got up the necessary courage I carefully tore open the envelope, revealing the pages (there were four of them covered with a tiny and beautiful handwriting). In the first paragraph she asked me to forgive her for not having written before and confessed that she was thinking about me all the time. If I had been Pato at that moment I would have swayed back and forth so much that I would surely have fallen on the floor. I took a deep breath and prepared to go on reading.

"Betto, dude, look at me," someone said from outside the window.

It was Nino. I left the pages on the bed and went over to the window, trying to hide my stupid grin.

"Did Ingrid write to you?"

I nodded yes.

"Great, tell me about it later, but right now I don't have good news."

I looked at him in surprise. Ingrid had written to me, it was a long letter and in the first paragraph she told me that she was always thinking about me. So what could this business of bad news be all about?

"Lucho is at the end of the street, waiting for you."

I looked out the window and saw him quietly walking from one side to the other.

"What's he want?" I asked, the grin no longer on my face.

"He told me to tell you that he wants to talk to you."

"He must have found out about the fight."

"I guess."

"And Pato?"

"When I got here I saw Lucho fussing with Pato and he sent him home."

I looked outside again and nothing had changed.

"I'm done for."

"What are you going to do?"

"I'm going to go talk to him."

"Don't be crazy. He's going to knock your block off."

"I don't think anything will happen."

"I'm going to back you up, just in case."

I thanked my friend for his words with a smile and went back to the bed. I left the pages of the letter in order on the bedside table and went out into the hall. As soon as I shut the door, I took the lucky stone out and kissed it three times, but instead of putting it back in my pocket, I kept it in my fist. I saw that Nino was biting his nails and didn't give me a lot of confidence. I walked to the end of the street and saw how Lucho stopped walking back and forth as soon as he saw me. I wanted to stop, but I didn't, in fact, I sped up.

Interview with Roberto Fuentes

What role did football play in your youth?

They say that football is the opium of the people. I lived in a poor area of Santiago and since our yards were small, my friends and I would get together in the alleys. There all we needed was a ball to cheer up the long afternoons. When we were fifteen we joined a football club and that was the first time we played on a large field. We were lost for several games until we got used to them. In summary, football helped me kill time and meet new friends.

Do you support a particular team?

I've always been a Colo Colo fan. I have a membership card and go to the Monumental stadium to cheer my team on. To be a Colo Colo fan is to be Mapuche, to be one of the people and helps me remember where I come from.

Which is more important to you as a fan, a good result or a good game?

When I play, I prefer a good game. Fun, tight, heated. The result isn't that important. But when my team plays and I'm just a fan, I'm happy with winning. We Colo Colo fans are spoiled, used to getting those three points every Sunday.

What motivates you to write fiction that takes place within a Chilean context?

I tell about my world. I write about what I know. About my awakening to life in a poor area of Santiago in the 80s. In the middle of the dictatorship on top of that. I feel committed to a world where people ride the bus and go to public schools. The idea is to show, to teach, hopefully to excite. There's no wish to propagandise or make demands.

How do you view the recent developments in the scandal surrounding corruption in FIFA?

FIFA has always been corrupt. The fact that it's come to light now is something else. But it's not a lot of light and it's coming through a tiny hole, but still enough to look inside and see the worst aspects of this mafia-style organisation. I hope that everything will change and that we stop being afraid that if FIFA falls, the world comes to an end, because it's precisely that fear that has resulted in the fact that they, the bosses, hungry for power and money, along with large consortia, have remained untouchable up to now.

How do football and politics intersect in Chile?

Oh. A lot. The dictatorship managed Chilean football. And you can still smell that. Today the owners of the clubs are all right-wing businessmen who at some point amassed their fortunes thanks to the dictatorship. I hope that soon we fans will manage to take the clubs back.

What is the place of football fiction in the literature of your country?

It's not that important because the market, which sticks its nose into everything, is small. People don't read much, few books are sold. There are more journalistic football texts than fiction. It's a shame. Football is a small world that reflects all of society.

Do you see any lingering reluctance to incorporating football or sport as a dominant theme or plot driver among your generation of authors?

I don't see it that way. Everyone writes about what he knows. And maybe football isn't very popular in the intellectual world, but now it's more respected, as are other sports. Many of my writer colleagues won't touch the topic simply because they know nothing about it. It may be that someone will look down on the plot of a story or a novel centred on sport, even more for a sport as big as football, but that's to be expected.

Victor Jara used to sing that "Life is so short in five minutes" – it can also be short in ninety.

Did any writer of football fiction influence this story?
Maybe Benedetti. He has a story where the attacker plays well even though it costs him a beating or even his life. If the ball's rolling around the box, it's impossible to repress the impulse to kick it in and, as in my case, to narrate it.

Is there a particular identity or style associated with football in Chile?
They used to say we were tacticians. That was a euphemism. In reality we were just mediocre. We didn't play well at all. Now with Sampaoli and thanks to Bielsa's legacy the Chilean national team goes after all the games, it doesn't matter who the rival is. Chile runs and attacks hard. Now we don't know how to play any other way. It's about time.

How would you describe the impact in Chilean society of having hosted and won the Copa América in 2015?
I want to believe that being the host country has an important economic impact. Provincial cities have the opportunity to show themselves to the world. We've organised important events before, and carried them out successfully. This Copa América wasn't an exception.

The impact on an emotional level has been tremendous. It has generated widespread enthusiasm, which has been maintained even as time goes by. Now I've been able to understand that we're a small country that hangs at the bottom of the world. Nothing is easy for us on any level. Everything is an uphill climb. Football players from the rest of the world are taller, faster and stronger. Only a very professional golden generation, with the support of two insane coaches (Bielsa, first, and then Sampaoli) enabled us to have a great team that could face any opponent on equal terms; besides this had to be combined with a bad afternoon for a world powerhouse, and only that planetary alignment could take us to victory. And it was fair. Precisely because we're a small country, a FIFA lightweight, we could never have won a fraudulent title. We sell fewer tee-shirts than Argentina or Brazil, just to offer a random point. We won, and in spite of the fact that it's still clear that we're not a world power and that we're small, now it's understood that distances are shorter and no one will be calling us "Chilenitos" any longer.

Colombia
RICARDO SILVA ROMERO

Ricardo Silva Romero was born in Bogotá, Colombia in 1975. He studied literature at the Universidad Javeriana. Between 1999 and 2000 he pursued a Master's degree in film at the Autonomous University of Barcelona. He is the author of a play, *Podéis ir en paz* (1998); a volume of poetry *Terranía* (Planeta, 2004, National Poetry Prize); and of a biography, *Woody Allen: incómodo en el mundo* (Panamericana, 2004). He is also the author of several volumes of short stories, including *Sobre la tela de una araña* (Arango, 1999) and *Semejante a la vida* (Alfaguara, 2013), and of two volumes of illustrated short stories, *Que no me miren* (Tragaluz editores, 2011) and *El libro de los ojos* (Tragaluz, 2013). He is also the author of several novels: *Relato de Navidad en La GranVía (Alfaguara, 2001), Tic (Planeta, 2003), Parece que va a llover (Planeta, 2005), Autogol (Alfaguara, 2009)* and the diptych *Érase una vez en Colombia,* made up of *El espantapájaros* and *Comedia romántica* (Alfaguara, 2012). Silva Romero is also a journalist, screenwriter and film critic. He is a fan of the Millonarios team and resides in Bogotá. "Cucho" (El Cucho) first appeared in Spanish in *Semejante a la vida* (Alfaguara, 2013).

Cucho

The game started forty minutes ago, but the score's still 0 to 0. As usual the locals are on edge. Cucho, who's the coach, the technical director of the Retiro School's team, is biting his nails because they're going to fire him, because the principal, under pressure from the Board, will not tolerate the boys getting scored on again or losing another game. This is his last chance.

Yes, sir: they have to win this time. By any means necessary. This year the Retiro has lost everything: the band festival, the maths contest, a place in the ranking of the best schools in Bogotá. Are they going to be shut out of the second round of the championship as well? Are they going to have to face the fact that it's not just their brains that don't work, but their feet too?

That's what Cucho thinks. That is, he's convinced this is the worst football team he's ever seen in his life. He'd like to laugh at them, but he can't because he's their coach. The supposed goal scorers are nodding off with their eyes closed, the defenders are stomping the ground and the midfielders are trying to finish a conversation they started during the lunch recess.

The substitutes are tall guys, really tall, who didn't make it onto the basketball team and don't even have boots. The goalie is afraid of the ball and has just flunked the final exam in chemistry, and the best player on the team, the one who brings form, tactics and strategy to the team, Mateo Delgado, son of Roberto Delgado, the distinguished president of the school's board, suffers from asthma attacks all the time and up to now hasn't touched the ball even once.

"We're screwed," comments Cucho, "I'm going to have to ask my brother-in-law for a job."

"Teach, what's your brother-in-law do?" asks Chino Morales, who's useless not only for football but also for everything else, academics, social life, family, everything, and for this reason, because he inspires compassion and a lot of pity in Cucho, has become the team's assistant coach.

"He has a chain of hardware stores, Chino, and just so you know he doesn't do so badly, not badly at all," Cucho is saying, just when Mateo Delgado, in the team's first play in counterattack during the entire game, passes one, two, three defenders, dribbles past the goalie, and is knocked down by a bastard from the other team, because, of course, these kids from rich schools like this one swear that a kick doesn't matter and you don't even get a scrape: "Penalty! Penalty! Come on, ref! Penalty!"

The band furiously plays the school anthem. The principal embraces the senior students. The philosophy teacher, Londoño, smiles ironically. The referee, terrified, says nothing happened, keeps on playing, and looks out of the corner of his eye toward the stands where the crowd is starting to move, in unison, as if they were about to lynch him. Cucho collapses onto the bench. He loosens his tie. He could be on the verge of a heart attack or a bout of gas. Either one. Anxiety and Coca-Cola are doing him in.

"I'm sorry, Chino," he says: "Coca-Cola blows me up."

"Got it, teach, my little sister lives with amoebas."

"Amoebas? Listen, Chino, those guys can bury themselves in the brain, you hear me?"

"No, no, no: amoebas," says Chino and he begins to think about the possibility that Cucho may not be as brilliant as he thinks.

Jaime Venegas, the team captain, famous for his tiny feet, hurls himself against the giant defence player who committed the foul not only because Mateo Delgado is his best friend but also because they had made plans to go rafting at Barichara this weekend, and now, seeing him groaning on the ground, kissing his knee, he's pretty sure there'll be a change of plans. What'll it be? Seeing a movie in El Andino Cinema?

The linesmen run onto the pitch to prevent a fight. The referee, his eyes as red as raw meat, covers his face with his hands.

Cucho and Chino go onto the field. The guys in the band try to strike up a tune, but they all seem to be playing a different song and end up just looking at each other in bewilderment. The school principal orders the spectators not to move. Not one more step. Londoño, the philosophy teacher, helps control the situation.

"We're not going to come to blows over a football game," he tells them. "Hey, you over there, take it easy."

"What school do they think they're from?" asks the principal. "The Richard Nixon Lyceum?"

The *Plays*, headed up by Rodrigo Peña, who has an amazing little airplane and knows how to fly it, all laugh because they've never heard of such a ridiculous name for a school. The other team's supporters from a school for boys up north, another one that, to be honest, would rather not be mentioned in this account, provoke the ire of the local fans with their gestures.

"O.K., OK, behave yourselves, show them who we are at this school," shouts the principal and points at the fans from the other school, "leave the rudeness to them, meanwhile, let's be polite."

While Chino Morales separates Venegas from the giant defender, the assailant, the captain of the other team, a guy about twenty-four who's probably been trying to pass calculus for the past six years and who's watched the last six graduating classes leave him behind, Cucho berates the referee even though the linesman, who has his pants pulled up to his neck, and is gesturing endlessly with both hands, curses him and orders him to go back to the bench and stop trying to start problems.

The referee takes his hands away from his face. And Cucho realises that he knows him from the Korean War and that he's crying inconsolably, like a little child.

"What's going on, ref? Why are you crying, brother?"

"His mom died this morning," states the linesman.

The referee concurs and begins bawling again. That's going to be an indelible memory from now on. His mom's no longer here and everybody in the stands insists on reminding him of that fact. The poor man's in mourning. Cucho snatches the whistle from his mouth so he won't blow it now, while Chino Morales prevents the veteran defender from beating up Venegas and the principal, along with Londoño, the philosophy teacher, holds back the rabid fans in the stands.

Mateo Delgado is about to lose consciousness and, in the middle of the fight, at the same time that he has a major asthma attack and his father runs onto the pitch to save him with a dose of Bitolterol, but all he can think about is the philosophy class where Londoño, the teacher, had said that there was no way to prove that we existed, and that all this, the fans, the ball, the goalie, even Cucho, could just be part of a dream.

But if the world is a fiction, why is his knee hurting? Why can't he get his breath? Could it be like Londoño said, that he was taught to be afraid and to feel pain? Could it be as Plato said, like a hundred years ago, or something like that, that ideas are the only things that exist, the idea of pain, of fear, or even of asthma? Could it be that all we have is the word "fear", and the word "word", and that we have to accept those codes and pretend that, yes, we really do learn about the world? Or what was it again the teacher was saying this morning?

Now he opens his eyes and sees his father. He's not dead. If he were, his dad would be wearing black. Like the referee. And he wouldn't be hearing the school band, but the church choir instead. Although, if he really thinks about it, it would be great if they would bury him at the spot of the penalty spot on the field. With the band and the whole nine yards.

Cucho, a few yards away, puts his hand on the referee's shoulder. Life has to go on. The game must continue and the team has to win. He can't lose his job. Not this time. His pension, with his rotten uric acid, with his seventy-three-year-old prostate, and his lame leg, a result of Korea, are no longer good for anything, and it's not just that the owners of his apartment are pressuring him to pay the rent nor that his wife's lover needs a little more money to buy whisky, nor even that he has to support his only daughter, an unwed mother, who has already accused three innocent guys of being the father. As if all that were not enough, he somehow has to pay off a gambling debt. He could refuse to pay it, of course, but sometime in the future he might need his arms and his legs for something. Better pay it.

"Brother," says Cucho, "do you mind if I ask you a question?"

"I didn't see any penalty," the referee says, "the little shit took a dive."

"You're kidding, he's got no knee left," replies Cucho.

"Nothing happened," says the referee, sniffling, "they pick up all this stuff watching too much TV."

"That wasn't my question," Cucho clarifies. "I know you can't back down. My question was were you in the Korean War?"

"Why?"

"Because I believe you're Atanasio García, and I think I saved your life."

113

"In Korea?"

"On the plane. You were about to fall and I reached out and grabbed you in the air. A little more and we were both goners."

"You're Ramiro Carranza?" he says, as if he were regressing to childhood.

"Such a long time ago, right? You save someone's life and then they disappear."

"No, don't say that," sobs the referee. "It's just that one thing and another comes along, you get married and the wife turns out to be no good, then your mom dies, and the kids leave, and you end up in the middle of a game just wanting to die."

"I'm sorry about your mom," says Cucho. "I know she was the apple of your eye."

"Really a great lady, wasn't she?"

"No, I mean I didn't know her, but you always talked about her, even in your sleep."

"Son-of-a-bitch referee!" shouts Peña, leader of the *Plays*, and then clowns around imitating some type of redneck fan. "Start the game, Pops."

"Out," yells the principal, the poor guy, who when he began used to insist that the boys had to be well treated, that, in fact, the school should become their second home, and rather than teaching they had to educate, but now, six years later, he's convinced you have to pick these spoiled little bastards up by the collar, shake them and force them onto their knees to beg forgiveness for how stupid they've become. "I don't want to see you again."

"So why don't you leave then?" Peña tells him.

The spectators give a collective "Oh" and then become quiet. The principal stares at the ground, at his untied shoe, and thinks to himself that he ought to go live in another country, or set up a business, and disappear, or become a spy for the guerrillas and begin by telling them that the Peña family has a splendid little airplane.

"Get going. Don't be insolent."

"And if I don't, what are you going to do?"

"Now, now, Peña," says the philosophy teacher. "You're not going to win any medals for being a smart-ass."

"And you, why don't you just shut up?" Peña tells him. "Isn't there some student you want to flirt with?"

A second collective "Oh". The rest of the *Plays* are beginning to have had it with Peña. He's no longer funny. Now he's just offensive. Poor Professor Londoño may be a little effeminate, and dress in tight jackets, but just because he invites students to join him for coffee at fashionable places, or brings them over at night to see his apartment, or asks them about private stuff, doesn't make him a fag. And even if he is, so what? Weren't Plato and Aristotle homosexuals? Didn't those Greeks run around half-naked, talking about whether we're more real than our own shadows?

"I'll expect you in my office the first thing Monday morning," states the principal. "If you don't show up, you can consider yourself expelled from the school."

If the game doesn't get started, if Cucho can't get the referee to get it going again, it's a sure thing that Peña, who at the moment is laughing at the principal's threats, and putting his forefinger in his mouth as if saying that he's going to throw up at any moment, is going to instigate a tragedy.

"Teach, did you know the ref before?" asks Chino Morales on the other side of the field.

"We knew each other during the war."

"The Korean War?"

"Korea, Chino, yeah, Korea, but now get going and get the team together. I've got something to talk over with the ref, with

115

Atanasio. Stir them up, get them in the right mood, remind them they're men."

"Right, Teach. Thanks," responds Chino and runs off, since for him, this is the World Cup, the opportunity of a lifetime. The referee, who's very sad, but no dummy, asks the linesman, with a symbolic gesture, to declare the first half over. And so he does. And the dismayed crowd of about two hundred people breaks up. And they're hungry.

"So, Atanasio, when did you get out of jail?" asks Cucho, in a matter-of-fact tone directed at the air around the referee. "Weren't you supposed to serve about thirty years?"

"I didn't lay a hand on that girl," replies the referee and he plants a kiss on a circle formed with his thumb and index finger. "As God is my witness."

"It's a shame *he* didn't testify at the trial, man," declares Cucho. "He could have saved you from jailtime, and you wouldn't have had to escape three months ago."

"What do you mean escape? I didn't do anything to that kid."

"O.K. Calm down, man. Lots of people have served time," states Cucho. Nothing that horrible had ever passed through his mind. "Take it easy; I'm not going to say anything, I know what these girls are like when they're in school. All I care about is that neither one of us loses his job."

The referee opens his eyes wide. He's not done anything bad, and he misses his mom. That's what goes through his mind.

"You know I've always been ready to save your life."

"I know, I know," wisely answers the referee. "Don't worry."

"It's a pleasure to see you, Atanasio."

"That goes for me too, Ramiro."

And Cucho doesn't turn to look at the referee even once as he walks over to where the team is, which at the moment is making fun of the speech, plagued with trite phrases that Chino

Morales has embarked on.

"O.K., O.K.," Cucho says as he takes a newspaper clipping out of the pocket of his plaid jacket with leather patches on the elbows. "Let's cut the bullshit and concentrate on playing a little football. I just don't know what's going on with you guys. Fuck! There's more guts in a frog's leg! Even I would be running circles around those little pricks."

"But Cucho, don't you see they're playing dirty? They put that fucker in defence and he almost killed me."

"Sure I know they're playing dirty, Delgado, sure, even your dad believed they had killed you, but I'll tell you one thing: here where you see me I worked in a garage, went to Korea, played with the lower division Santa Fe teams, had a restaurant and lost it, managed to produce a daughter, and it hurts me to piss, but at seventy-three I still get a hard-on when a girl goes by in a miniskirt, and I can still pass the ball and place the goals where the carpenter put his square (just where they're needed). And how old are you? Seventeen?"

"Seventeen."

"And kid, not a damned thing down there."

"I don't understand you, Cucho."

"You're acting like a little fag, Delgado, a little faggot. Can't get your breath? You want that windbag philosophy teacher to give you mouth-to-mouth?"

The team laughs. Cucho looks at them one by one, and thinks, with a touch of tenderness, that in the end they're like the fuckin' sons he never had. Delgado knows the coach didn't mean to offend him, and that what he's telling him is, in fact, that they all depend on him. That he has to play the game of his life and help save his job because neither his father nor the principal are ready to lose another game.

"But if we don't even have any proof that we exist," says

Delgado, "then why kill ourselves playing?"

"What?"

"Prove to me that we exist, Cucho. Give me proof that all this really is real, that we're not just a computer program, or a play put on by an evil god."

"Shit. This boy has gone crazy."

"You mean like in *The Matrix*?" asks Chino Morales. The others, naturally, have lost interest because, whether we exist or not, whether we're living in a game of PlayStation or not, the truth is that, over there, look at her, there comes a spectacular beauty.

"Exactly. Like in *The Matrix*."

"Did you see it, teach?"

"No, Chino, the last movie I saw was *El último cuplé.*"

"Cucho, do you mean that you've never thought all at once that everything is just a dream?"

"It's a nightmare. If it was a dream, we'd be winning."

"I mean it. There's no way to prove that all this isn't just fiction, and if it is, then everything depends on us wanting to play the game."

"But I think, I eat, I feel hunger," says Chino Morales. "That doesn't count for anything?"

"Nothing. Somebody's tricking us."

"But everything is meaningless."

"Everything."

"Everything's like a film."

"Or like a football game," says Cucho. "Like this one, and we're going to win; we're going to soak these shirts in sweat and sprint all the way up to the last line of defence."

"But if it's all just a game, we don't need to invent another one. Winning or losing, it's all the same."

"No, Chino, no. You have to win," replies Cucho. "Or is that

the way they made you? Huh? Are you cowards? Are you going
to come to me with foolish bullshit? You know what I have here?
In my hand? No?"

No, you don't know.

"This is my horoscope, the one for Leo. Want me to read it to
you? No? Yeah? You don't care? Well, it says 'you always think
about others, but today you need to come first, enjoy yourself
and take those trips you've put off. You'll be guided by your
intuition and make the changes it dictates, you'll relate to the
people you feel close to. Thanks to your intuition, an ear to the
ground, you'll find a sure way to invest your money. With your
intuition, shrewd like a fox, you could predict electoral results
or football games.' What kind of games, Chino?"

"Football, teach."

"Not hopscotch, basketball or tennis, right?"

"No, sir. Football."

"That's right. You've got an old fox here, older than the devil
and wiser. That's me. I exist, have heartburn all the time, and
I go, stand in line, pay the electric bill, which exists, and keeps
going up, so don't you come to me with it's all a trick of the
senses, because the trickster there is the government, and I
know that now is the moment, the only moment, that either we
win or we win, and if we don't, then you guys are going to lose
one of the best memories of your lives, and, as for me, I'll lose
the only job left for me. Delgado, we have to play the game,
where are your balls, get with it. You want to think nothing
exists? So think it, my boy, what difference does it make? It's
all the same. If all this is a game, a farce, you don't have to have
asthma; all you have to do is play, right?"

"But this is my last game," says Delgado.

"Whatever you say, kid, but get moving, for God's sake. Play
for that chick," he says, pointing to the woman passing by the

edge of the campus, "for that ass, that smile, do you have a girlfriend?"

"Sure, Cucho, sure. So what?"

"It's real important, kid. Is she in the stands?"

"Yes, sir," answers Chino Morales. "That's her."

"And don't you want to eat her up?"

"Yeah, sure, no, I wouldn't put it like that."

"What then? Do you want her to be yours?"

"Maybe, Cucho, I don't really care. It doesn't matter."

"It matters a lot, kid. If you don't want to play football because you don't see any meaning in anything, you can play because you're turning into a fag in the eyes of your dad and your girlfriend."

The players nod their heads in agreement, as if they were about to go into battle and the general had just yelled out a magnificent speech to stir them up, to make them mad, to fire them up. The referee, tired of it all, blows the whistle and points to the centre of the pitch to start the second half. Cucho looks at all of them and says, with a gesture, that his life depends on the next forty-five minutes.

"I'll see, Delgado, I'll see."

"Ready, Cucho," says Mateo Delgado, as he stands and does some stretching movements to recover his flexibility. "If we lose, I'll tell my dad it was my fault."

Cucho smiles. It reminds him of himself when he was that age. Irreverent, a skilled lefty, brash. Sometimes he wishes he were younger. To have the wisdom of age with the fire of youth. But no, not now, why, when he feels fine most of the time, seventy-three years old, still strong as a bull, and he mostly never regrets being old.

Chino Morales is nervous. He doesn't want to lose Cucho. He glances at him over there, with his tie loose, wiping his forehead with a striped handkerchief, breathing hard, picking at his nose a little, and he wants to be his assistant coach forever. That's his teacher. Nobody in that school had been able to motivate him like Cucho had.

So the second half of the game gets started. And the twenty-four year old guy, the defender on the other team, sticks to Delgado like a bodyguard, doesn't let him move, not even breathe or anything, and then Cucho shuts his eyes and devotes himself to listening to the insults from the stands, the principal's reproaches and Chino's shouts, which vaguely remind him of Robin's, Batman's sidekick, in that series from the 60s.

They're going to lose. Cucho opens his eyes and over there, to the right, a long pass, and the forward on the other team, running like crazy, is about to centre the ball, does it, then the twenty-four year old runs up and hits the ball so hard with his head that it seems as if he hit it with his foot, and the goalie, terrified, shuts his eyes, and it's a goal. My God, that leaves the score at one to nil, or better yet nil to one, and there's still a half hour left in the game. And it won't even do Cucho any good to tie. No, he can't. He has to win, because, otherwise, they'll be out of the tournament. The only time they're the home team. The competition they themselves organised.

Something's got to be done. He takes off his plaid jacket, hands it to Chino Morales, who carefully folds it and drapes it over his arm, like a mother in the 1950s, and he pulls the shirt out of his pants, and against the backdrop of laughter from the stands, the distress of the subs on the bench, and the disgust of the supporters of the other team, he starts to shout out every saying he knows.

"Stir it up," he yells to Delgado, "that way, that's it, that's it, go on, go on, no, no, not like that."

Delgado, closely watched by his father, and assaulted by the loud mouth of his girlfriend, asks God, if perchance He exists, if he's not just part of the farce, or if maybe He's the director, to take away his asthma, to let him run like a thief, a pickpocket, to give him legs to get away from this guy and from the one that's coming, and let him make the pass to Venegas, who's with him, but when his friend is about to kick the ball as hard as he can into the net, the same bruiser from before, veteran of a thousand battles, deliberately launches himself at Venegas' ankle.

It hurts the spectators more than the player. They shout like a Gregorian choir, and syllable by syllable, the word *bastard*. The principal, beside himself, tells Roberto Delgado, the president of the Board, that he can't believe it. Londoño, the philosophy teacher, is paralysed, as if he had been on the receiving end of that kick. Cucho spits a few inches from Chino Morales' shoe and rushes onto the pitch to defend his kids.

"I hope this penalty weighs on your conscience, ref," he shouts, "I hope you take it to your grave."

The referee signals to the penalty spot, turns around and winks at Cucho. He couldn't be more shameless, for sure, but that gesture, that thousandth of a second of his life, returns the coach's soul to his body.

Of course, now there's another problem. Not just one, but two. First of all, Venegas is in so much pain he can't get up and a bunch of the subs led by Chino Morales, grab him, pull him up, while he's telling God that it's not, it's not fair, that now he won't even be able to go to the movies at the Andino, nor rafting nor anything else.

"What a motherfucker!" he cries. "What a chicken shit, faggot, cocksucker!"

And then, the philosophy teacher, Londoño, has come down onto the pitch and is talking with Delgado and is surely filling the poor kid's head with more nonsense. He doesn't like that friendship one bit. If he had told one of his teachers in high school that the world was a farce or that everything was meaningless, for sure they would have given him a good slap in the face.

"Delgado, get yourself out on the pitch to take that penalty," Cucho shouts to him.

"Yeah, Delgado," yells Peña, the king of the *Plays*, as loud as he can. "Don't be 'promiscuous'."

The *Plays* laugh, although it looks like they didn't really know what "promiscuous" means, but Londoño, the teacher, can't take any more and heads for the stands, like an assassin.

"Why don't you hold hands, you shameless fags, now you can even adopt kids."

"Shut up, Peña, not another word," warns the principal.

"Yeah, shut up," yells one mutineer.

And there goes Londoño, ready to give him what he deserves. He won't stand for any more rumours that he's a homosexual. He's thirty-five years old now, and that sort of thing shouldn't bother him, but it irritates him that the students laugh behind his back, that they make fun of him in the yearbooks, that they won't leave him in peace to wear the jackets and shirts that he likes and the bracelets he brought from the Sierra Nevada. If they only knew. If they only knew.

"What? You gonna hit me?" Peña tells him. "What a big man!"

"Come on, come on, let's see if you're so macho," says the philosophy teacher.

"I'm macho, all right. Not like some others."

And everybody in the stands is stunned. The principal is about to get in the middle of things, but Roberto Delgado, president of the Board, takes him by the arm and suggests with a glance that it's not a good idea for him to interfere, that maybe it's better to just let the fight happen.

With his eyes closed, Peña launches a fist with his thumb tucked inside and against the teacher's shoulder, breaking his thumb as a result. Londoño twists his arm and forces him to his knees. Then he kicks him in the stomach.

"So, who's the fag? Who?"

"You are."

"Who?"

"Me, me, me."

Londoño releases him, and Peña, like Chuckie, the devilish doll, who turns and turns and neither gives up nor lets himself be done in for anything in the world, hurls himself against the teacher's back and rams a knee into his shoulder blade. Londoño, badly hurt, turns, butts him with his head and spits on him. And Peña, who sees the teacher as a monster, a man who has turned into the Incredible Hulk, the green man, covers his face as if a ball was about to hit him.

"Get going," says Londoño. "Out of here."

Peña looks at the principal, at the stands, at anybody, but nobody responds to him. He decides it's better to leave before he bursts out crying.

"I'll see you in my office on Monday," the principal states.

"Expect me, my parents and my lawyers."

"Come with whomever you want, but be there."

All at once Cucho remembers that there's a game. And he's got to send in someone to replace Venegas. The problem is that not one of those on the bench has boots, and that the injured party, Venegas, has tiny feet. Who could play? Who?

"Teach, we can beat them with ten," says Chino Morales.

And just like in the comics, the light goes on over Cucho's head: his assistant's feet are small.

"Chino, try on Venegas' shoes."

"No way, teach, they're disgusting."

"You don't want to play? You don't want the team to win?"

"Yeah, but I don't play very well."

"Don't be a sissy, Chino. Get over there and leave them in the dust, try on the shoes and make us a goal."

Chino gets goosebumps. The statement "get over there and leave them in the dust" will go down in history as the one that gave him the strength to overcome himself. That's the battle. He nods his head "yes," takes off his terry cloth sweat-shirt, and the subs discover that Morales, the assistant coach, always wears a kit under his clothes. Like a superhero. Ready to serve.

He measures the shoes, and, like a modern-day Cinderella, discovers that they're exactly his size. Yes, they're sweaty. Naturally they smell. But they're going to take them to a victory.

Delgado takes the penalty. And, although the goalie hurls himself in the same direction the ball is coming from, it's a goal, the spectators hug each other, and Cucho can breathe again. There are still twenty minutes to get another goal and move ahead to the second round.

Chino Morales keeps it simple, making fast passes, thinking about solutions before confronting problems. He wants Delgado to be the star of the team, and therefore always passes the ball to him. But the game is getting complicated, and the players on the other team are constantly sending the ball in any direction possible to kill time.

And time is running out. The linesman yells to the referee that time is running out. And the referee, Atanasio, the ex-convict, the fugitive, feels like everything is going to hell. And Cucho already sees himself back in the hardware store behind the counter, putting up with his dickhead brother-in-law's sarcastic remarks. And Londoño is seeing a future ahead of him far from any school, far from everything. And the principal is now expecting the Peña's lawsuit, a reprimand from the Board and a lack of respect from the students.

And the team tries and tries, but there are only five minutes left, and nobody even dares watch the field. And when everything is about to end, Chino Morales passes the ball to Delgado and Delgado returns it to him, and then Chino confronts the twenty-four year-old sweeper, face to face, and even though no one would give a nickel for him, Chino manages to nutmeg the defender and take on the goalie all alone.

Delgado comes in from the right, marked by two, or three defenders, half-dead from asthma, and Chino pretends he's going to pass to him, so they all turn in that direction and that allows him to go the other way, catching the goalie off guard, and he fires away at the net with all his strength. Goal.

The referee raises both arms as if the war had ended. It doesn't matter to him that they realise he's happy. He's been saved from jail. And he hasn't had to blow the whistle for another penalty or anything or even add ten minutes of injury time. He celebrates that goal like he did when he was young and still happy watching football games. That two-to-one has totally rejuvenated him.

Everybody hugs everybody else. Everybody. As if calling warriors to battle, the band plays a *pasodoble*, the spectators clap their hands and the principal and Dr Delgado shake hands. Chino Morales, for the first time in his life, hugs his teammates, and now he has a story to tell at home and a way to introduce himself to the schoolgirls and an excuse to offer for his poor grades. He runs around the pitch and lifts up the striped shirt of his kit so the cameras, that don't really exist, can see the sign he wrote with a marker on his flannel undershirt: "God is our schoolmate," it reads.

The supporters of the other team have turned into statues.

The veteran defender, exhausted, takes out a cigarette and smokes it in honour of the defeat. Professor Londoño waves goodbye to Delgado from afar. And slowly walks away forever from the Retiro School, the last school of his life. And even though that image is really sad, because it leaves us wondering what the supposed philosopher is really feeling, what kind of relationship there was between himself and the star of the team, on the other hand, Cucho, as happy as can be, with tears in his eyes, thinking that that reason, that kind of emotion, is why he loves football.

"Now nobody can stop us," he tells the reserves. "I only ask to be able to give the first kiss to the trophy."

He puts on his plaid jacket. Tucks in his shirt. Tightens his tie. And, slowly, exits the scene.

Interview with Ricardo Silva Romero

What role did football play in your youth?
First of all, football, for me, was a way to stand out: since I played well in elementary school, and was a good forward who kicked the ball with my left foot, I was important to the class. Later, during adolescence, I used football to limit the topics of conversation to one that everybody was interested in (the World Cups, the Colombian league championships) and at the same time to avoid any confessions about my life and way of being, which has always been somewhat eccentric. Football and movies have been my passions, my parentheses. It's always brought me happiness and relief.

Do you support a particular team?
I'm a Millonarios fan. Only Millonarios. It's the Bogotá team that my dad and my brother taught me to love. Of course, I like it when the Colombian team wins. And, as proof of how strange football can be, I support Germany in all the World Cup games.

Which is more important to you as a fan, a good result or a good game?
That's a difficult question. But I'm afraid that being a fan means to completely lack any capacity for self-criticism. Supporting a team is irrational, crazy. So I think the answer is that what interests me, as a fan, is that my team win.

Do you see any connection between the creative process and the way in which someone plays football or behaves as a fan?
In football I see a structure similar to that of a play. A structure

against time, which is the essence of suspense: there are 50 minutes left, 30, 20, 10… And I see a question, who's going to win?, that moves the story along as happens in any story. Telling a story is being coach, player and fan all at the same time. Planning, setting the scene and enduring the tale at the same time.

What motivates you to write fiction that takes place within a Colombian context?

It seems to me that it's more interesting for everybody. On the one hand, it's what I know best: what's happening in Colombia. On the other hand, although I don't feel obligated to narrate a Colombian experience and I believe that interesting things are always revealed when a foreigner writes about a country he can't know completely, in my opinion it's better for the readers: as for me, if I were Swedish, I'd like a Colombian first of all to tell me good stories, well written, and second, stories about Colombia, stories I don't know in a language in which I've never thought.

How do football and politics intersect in Colombia?

That's a complex topic. Semester-long courses are dedicated to it. But, in summary, football has been used in Colombia to create a nation (so that in any part of the country we feel like we're part of a project, part of the same project) and it's been used by politicians to put off the urgently needed solutions to our society's problems. Football has always been a good test of what's happening in Colombia: yesterday, in the times of Pablo Escobar, it showed how society was shaken up and redrawn by druglords, and today, it demonstrates the pace at which we have been living so that the rights of Colombians aren't buried under the resurgence of the worst of the political right.

Your novel Autogol fictionalises the death of Andrés Escobar. How would you describe the impact of this tragic chapter in history on Colombian society?

I believe that it was the end of the craziest period in Colombia's recent history. The period when Pablo Escobar tried to rule but ended up dying the way he lived. The period when Andrés Escobar wanted to play football, but ended up executed by the bookmakers and the *mafiosos* because, yes, he made a mistake and so what. I think that for many, myself included, it was the first time that we felt ashamed of being Colombian. You don't feel either proud or ashamed of being from your country, but that day, yes, that time, yes: how do you explain to the world inhabited by the same species from one end to the other, that in this corner of the planet we kill players for committing an own-goal? To what extent can we take on this tragedy, or tell about it? It was horrible that they killed Andrés Escobar, a stain on a stained history, but we have to live telling it.

Do you see any lingering reluctance to incorporating football or sports as a dominant theme or plot driver among your generation of authors?

I don't see resistance, but I don't see interest either. There are some who do it and those who have done it, in any case, especially in the area of children's literature. But I don't believe that many are interested in doing it. What does this say about football and about literature? Perhaps that they're too similar, I don't know.

How would you describe the impact in Latin America of Brazil having hosted the World Cup in 2014?

I believe that it was very important: every country from Brazil to Chile, from Colombia to Argentina, was going through a political crisis worthy of study. Well, in Latin America it tends to be like that. But I mean that the citizens of all the countries took the World Cup as a way to reaffirm their nationality, to see it as meaningful. Brazil, on the edge as a society, received that 7-1 score like a bucket of ice water, like a wake-up call, to which it still hasn't been able to respond. Colombia, on the precipice of elections, which could have returned the recalcitrant right to power, had a tremendous participation in the World Cup, which returned a kind of unity to the people who tend to hate themselves if they don't find a good pretext for it. It was, in short, an important and telling World Cup.

How do you view the recent developments in the scandal surrounding corruption in FIFA?

That it was just a matter of time that someone would dare to investigate the shady dealings that the bosses of football have been conducting in the sport and the business. Football, as a business, is a lot like the mafia, like "family" in quotation marks. It's a secret out loud. And investigating it and finding proof can return a certain illusion to the fans, a kind of relief at the moment of going to the games of their favourite teams. Now the only voice missing is the Vatican.

Is there a particular identity or style associated with football in Colombia?

There's a beautiful kind of game, which comes from nostalgia for Brazil in its better times, that's still what Colombian teams are looking for. But now, in these years, as has been happening with so many teams around the world, it's being mixed up with the need for results, with commercial success, which is today's reality, and it's been losing a lot of its personality.

What is the place of football fiction in the literature of your country?

I believe it's a subgenre. And I think it's been growing so much that now theses have been written and anthologies of football stories published. As in every country, it's a very individualised fiction. And I believe that many marvellous football stories are lost, lost to the reader, I mean, because people tend to think (as happens with children's stories) that they're only for a certain kind of reader. I repeat: football fiction is a compassionate and humour-filled way to summarise what is happening in the world.

Ecuador
JOSÉ HIDALGO PALLARES

José Hidalgo Pallares was born in Quito, Ecuador in 1980. He is the author of two volumes of short stories, *La vida oscura* (El Conejo, 2003) and *Historias cercanas* (El Conejo, 2005, Joaquín Gallegos Lara Prize) and of the novels *Sábados de fútbol* (Paradiso, 2007) and *La búsqueda* (Paradiso, 2013). His work has been included in *Quince golpes en la cabeza* (Editorial Cajachina, 2008), an anthology of new Latin American writers, as well as in other anthologies published in Ecuador and in other countries. Currently he lives in Buenos Aires and writes for the newspaper *La Nación* in that city. He's a fan of the Deportivo Quito team, watches their games on the internet but, out of superstition, he does it wearing a blue and scarlet jersey. An earlier version of "The Idol" (El Ídolo) first appeared in Spanish in the anthology *Cuentos de fútbol*, published in 2011 by the "Quito Reads" program of the municipality of Quito.

The Idol

It's almost certain that the press and the general public will end up forgetting him, like everyone else (not us, until the last one of us dies, there'll be somebody who'll remember him). But it's also possible that some visionary will begin to put him up as an example of patience and tenacity, even of the power to overcome. Could be. After all, never before in all the history of football, and I'm not just talking about national football, has there been a player as cursed by the fans (the rival fans and, often enough, his own), as sneered at and as trashed. So much so that he started to arouse pity, a not very frequent sentiment in a stadium, where you can feel anger, hatred, euphoria, grief, desperation, but pity, hardly ever, unless it's for yourself, for having chosen the wrong team.

I don't think I'm exaggerating when I say we were the most hostile, or to be more precise, the most hurtful. We made fun of him, setting his nerves on end, inciting him to commit fouls became a true pleasure, one of the few sources of happiness that we could experience, being, as we were, fans of a team in the middle of the league standings or lower. Those jokes were our way of venting for the way the fans of the other teams (not all of them, there was always some little rural team that had recently climbed up in the league standings that we could look down on) made fun of us. They had good reasons: the Rumiñahui team, our beloved "Black and Yellow", besides being the team that drew the smallest public in the country, year after year dashed our renewed hope of achieving something half-way important (even though in our chants we pleaded for them to pull off a championship title, we would have been satisfied if we had classified for any tournament on the continent). But we fans – a thousand, fifteen hundred, two thousand at the most –went on being there every Sunday, with our patched up drums and our faded black and yellow banners, jumping up and down and cheering until we were hoarse; and that untiring spirit, that inexplicable loyalty was, at the same time, our principal source of pride (not to say the only one), our major argument against the fans of the winning teams, who we liked to call posers, because they only filled the stadium for the important games. And that's the way it was with him, Edwin Arnulfo Guerra, Sunday after Sunday, he received the no less inexplicable confidence of his coach (who, according to the rumours, he was screwing) and leaped onto the pitch as a starter, only to receive a wave of insults and mockery from the stands and to make the hairs of his fans and of the players on his own team stand on end every time the ball rolled into his box.

To be frank, even in his worst moments, no one dared say that he was a terrible goalie, you couldn't even call him bad. In fact, his reflexes were great and several times he stopped sure-fire goals. His problem was that every once in a while, a lot more often than you could consider acceptable for a professional goalie, something short-circuited in his brain and he allowed goals (or put them in himself) that were way more than just ridiculous. Of these absurd plays, also known as "Arnulfisms", the ones that I remember best are two: the one scored from goal to goal that our pathetic goalie scored on him one rainy afternoon at the end of September (that was the first time the name of our beloved Rumiñahui appeared on international sports pages) and the other one, while playing against a team from Manabí, when a teammate sent him a sloppy pass backward and he, to avoid a corner shot, ran after the ball so clumsily or with such bad luck that when he stepped on it he fell head-first against one of the advertisements near the backline, "while the ball made a whimsical journey to later slowly cross the goal line," as expressed by one of our flowery football commentators. Videos of both goals went round the world, either on sports reports, comedy programs or on YouTube, where a Uruguayan, whose national squad would be facing ours in a few days, wrote: "PLEASE INCLUDE THIS ANIMAL IN SUNDAY'S GAME!!!!!!". Obviously, the Uruguayan's request was not honoured, but Guerra's name became even more famous than that of the top goalie on the "Tricolour" team and of every other Ecuadorian sportsperson, including the winner of two Olympic gold medals and three-time world champion, Jefferson Pérez.

When the storied coach of his team, after not having fulfilled his goal of classifying for the Copa Libertadores, handed in his resignation, we all took it for a given that Guerra's career had reached its end, that no other coach would have the confidence or the affection or whatever it was, to keep him on the team. Ironically, if anyone lamented that situation (although perhaps the word lament is excessive), it was us, since between making fun of him time after time, we had come to feel a kind of gratitude toward Guerra, for having delivered those great moments that our own players couldn't give us.

Nevertheless, that kind of gratitude didn't mollify our indignation when, with less than a month to go before the start of the new season, the management of our team announced with great fanfare that they had signed Guerra to a contract for the next two seasons. *"The Club Atlético Rumiñahui Football Board,"* said the official communiqué, *"is pleased to notify its loyal fans that we have reached an agreement with the experienced goalie, Edwin Araulfo Guerra, whose integration into our glorious institution was sought by the coach, Gastón de Santis, himself."* At least the use of "experienced" was beyond any argument, since at that time Guerra was nearing the age of 38. Even so, the decision was not well received by the fervent Rumiñahui fans. The opinion page of the official website of our team, generally used to unload the oft-repeated frustrations of the previous weekend, to underscore the coach's mistakes in making substitutions or in the starting line-up or for how the trips were coordinated when the team played outside Quito, had never received such high volume of comments. These ranged from the astonished but still respectful "ARE THEY CRAZY???????? WHY DON'T WE LEAVE THE GOAL EMPTY ONCE AND FOR ALL?????????", to the ardently fired up "YOU'RE ALL A BUNCH OF IDIOT SONS OF FUCKIN' BITCHES, FROM THAT NUT-CASE RODRIGUES [(Vicente Rodríguez, our team's president at that time)] TO THAT FAG DE SANTIS, WHO CAN ONLY WANT THAT ANIMAL GUERRA TO FUCK HIS ASS". The two or three fans who were imprudent enough to defend the contract received every kind of insult imaginable; one of them who stuck to his position was even warned it would be better for him not to show up at the stadium again. Despite the protests, the contract had been signed and, for our part, nothing could be done about it, except to stand up like men to the charges of the fans of the other teams, who now had yet another reason to make fun of us.

In the first game of the season (in which we were accustomed to chanting the names of our new reinforcements to see if that way they would fall in love with the jersey they were wearing and would play with a little more commitment than could be expected in exchange for their modest salary), Guerra, whose name we apparently did not mention, was doing all right. Nevertheless, the first "Arnulfism" (which, fortunately, did not end up in the goal) caused a stream of jeers and insults of the nastiest kind; it was as if a good part of our fans had no idea that Guerra now played for the Rumiñahui and that our obligation, however much it cost us, was to support him. The hostility continued through three or four more games, in which Guerra showed himself to be visibly nervous. From then on, his usual errors (fake goal kicks, rebounds inside the box, weak blocks) became more and more sporadic. In the eighth game of the season, a really memorable game, the aversion for Guerra began to turn into romance: our "padlock" as we started to call him after that saved two penalties against our traditional rival, which allowed us to win the classic for the first time in five and a half years and, above all, we took control of the first position in the league standings, a truly memorable achievement for our modest institution.

The rest of the first phase of the season seemed like a long dream: we defeated the three most popular teams in Quito (even thrashed one of them); we tied as visitors with the two powerhouses of Guayaquil and we took pleasure destroying provincial teams in their own stadiums, and several of them had owned us until then. After several weeks of scepticism, the sports press began to put the spotlight on our team. ***The yellow and black miracle*** was the title of one special report in *El Metropolitano* on June 26, 2005, the first paragraph of which I reproduce below:

With the first phase in the Ecuadorian football championship behind us, the humble Rumiñahui team is at the top of the league standings, accumulating 43 of the 66 possible points. The architect of this miracle, the Argentine coach, Gastón De Santis, points out that the results are due to his players' humility and to the team's unity. "The guys have understood what I've been trying to communicate to them in practices and have played each game as if it were the last, they deserve all the credit," insists the gaucho coach. For his part, leading goal scorer, Christopher Chalá, who has made nine goals so far this season, affirms that the support of the fans has been fundamental throughout the campaign, a historical one for one of the capital's oldest teams.

The delays in the payment of salary to the players and the arrest of our central defender, Jacob Ayoví, accused of running over a pedestrian for driving while intoxicated, made the second phase of the season seem a little more like what we were used to. Even so, the first place reached during the previous phase assured us of a place in the playoffs, for which, with the help of raffles, fan clubs and personal contributions, we had raised almost $20,000, which would cover the salaries of the team members and the coaching staff for a month.

If in the first two phases of the season Guerra's ability as goalie had allowed him to gain our esteem and respect, his performance in the playoffs unquestionably consolidated his reputation as an idol. Playing against our most difficult rivals, the ones that could steal our dream of being champions, he saved penalties and open-pitch "one-on-ones" and his extraordinary ability to feign injuries and kill time when the adversary had us trapped gave our defence a breather, and the players on the other team lost patience and got yellow and red cards. Our fans started to hang banners with his image on the fence that separated the stands from the field, and someone wrote on a yellow and black striped banner in fancy medieval calligraphy a rhymed acrostic intended to show the adoration (that's all it can be called) that we had begun to feel for our new hero:

Goalie
Universal

Ecuadorian
Raider
Rumiñahui
Applauds you

Even rival fans started to look upon him with a certain amount of admiration: it's not that they stopped insulting him, but when one of our defenders passed the ball back to him, you no longer heard that humiliating murmur "gooooaaaaal", that we ourselves had started in his lowest moments, to make him nervous. For his part, he pretended to preserve his simplicity. Before beginning every game, when we were chanting his name, he would just raise his right hand in our direction and keep on walking toward the goal, with his head down and his gaze fixed on the turf.

Right after the next to the last round of the playoffs, Rumiñahui was first in the standings, with 19 points (the result of five wins and four ties) and a goal differential of +7. Our hosts, the Guayaquil Sports Club, which –the whims of destiny – would face us in the last game, had 16 points and a +2 goal differential. To deprive us of the championship, therefore, not only would they have to win, but give us a thrashing, which in a regular season game, to be honest, would not have surprised anybody, even less considering that the game would be played in Guayaquil.

Although in the interviews and press releases prior to the grand finale (which the press, always so imaginative, baptised as "the battle of David and Goliath") our players proved to be cautious and chose not to speak of celebrations or victory laps; we were confident. After all, we had played nine games without losing and in the entire playoffs they had only gotten four goals on us; that is fewer than half a goal per game. Since there was no other way, we organised a caravan of thirty buses to cheer on Rumiñahui in the most important game of its history. The tour, subsidised in part by the management, cost $20 dollars per person and included round-trip transportation (leaving at 10:00 pm on Saturday and returning on Sunday at 7:00 pm, after the game and the lap of honour, general admissions ticket and two meals consisting of a tuna sandwich and a glass of soda or juice). The wealthier would go in private cars or directly on the plane with the team. We had a banner made, measuring 19'×32' for the occasion, the biggest one we'd ever had, with the inspiring slogan "Thanks for this Christmas" and we collected eight bags of confetti; besides which, we'd be carrying forty small banners, twenty sparklers and our eternal and much mended bass drum, which we pounded on by turns, with a half-full bottle of water.

I can still remember the days prior to the game: my anxiety didn't let me sleep at night and during the work days (not so busy since it was December) I read the team publication and the newspapers to see if there was anything new on our team or on the rival team (injuries, suspensions, arrests for drunk driving); I was so nervous I lost my appetite and there were many times when I had to pinch myself to be sure I wasn't dreaming. It's that getting to see the Rumiñahui as champions was something that not even the most optimistic among us could have imagined.

The longed-for day finally arrived. Except for a blown out tyre on one of the buses in the caravan, the trip to Guayaquil was uneventful; it even seemed shorter than at other times (no doubt because we were all drunk). We didn't even have any problems during the much-feared arrival at the stadium, where we expected to be greeted with a shower of insults and stones. In fact, what bothered us most was how little importance the rival fans gave our arrival. It was as if, being so few, we weren't even worthy of insults. Once in the stadium we had to wait more than three hours until the beginning of the game; under a merciless sun, we begged for a little water to survive the hangover and we recriminated each other for spending the little money we had to buy a case of anise-flavoured liqueur. But when the zero hour arrived, we put all our discomfort aside and joined together in a single chant. Even now, when I see the videos of that afternoon on YouTube, I get goosebumps.

From the opening whistle, the game was what we expected: Guayaquil attacking with everything they had, keeping us in our half of the field, and our guys putting up a defence with more heart than order. Even so, we managed to start a couple counter-attacks that were, lamentably, unsuccessful. At the end of the first period, the score was still nil to nil, which, for us, was enough to earn us the champion's crown. At the start of the second period the Guayaquil players maintained their strategy, but after the first fifteen minutes, they all became desperate and started to take long shots that our defence blocked with confidence. Only then, from the suites and boxes did some projectiles start to fall on us (half-eaten sandwiches, empty bottles or bottles containing something we preferred not to know what, and even a practically new shoe), all of which encouraged us even more to keep on chanting. It was incredible: numbering barely a thousand, we had silenced more than eighty thousand people. But after thirty-two minutes, when the situation seemed to be under control, "*A stupid move in the back line of the yellow and black team*" (so said the report in the next day's edition of *El Metropolitano*) "*made it possible for Crespo to confront the goalie Guerra one-on-one and subtly finish the goal at the left post, raising the hopes of the until-then-drowsy fans of the coastal team. Five minutes later, Jiménez tried a shot from outside the box, which didn't seem to represent a problem. Nevertheless, Guerra couldn't control it, and Antonini took advantage of the rebound causing a frenzy among the local fans."*

Even though at that time our obligation as fans was to go on cheering on our team, our nerves kept us from it: one more goal would leave us without the championship. Chewing our nails, looking at our watches every two seconds, we prayed that the game would end and, above all, that Guerra wouldn't commit another "Arnulfism", those gross errors that, thanks to his good season, we had managed to forget.

And he didn't do it. Because what he did can't be qualified as an "Arnulfism", it was something far worse.

Playing in the extra minutes (here I'm copying the version in *El Metropolitano*, because I don't consider myself capable of telling what happened without getting carried away with emotion and letting out some insults that might wound someone's sensibilities), *a desperate Antonini tried a shot on goal, but in his eagerness put everything he had into the shot, he also kicked the turf, spraining his ankle, according to later statements by the club physician. The ball continued slowly on its way toward the goal. Guerra seemed to have the situation under control. Nevertheless, to the surprise of his own team and everyone else, the yellow and black goalie took a step to the side, allowing the sphere to cross the goal line.*

What the newspaper doesn't say, perhaps because they couldn't find an elegant way to say it, is that after the goal and the almost immediate whistle ending the game, Guerra turned towards us and, with a smile painted across his face, grabbed his balls, with both hands, as if to leave no doubt about what he wanted to say to us. The only reaction we could come up with was to begin cursing him, swearing revenge, throwing out insults with a rage that at times was transformed into nausea. One of us tried to jump onto the pitch to redeem our team's honour, even if it were by delivering kicks, but the police stopped him and put him under arrest (along with dozens of Guayaquil fans, who had also invaded the field, but in their case it was to hug their players and to try to snatch some piece of their kits). When Guerra had disappeared from our view, I turned to look at the stands and the scene I beheld was simply heartbreaking: children, youth and adults were crying inconsolably, their heads between their hands; others were still cursing, I don't know whom, their faces distorted by hate; and a few were fighting with the police or with Guayaquil fans, trying to make up for the biggest frustration we had lived through in our already frustrating lives as Rumiñahui fans. I, who had pinched myself again, but this time to be sure it wasn't just a nightmare, knew that that was the last time I would go to the stadium, because the grief I was feeling at that moment (and the remnants of which are still present today) was far more than any person is prepared to suffer for a football team. The next year, reading the sports pages, I realised I had not been the only one who made that decision and that the Rumiñahui team, with their unsponsored jersey and their now much reduced and disgraced fan base, would soon disappear. I wasn't wrong: in that season they dropped down to the first division B league and in the next to the second division. Not long ago someone told me that there's a team called Rumiñahui that wears a jersey with yellow and black stripes in the Sangolqui neighbourhood league.

We've never heard anything about Guerra since. Several newspapers, TV channels and radio stations searched for him assiduously for an interview, but none of them could find him. Everybody presumes that after the game he left the stadium, as if he were just another fan, grabbed a taxi and went to some acquaintance's house to hide. Anyway, he didn't show up in the team locker room, where De Santis and his teammates were waiting to massacre him. Some say he went to live in Spain and established a restaurant that served Ecuadorian food that allows him to live comfortably. Others say that with the money the Guayaquil management paid him to let them make the three goals he has enough to spend the rest of his life scratching his balls. I don't believe they paid him off. It's perfectly clear to me that everything he did was done to take revenge on us, for all those years when we cursed him. And in order to do that it wasn't enough to allow goals in some little game of no importance; he had to let us build up our illusions, climb up to the clouds so that our fall would hurt more, although to do that for a year he had to wear a jersey for which he no doubt felt a hatred like we now feel for him. Looking at it that way, it's not so wild to think of him as an example of tenacity or victory. Yes, the son of a bitch won and, above all, he defeated *us*. A real thrashing.

Interview with José Hidalgo Pallares

What role did football play in your youth?

I always liked to play football, to go to the stadium and to see games on television. Like many Ecuadorians, when I was a child I dreamed of being a football player, unfortunately my aptitude for the game precluded it. Anyway, football was important as a recreation, as a connection with my friends and with my brother and, often, as a cause of suffering from my team's poor results.

Do you support a particular team?

Yes, I've been a fan of the Deportivo Quito since I was six years old, but I saw them win a championship only recently when I was twenty-eight. Throughout all those years we had almost achieved it several times, but in the end something always happened. In 2008, when finally – after 40 years without a title – Quito won the championship once again, it was like a dream. My wife gets annoyed when I say that that was the happiest day of my life.

When I'm in Quito, I try to go to the stadium every weekend and when I'm out of the country I watch the games on the Internet.

How do football and politics intersect in Ecuador?

Currently in Ecuador, as also occurs in other Latin American countries like Argentina or Venezuela, politics stirs up lots of passion. You're either for or against the government with almost the same fervour that you're a fan of one or another team. Beyond that, in Ecuador the governments usually take advantage when the national team has good results in order to promote themselves.

What are your views on the current state of freedom of the press in Ecuador?

Ever since the beginning of President Correa's administration the media and independent journalists have experienced pressures and attacks (verbal and even physical). The situation has been getting worse with the passage of time, despite the fact that the government has newspapers, TV channels and radio stations under its control. The institutions created by the regime to control the press seem to be more and more intolerant of any news and investigations that affect the government. It's common in Ecuador for high public officials to demand their "right to respond" to news and even opinions that they don't like.

How would you describe the impact in Latin America of Brazil having hosted the World Cup in 2014?

I believe it was a special World Cup, not just for Latin Americans but for all lovers of football in general. Having it in a country with a tradition of football adds something special to the World Cup. Anyway, for Latin Americans it was even more special because many could travel to Brazil to cheer on their respective national teams, which raised the expectations of achieving something important. I was still living in Argentina during the World Cup and the mood and atmosphere lifted more and more as the team advanced. Unfortunately it didn't end well. As far as Ecuador is concerned, its participation was a disappointment because the teams in the group stage were beatable.

Is there a particular identity or style associated with football in Ecuador?

No, Ecuador has no equivalent to the *jogo bonito* of Brazil or the Italian *catenaccio*. For now, the national team is trying to demonstrate a fast game in Quito and well-organised play when the games are outside the country, but our major weakness is still the lack of goals.

What is your evaluation of the Ecuadorian national team's performance in the 2015 Copa América?

Another disappointment. Frankly, a real failure. We were the worst South American team in the competition, which places the strength of the Ecuadorian team in doubt when it plays outside the country.

How do you view the recent developments in the scandal surrounding corruption in FIFA?

I believe that the judicial procedure initiated by the justice system in the United States and the arrest of high-ranking officials in world football revealed something that many already suspected: corruption in the negotiations for TV rights and in the designation of host countries for the World Cup. This is all a consequence of FIFA's policy of managing football more and more like a business and not as a sport. I ask myself how many of FIFA's high-ranking officials as well as those in the national and regional federations have ever played football or gone to a stadium as fans. I hope that the process moves forward and that the judicial systems of every country where corruption is suspected will do their part.

Did any writer of football fiction influence this story?

I don't know if Roberto Fontanarrosa influenced the style of this story, because he's not one of my favourite authors, but I would like a football fan to react to my text the same way I felt when I read "19 de diciembre de 1971" ("December 19th, 1971") by Fontanarrosa, which is the best football story I've read.

What is the place of football fiction in the literature of your country?
As in all Latin America, in Ecuador there are short stories and novels that have football as a major theme, but those texts don't occupy a central place in Ecuadorian literature. The great points of reference are still authors like Pablo Palacio or José de la Cuadra.

Do you see any lingering reluctance to incorporating football or sport as a dominant theme or plot driver among your generation of authors?
I believe that many authors of my generation see football or sports in general as a minor theme that cannot lead to a relevant literary work. That's probably due also to the fact that many stories or novels about sports treat the characters' conflicts so superficially and unrealistically. In that sense, I believe that novels like *The Art of Fielding*, by Chad Harbach, underscore the path that any literary work that centres on sport should take.

Mexico
JUAN VILLORO

Juan Villoro was born on September 24, 1956 in Mexico City. He has a degree in Sociology from the Universidad Autónoma Metropolitana, Unidad Iztapalapa. He is the author of several volumes of short stories: *La noche navegable* (Joaquín Mortiz, 1980), *Albercas* (Joaquín Mortiz, 1985), *La casa pierde* (Alfaguara, 1999) and *Los culpables* (Almadía, 2007). His novels are *El disparo de Argón* (Alfaguara, 1991), *Materia dispuesta* (Alfaguara, 1997), *El testigo* (Anagrama, 2004, Heralde Prize), *Llamadas de Amsterdam* (Interzona, 2007), and *Arrecife* (Anagrama, 2012). He has also written plays, essays, children's literature and football-themed *crónicas*, including *Los once de la tribu* (Aguilar, 1995) and *Balón dividido* (Planeta, 2014), as well as the football-themed essay *Dios es redondo* (Planeta, 2006). He has been a professor at the Universidad Nacional Autónoma de México and a guest professor at Yale, Princeton and Boston Universities. He loves football and is a fan of the Barça team. "Ghost on the Edge" (El extremo fantasma) first appeared in Spanish in *La casa pierde* (Alfaguara, 1999).

The Ghost on the Edge

"The only thing real here is this heat," – Uribe shoved the envelope across the desk. "You were way too ambitious; you were fuckin' dreaming," his asthmatic voice was just one more thing that made a person want to leave the room: the mouldy wall, his dirty shirt, the cigar stump and the ashes that were starting to smell like something else in this courtyard where the absurd Rayados team logo stood out.

Hours later Irigoyen was walking toward the dock. His suitcase was so heavy it felt like he was lugging a body to toss into the sea. For some reason the idea of a man's slashed cadaver (whether a 175-lb. defender or Uribe's 265 lbs.) entertained him until he reached the shore. The calm waters of the river, mud-coloured even in the moonlight, emptied into the equally tranquil sea. In the distance he could see gas flares from the petroleum platforms as well as the red lights of a passing tanker. Irigoyen turned to the right: it was like tossing down the last swig of a drink that made a man forget all of the previous ones and diverted them toward some chosen tragedy. He saw the tiered silhouette of the stadium, *Vasco,* Uribe's powerful delirium.

The moon disappeared for a moment, hiding the road that descended among brush and Sunday's trash. Irigoyen sat down on top of his suitcase. He breathed in the night air, a heavy odour of distant gasoline and decaying shore plants.

He was carrying all the weight on his right side, and his ankle was starting to bother him. He would have liked to get rid of that tingling sensation, to erase it the way he had erased that memory from his youth (the time spent with a woman who had spread her legs for him in exchange for a few pesos). That's the way it always was with injuries; they showed up again whenever they felt like it. He saw himself at age fourteen, his nose broken by a blow from a right-winger's elbow, in bed with that woman who smelled like wet plants; he saw himself a little while later, crying on a park bench, like a coward, yet one who dared to cry even with a broken nose. As he walked down the road he remembered other less significant injuries, the toenail smashed when a Uruguayan player whose name he no longer remembered stomped on it, the stretcher that carried him out of the Torreón stadium under a shower of beer and piss, the two teeth he left behind on the pitch in Tegucigalpa; he couldn't complain too much, it all went with the job, but the injured ankle represented something very different. He came out of the operating room only to hear the sing-song voice of the doctor: "Soria went for the ball." Feeling awful, he'd stayed behind in Guadalajara, with his ankle held together by a pin placed there by a surgeon who was a Chivas fan, capable of justifying the action of Soria, the most competent enforcer in the whole first division. "Same as Onofre," added the doctor.

When Irigoyen abandoned his childhood, along with the broken nose, he had found out about those strange bones: Alberto Onofre fractured his tibia and his fibula a few weeks before the World Cup in 1970. He was never the same again and passed into legend like a bitter hypothesis, like those gentle and carefully measured diagonal passes that he was not able to make in the World Cup.

"At least you're already old enough to go into coaching," commented *Zorri* Mendieta while he was signing his cast with the miserable handwriting of a goalie whose hands have been stomped too many times.

It was looking at Mendieta's hands that led to his decision to retire. Thirty-six years old and no chance to play till the next season. He could just imagine the sarcastic remarks of the sports announcers welcoming his return: "Methuselah's back on the field!" *Deaf* Fernández, his coach, told him with the voice of experience gained in the five countries that had ended up throwing him out.

"Learn to chase down the balls."

He couldn't stand the idea of becoming no more than a useful nuisance in the crowded midfield, of running in opposition to his own history as left-forward. Ever since he learned how to play from old man Scopelli, he hadn't been able to move any other way: the ghost on the edge of the pitch who nodded off during most of the game only to appear unexpectedly in an empty space.

He chose a farewell without fanfare, in keeping with his humble record: two national championships, 32 caps with the national team, a good, average player, with no magic nickname, no spectacular plays, but he was there, packing the area to allow some show-off to score with a bicycle kick.

The smell of pitch and rope that came in on the breeze suggested that boats were passing close by, but the barge only made two trips, so the dock smell must have come from the tanker and from the petrol platforms to which the workers had returned, fired up by the game. He thought about Olivia, the vague smile that seemed to mean two things at once: "If you win, we'll see each other at the bar." Olivia entered into other people's lives as if through a window. Maybe he resisted the wonder of having her near because the heat resisted any possible surprise.

Zorri Mendieta was the first one to mention Punta Fermín to him; a town whose life revolved around oil and that could only be found on the most recent maps. A businessman had bought the franchise of a third division team; now the Rayados were in the second division and needed a young coach.

"He liked your name," said *Zorri*, as if he were in the same conversation with Lángara, the Reguiero brothers, Cilauren, Zubieta, those mythic Basque players who had stayed in Mexico and were still the idols of the well-informed fans.

After a routine course (with the usual vague descriptions of any night class), Irigoyen was certified as coach. But it was in the Brindisi, an Italian restaurant near the Atlante's Stadium, where he really began his second life. He was dining with *Zorri* and *Deaf* Fernández when somebody straight out of a newspaper article showed up. When the guy sat down at their table, Irigoyen had a funny feeling: the fellow's gaunt face, the well-known nose, the long grey hair, all seemed purposely accentuated; the fourth diner looked *too much* like César Luis Menotti; there was something unreal about having the fabled coach so close. In one way or another – everybody said so – Menotti always had bad luck. His glory as world champion was sinking slowly into the sunset of teams that played beautifully and never won a fucking thing. At that table, overwhelmed by *Deaf* Fernández's introduction ("a new colleague"), Irigoyen listened to the Argentine coach. He had taken over the national team and figured on playing the offside trap in a country where Cruz Azul had snatched the championship from Atlético Español with three offside goals; he would defend the offside trap on fields where the tactic was to let the grass grow and then water it a half hour before the game. He found out that Menotti was just fucking around in Mexico; he also knew that his enthusiasm was contagious.

He was surprised that everything fit so easily in his suitcase. He hadn't accumulated much, and for some reason that struck him as the sure sign of a childless divorced man. He imagined Punta Fermín as a landscape as empty as his recent life had been. The fact that it had a man's first name but no surname professed its lack of a history. Nothing had managed to last there. The team, the stadium, the town itself were younger than he was.

Vasco Uribe sent a driver to pick him up at the airport in Cancún, and for three hours Irigoyen gazed out at a flat plateau, scrawny trees that didn't look like much, or perhaps like something out of an African film.

"I'll give you a little tour," the driver said, slowing down as he came into town. The heat was even more intense.

They drove down a long street, lined by black market shops. One shop boasted a live alligator in a wooden cage. A little further along, a pig almost ran under the pickup. They passed some girls eating blue snow cones.

"How about those girls?" the driver asked. Irigoyen noted their skinny legs, feet in clear plastic flip-flops. "They're waiting for the workers from the platforms. They come into Punta every two weeks. They say that working close to oil makes you horny. You think so?"

Irigoyen asked about the blue snow cones.

"They use a syrup that comes from Panama. Everything here is imported. Even us. Who would bother to be born here?"

There was no church, no town square with a bandstand, not even a basketball court. The town hall was a rectangular building almost indistinguishable from the black market shops.

They passed through a residential area that seemed to have sprung up recently and been abandoned just as recently. They then took a highway across the rocky plateau. The almost motionless sea on their right added to the heat.

Irigoyen saw a flock of parrots: the green birds accompanied them briefly and then alighted in a place where there must have been some trees. A little while later they saw the first signs of foliage.

"There are plants here because of the *cenote*," the driver explained.

Two subterranean rivers flowed into a deep pool. *Vasco* Uribe had purchased all the wetlands around the *cenote* to build his stadium, the clubhouse and a villa overlooking the Caribbean.

They passed under an arch with green and white letters that spelled out: Rayados Football Club. The name of the team came from a tribe that used to live in the area, nomads who had marked their bodies with white stripes of lime and had disappeared, leaving neither pyramids nor altars. The only thing that recalled their shadowy passage through the peninsula were the team's tee-shirts.

"A team in Monterrey has the same name," Irigoyen mentioned.

"Doesn't matter," the driver replied. "They're a long way from here. Just look at that beautiful sight!"

They had entered Uribe's property. The driver was pointing out something that might be a pond surrounded by rocks, an impeccable lawn and a villa with balconies.

Irigoyen got out of the pickup. A giant of a man was waiting for him. His huge fingers made the expensive, thick cigar they held appear slender.

He shook Uribe's hand, a calloused hand that seemed to have come from the land itself.

"You're gonna be happy," *Vasco* spoke to him familiarly, with the winning air of so many executives, and without expecting the same familiar treatment in return.

They entered the house and crossed a large living room with a marble floor. An abundance of oriental rugs overwhelmed the space. Fortunately they didn't stop there, finding their way onto a terrace at the other end of the room. It occurred to Irigoyen that the view from there justified the design of the building:

from the wicker chairs he could take in the stadium and the pitch itself (the stands surrounded the pitch in a horseshoe shape, leaving the side facing the owner's villa open). Irigoyen could see the silky goal nets at the south end.

"How about a cocktail?" Uribe was out of breath, and his tongue made a raspy sound; a drink appeared to be a matter of some urgency.

Irigoyen turned around. A young girl had entered the room soundlessly. She was barefoot, had oriental eyes and the same straight hair he had seen on the girls licking the blue snow cones.

"Olivia," exhaled Uribe.

Irigoyen saw that ambiguous smile for the first time, as if she were looking at something disgusting and yet pleasing at the same time.

They drank a green liqueur, cool and dense. The trip, the heat and the liqueur carried Irigoyen into a dimension of unreality. As the sun set, the lawn took on a rare radiance, as if it were absorbing the last reserves of light.

"I'm exhausted," complained Irigoyen.

"Take him to his cottage, *m'hija*," Uribe spoke to the girl in a tone that was both affectionate and commanding at the same time, as though his authority were not based on salary alone.

The cottage intended for the coach turned out to be comfortable. Television with channels from Miami, ceiling fan, a massage showerhead. The team included five first division veterans, a dozen rookies and Marcelo Casanueva, on loan from the Cruz Azul team, a condition he had insisted on in his contract. The smell of mud, sweat and bodies worn out on many pitches pervaded the locker room, a reminder that football had always sprung up out of poverty. Maybe because they hadn't seen anybody in some time, the players listened closely to what he had to say, as if he were talking about things from the other side of the ocean.

After seeing Punta Fermín's semi-desert landscape, he was surprised that the stadium filled up every second Sunday. In spite of those suffocating bus trips that that they had to endure when they had to travel for games, the team worked well together, and Marcelo Casanueva soon became the leading goal scorer. During the previous season Marcelo had started on the Cruz Azul team, but he reported his coach for skimming money off the entrance fees and was sent back to warm the bench. He wanted to play so much that he accepted the invitation to go to this end-of-the-world place. He was the kind of player that Irigoyen admired and detested at the same time: a religious fanatic with greasy hair and a bundle of superstitions, who always stayed behind to practise free kicks after the training sessions ended without being asked by anyone. Although his goals were a clear triumph of will, he couldn't answer a reporter's questions without mentioning God. In the way he looked at the others and in the way he played the game, with a puritanical efficiency, there was an inability to enjoy life that brought attention to the fun sought by his teammates. Even his eating seemed to be governed by a superior self-restraint; he would chew his food to the point of tedium, never adding salt or hot sauce. After ten games it was clear that his ability was far beyond the second division; still he refused to meet with the scouts from Atlas that came to watch him play. Irigoyen told him that he appreciated his loyalty, and Marcelo glanced up at the sky with an expression of disgust, as if God were his coach.

During the week, the vegetation and the sea isolated Irigoyen and his players. For a football team, there are endless lost hours spent playing cards or running laps. Sometimes it's harder to overcome the tedium of team meetings and training sessions than it is to deal with the pressure on Sundays. The players on the Rayados had left their families behind in cities where there were schools and where a teammate didn't share their bedroom. The only one who had the right to bring his wife and children along was the coach. His cottage offered more space than Irigoyen needed; he began to scatter clothes and towels on the floor so it would look lived in. He refused to think about what that permanent isolation would mean for him and for his team at the end of a year. In football the future was next Sunday.

The Rayados bus went into Cancún every Monday for R & R. The players sought out more or less imaginary *gringas*, video-game parlours, cybercafés where they could write letters without worrying about spelling, or street fairs from which they would come back carrying ridiculous stuffed parrots. He preferred to stay behind in the team's empty quarters. He would kill time reading outdated magazines, tossing stones into the *cenote*, walking the lawns that were so green they punctuated the impression of being in an oasis besieged by the surrounding desert, staying up until the wee hours to watch the movies on TV, that at that hour were always the best ones.

One Monday when the team was away, he hiked through an area of low palm trees and came to a clearing. All at once something strange happened, like when he was running in the forward position and a shadow coming out of nowhere stole the ball. He turned to the right and came face to face with Olivia, leaning against a palm tree. A dog was licking her feet.

"He loves it. It's the salt from my sweat. Dogs need salt," said the girl.

Irigoyen stared at the tongue that was wetting her toes. Olivia closed her eyes, perhaps to focus on that wet caress or just so he could observe her at his leisure. Afterwards she raised her hands and hugged the trunk that was supporting her. Irigoyen hurried away.

What was Olivia doing in Punta Fermín? The driver had told him that she was from Veracruz, where the owner had coffee plantations and a chain of hotels. Irigoyen recalled the gleam in the eyes of the driver, obsessed with the relation between petroleum and sexual heat. He saw again the way he brought the index fingers of both hands together to demonstrate the relationship between Uribe and Olivia. He found it hard to believe the driver, who clearly had been marooned on this coast far too long. Irigoyen used other clues to try to decipher the vague situation with Olivia; he had seen her get out of the limousines used by the heads of the oil workers' union; he had observed her entering Uribe's box, wearing those flowery and colourful dresses that were considered elegant here; he had watched her crossing the fields at night with no discernable destination.

Ever since the first game, Irigoyen had grasped the hidden purpose of the stadium; in those stands the oil workers met women who came in boats and on rafts from the nearby villages and who didn't pay to attend the games. At five in the afternoon, the incoherent screams and the enthusiasm that had nothing to do with what was happening on the field, demonstrated that the spectators were absorbed in their own rites in the stands. The Rayados pitch was the public square that the town lacked. Sometimes there were fights, even a stabbing, arising from arguments that had nothing to do with the game. At seven at night it did little good to turn off the stadium lights; bonfires would appear in the stands, and radios would blare out the music of guitars and accordions. "When they were building the rigs, they had to bring in women from Chetumal; the guys were going crazy with this heat," Uribe commented over a glass of the green liqueur. Seen from his terrace, the fires in the stands suggested a wild celebration.

On Monday mornings the barge filled up with women only. Olivia was different; she had come from farther away, and she stayed on land.

There in that clearing among the palms Irigoyen felt for the first time that there was no mistaking the way she looked at him.

He went back to the cottage, got in the shower and the torture of the cold water pulled him away from those shining eyes, bronzed legs, and feet caressed greedily by the dog's tongue. He dried himself off in a rage.

It was when he dropped the towel that he saw Olivia:

"I wanted to see you."

From that moment on Punta Fermín was Olivia's slender waist between his hands, her dark nipples, the vegetable scent of her breath, her grass-stained feet, the occasional howling of the dog that waited for her outside the cottage.

Olivia didn't talk much, but her smile, on the other hand, said too much; as if contradicting her own motives. Irigoyen enjoyed comparing that expression of hers to a penalty: a feint to one side, then the shot to the other.

As she walked away, she said, "The boss is waiting for me," in the same tone of voice that Marcelo Casanueva used for his appointments with God in the goal area.

It was hard to keep secrets, living as close together as the Rayados did. *Vasco* had to know about, and deep down accept, his relations with Olivia. Irigoyen had more than enough time to think down by the polished stones around the *cenote*, as he watched the spins and turns of the swallows, and he reached a hypothesis which in any other setting would have worried him, but which in that timeless environment acquired a kind of easy normalcy: Uribe hired him because he was a loner and Olivia could keep an eye on him, an explanation that was as whimsical in its own right as the one offered by *Zorri* Mendieta: "He liked your name." Irigoyen ended up getting used to that irony: he, who despised man-to-man defence, was being watched even in his most private life.

Maybe the scorching sun and their distance from any city had something to do with his calm acceptance of that slow pace of life, the demanding schedules (sleepless nights during tropical thunder storms, unshakeable drowsiness on endless highways), noisy Sundays, empty Mondays, Olivia traipsing between his cottage, Uribe's villa, the local union office, the dances she sometimes told him about and which, depending on her mood, he imagined either as small town parties where they raffled off an iguana or as orgies with outrageous scenery: palm trees in golden pots, enormous beds fit for a Central American dictator.

Gradually he came to understand his surroundings by submitting them to a different logic. Besides which it always took Irigoyen some time to start to worry about what was happening around him; he knew it all too well and remembered it every time he came across one of his ex-wife's bobby pins stuck away in a corner of his suitcase. He imagined things in terms of his position on the field; his role was to run along the sideline, fill in a sudden gap on the far left, anticipate the direction of the ball, never be the one who is there, but the one who is going to be there, stay a little on the margins, as though he already knew back then that his destiny would take him off the pitch to the coach's bench, on that Caribbean coast where, to his amazement, the nation still existed.

The end of May brought torrential rains, and a suffocating steam took over the nights. Olivia's hair became even frizzier in that climate; it always looked damp, like a sign of what was happening outside. One day when it had started to rain early and she couldn't visit him, there was news of Menotti on the TV. His team had played as never before, but there were changes in the Federation, and the coach had resigned amid a wave of slander. Irigoyen remembered the words of *Deaf* Fernández, heavy with his own failures: "In this business if you think, you lose; be careful, that's the danger faced by goalies and forwards; they have too much time to come up with ideas." The goalkeeper was usually the eccentric in the group; his good luck charms by the foot of the post, his flamboyant sweatshirts, his prayers on his knees in the goal area, all separated him from the rest of the team. It was more or less the same with the left-winger; that's where the team ended, everything became leftward and acquired an absolute urgency. Even he didn't trust that space and would come onto the pitch stepping with his right foot first, which had never been any good at kicking balls. "The worst thing is to think outside the stadium, the guys in charge never forgive you for having a life somewhere else; at some point I considered myself an individual and I was screwed," *Deaf* Fernández went on and on about the problems with football, as if enumerating them somehow reduced them; he was speaking as if the number 11, instead of a position on the pitch, represented a form of conduct.

Irigoyen turned up the volume on the television:

"He came from far away, and he took advantage of us," an announcer on the payroll of the new officials of the Federation was saying. He was referring to Menotti. Would they throw him out of Punta Fermín as well? The world had become an impatient place where a coach should pack his bags if he lost three games in a row. The Rayados were playing well, but the ridiculousness on the television forced Irigoyen to remember that *Vasco* bragged about his tantrums ("I made them rebuild that wall seven times"), displays he used in order to underscore his authority. One Sunday he filled the stands with drumlines, and two weeks later he banned all musicians from entering the stadium. He could fire Irigoyen for any reason, and even if he didn't, how long could Irigoyen stand being in a place where the drinking water came in by boat and where nobody had any real reason to support the team?

Uribe was the boss and had to take care of business in Veracruz and in the capital, and so was often away from the villa for weeks on end. When he returned, he always complained about the vegetation that had invaded its rooms, and with tirades worthy of the theatre, would tear into the Mayan gardeners, who barely understood anything he said.

On one of those returns he barged into Irigoyen's cottage and confronted the coach as if he were personally responsible for the vines that had gained terrain during his absence:

"How does the team look to you?" From the tone of his voice it was clear that it didn't look good to him.

They were in fourth place. What more could you expect from a team of novices?

"The top teams don't always make it to the finals; they get worn down at the top, all that pressure. The way things are going we could make it to the playoffs and give everybody a surprise."

Vasco stared at him for several seconds. Then he said:

"I really liked that crap you just spouted, about getting worn down at the top... Take care of the boys. Take care of yourself. You've got one hell of a team," Uribe clapped him on the back and left the cottage.

Irigoyen didn't understand the previous scene and didn't even try; ever since he had been a player himself he had given up trying to argue with the bosses. Whoever paid the bills was always right.

Uribe's arguments wore thin one Friday about two weeks later: the players didn't get their paychecks. The owner blamed the drop in the price of oil. The union had to cut expenses. What followed were weeks when everything was in a muddle, talk of the Persian Gulf, of barrels that nobody had seen and which affected them all the same. When the salaries finally returned to normal, nobody was in the mood to protest the bad news the owner brought as he lit his cigar: there would be no bonuses since they were going to the playoffs.

"There's no money. The price of the damned oil has hit rock bottom."

Nobody felt like challenging him.

Irigoyen was starting to get tired of that distance where everything was happening in a different manner. The flames that marked the horizon became for him an irrational and well-defined frontier. Even if the price of oil went up, he would be gone soon.

One night while Olivia traced lines with her finger on his sweat-soaked back, Irigoyen asked her to go away with him after the championship game. She drew up her legs and hugged her knees to her chest.

"Only if you win," she said, as if it were impossible.

The sports pages consecrated them as the standout team in the second division, but Olivia was obviously looking at other clues. She blew a lock of hair away from her eyes, which sparkled in an unmistakable way as she stated:

"You should leave before. I spend a lot of time with the boss."

It took Irigoyen a while to get the relationship between the two statements.

"What did he tell you?"

"The top teams travel by plane."

Irigoyen thought about the clear blue sky that had covered

him all those months. You had to travel to Cancún to see the exhaust from a jet. They were too far away; the big teams would never agree to a trip that expensive and exhausting.

"Besides, a second-division team costs the union a lot less," Olivia drove her point home: they'd never let him win. "Get out of here now."

Irigoyen insisted that they go together. She repeated, with that smile that could mean anything, that for that to happen he had to win. Her emphasis on winning was depressing. Maybe because that meant he would be fired. On her lips winning the title would be a tragedy that meant going away with her, tying her to his bad luck.

The future was each Sunday leading to the playoffs. They won against teams that put their trust in their hounding defence and wanted nothing more than a chance goal, preferably from a free kick. Marcelo Casanueva played as if he had already moved on to his next team. It disgusted Irigoyen to see him leave the pitch as if he were unaware of his own prowess, but he also knew that that was his advantage: the cold striker, unshakeable.

TV took to the Rayados in a really big way; the team was always surprising, not so much in their games themselves as by daring to win out there in the sticks where nobody expected anything to happen.

The logical candidate to win the division playoffs was Tecnológico Hidalgo. Irigoyen had a vague memory of the infinite comings and goings of the Mexican teams and their players. He couldn't remember how many clubs *Zorri* Mendieta had played for. Had Atlético Hidalgo been in the first division two or three times? Anyway it was a bad team, but one with a tradition of being partly the garbage can, but also the nursery school for the big teams' old timers and their novices.

In the first games of the playoffs Irigoyen was interviewed by an immense number of sweating reporters. All of them let fly the word "surprise" in their first question. Football doesn't exist unless it's televised, and Irigoyen resigned himself to the tiresome monotony the sports announcers were using to describe the amazing performance of Punta Fermín. For years he had detested the announcers who attempt to "expertly analyse" the game after each goal (if the ball goes into the net, the idiot of the moment comments that the team is well trained). But with time, and perhaps with Punta Fermín's distance from the centres of power, he began to enjoy the unimaginative praise of the TV commentators. The long run to the championship had served that purpose, to get the imbeciles to screw themselves in their estimation of los Rayados. Before the stunned TV cameras the team turned the unusual into routine, and so they came to the final game against the Tecnológico Hidalgo as expected.

There was a week's rest and then on a Monday the clubhouse filled with reporters who had arrived in helicopters and rented jeeps. Irigoyen was expecting – although he didn't realise that until later, when it was already humiliating – idiotic congratulations on the "magic" of his Rayados. But from the first question he knew that the atmosphere had changed in the muddy minds of the reporters. What did it feel like to face an unbeatable team? Do you maybe believe in miracles? What virgin are you praying to?

Vasco Uribe presided over the press interview, behind a cloud of tobacco smoke, and allowed a flood of questions in which the unexpected presence of the Rayados in the final game, rather than a merit, seemed more like a petulant challenge or a disingenuous demonstration of arrogance. All of a sudden the Tecnológico team, with its stadium in Pachuca, only an hour from the capital, had come to represent a powerful and symbolic centre, invincible from the outer limits of the nation.

Irigoyen hated the press conference, not so much because those people talked about the Tecnológico team as though they had already won the championship, but because he had been infected with enthusiasm from their own earlier commentaries.

On Tuesday the sport tabloid *Esto* announced that the Tech would be getting reinforcements from the America, Atlante and Guadalajara teams. The signs were unmistakable: three powerful franchises were sacrificing their reserves to support the team favoured by the central powers. Irigoyen thought about those impossible airplanes Olivia had mentioned.

Uribe had gone to the capital to discuss the conditions for the final with the officials of the Federation. After learning about the last-minute loans the Tecnológico were getting, Irigoyen tried to speak with *Vasco*. He went from one cell phone to another without ever hearing his boss's asthmatic voice.

The night before the away game the disaster got even worse. The usual bus, decorated with ostentatious palm trees, was substituted by one with metal seats. The Rayados arrived in Pachuca two hours before the game, like shadows of themselves.

The referee took it upon himself to bring them back to reality: he blew the whistle when he felt like it, called a questionable penalty and only remembered that he was carrying a yellow card in his pocket when they broke the leg of the Rayados right wing. The 0-2 score came cheaply. Uribe went into the locker room to talk to them. After not having seen him for so long, he seemed to Irigoyen to be oddly rejuvenated:

"No way, boys, you did what you could." Although he was trying for a tone of resignation, he came across as nervous. Irigoyen understood his fear: he still thought they were capable of turning it around in Punta Fermín.

He spent the 26-hour return trip convincing himself that

nothing was in Uribe's interest more than losing the final game. He wasn't very surprised when the boss called him into his office the day before the event. He recognised the atmosphere in that room which he had rarely entered; the cigar had been put out hours ago, but Uribe still had it between his lips, incapable of thinking of anything other than the indecent ideas that he was going to communicate:

"The only thing real here is the heat," he shoved the envelope toward him; Irigoyen glimpsed the green stack of dollars. "Let's see if you can wake up: you were fuckin' dreaming. *Zorri* told me about you, and I took you to be one of those fools that risk their money based on the horses' names. You were a beginner with visions of grandeur that always sink a team. I figured with a little luck you'd have a decent season, but no more than that. I should have sent you straight to hell in the beginning. Sometimes a guy is just too generous. The team you put together was too strong. Didn't it ever occur to you that you can't play that way out here in the swamps? Subs for the wingers in this pigsty! Do you know how I got my franchise? People at the top, the ones that you can't even imagine, wanted some entertainment besides the local whores for the workers out on the rigs. Do you really think they'd let us make it to the top? Have you ever seen an airplane in this fuckin' sky? Do you have any idea how much it costs to broadcast by television from out here? There'll never be teams out here in the sticks. It's not the pitch that ends here; it's the country."

Irigoyen picked up the envelope with the money and looked at Uribe, as if trying to perfect his contempt for the man. He felt a stab of pain under his sternum, a profound nausea as he stared at the ashtray full of cold ashes. He thought about winning. Absurdly, that too meant getting Olivia.

He had a pounding headache when he got to the locker room before the game. He supposed his players had also been given money to lose. Some of them, the veterans about to retire, had no reason to refuse a big payoff. Others (for the first time he saw Marcelo as an ally) simply could not accept it; sooner or later news of the bribe would reach some reporter; it wasn't hard to imagine an exemplary and exaggerated reprimand, suspension for life for some players and a heavy but bearable fine for the execs.

His speech was long. When he had finished, they all looked at him with a respect that more than anything else was due to the fact that someone could string together that many words with so little air. They walked out of the locker room as if it were from a crypt inside a pyramid. The Punta Fermín pitch had never seemed that green to him before. "Don't play for Uribe; don't even look at the owner's box..." What else had he said? Once again he breathed in the strong smells of football; he spoke of money without glory, of childhood idols, the accounts they'd have to settle, all of it incoherent, passionate, and not a bit convincing.

Irigoyen was the first one to betray his own words; in the atmosphere that had again become stifling, he looked for Olivia's dark skin and black hair in the box with Uribe and the union leaders.

If they won, the team would be finished; it wasn't hard to guess the end of the story: Uribe would be obliged to negotiate with the Federation and to sell his franchise to executives with a team in the centre of the country. The fate of the Rayados was sealed; on the other hand, the afternoon would have unpredictable consequences for Irigoyen. He let himself be carried away by a disturbing, yet insistent thought: that Olivia's decision depended on the score, another reason to lose. "I'm gambling on it too," she had told him as he stared at the scar on her thigh. For months he had kissed that wounded skin with passion, as if that were the way to find yet another key to the enigma of Olivia. "Acid spilled on me," she told him to explain the scar. It was hard to believe her; that scar made him think about the petroleum workers, about how they would punish her if she tried to disobey them. Yes, Olivia did run other risks. Those nights that Uribe had paid for were turning out to be a gamble for him. Irigoyen knew, better than ever, that he was out of the game.

The match was a comedy of errors: veterans who got to the plays late were hardly distinguishable from the nervous kids whose slide tackles were poorly timed. For the first time Marcelo let himself be carried away by his emotions; he missed simple passes and took wild shots that ended up in the stands. Slowly, as he sat on the bench in his sweat-soaked clothes, Irigoyen came to grips with his mistake. His speech had irritated them all; it insulted the ones who had accepted the bribe and was a source of tension for the others.

At half-time with the score at 0-1 and the aggregate at 0-3, he tried to calm their nerves: they were playing against themselves, not the Tecnológico and their reinforcements; they had to make more touches, show their enthusiasm for the game, after all, in football if you aren't enjoying yourself, you don't win. He read the disillusionment in their eyes; his players didn't believe him, or in any case, believed that Uribe had visited him on the bench with a check intended to change his opinions. The younger players glared at him as if his calm appearance were a bribe, and the veterans' sympathetic stares were just as annoying. He added another piece of advice, telling them to open up the pitch and to keep an eye on that evasive number 9. Nobody was listening.

It was twenty minutes before the end of the game when Marcelo was buried in the box. Even the referee, who considered violence a requisite of the sport, had to call the penalty. The designated shooter was Marcelo himself. Irigoyen knew only too well the effect of adrenalin on the body of a recently fouled player; still a substitute could miss on purpose. He let him shoot. As soon as he saw him run up, much too fast, he knew the ball would end up far from the net. Marcelo had so many reasons to score but not one would find its way into the net.

It was dawn. The tanker stood out against the backdrop of a yellow sky. Irigoyen could see the rust covering the sides of the prow. The envelope padded his shirt pocket; he still had a chance for greatness: he could tear up the money. However, ever since he packed up his things, he knew he wouldn't do it; little by little he was accepting the idea of a settlement, exaggerated, perhaps, but everything had been muddled by that heat; he chose a lesser drama, a negotiated defeat.

On the dock he felt the tug of the old break in his ankle. He waited until he heard distant laughter. After a few seconds he saw the exhausted faces of the girls returning from their night in Punta Fermín. They fell silent in the presence of the coach. One of them offered him a blue snow cone. For the first time he tasted that syrup that smelled like some exotic flower. Almost all the girls were barefoot. He saw them yawning, shielding themselves from the sun with their forearms. None of them could have been more than twenty years old. Shortly the motor of the barge started up. Irigoyen stepped on the rotten wood, with his right foot, and felt the push that would take him away from the coast.

He looked for the stadium behind some mangroves. It was only then that he realised that he still thought Olivia might come with him. Irigoyen had lost the bet; the team would remain there, and she was in no rush to leave. Maybe it was just another feint; with her you never knew. Minutes later he thought he heard someone calling him. He was wrong; it was the wind bringing disjointed sounds from somewhere.

Travelling down the river, surrounded by sleepy women, he got an unmatched view of the stadium. A little community of happiness, vegetation, perfect lawns. Then he saw a silhouette standing on the shore. The dog was licking her feet. Olivia didn't wave goodbye; she watched the boat on the scorching river, as if he had come there only to leave, to detach himself toward some empty place, the point that meant the end of the game.

Interview with Juan Villoro

What role did football play in your youth?
My parents divorced, and my dad took me to the stadiums, because he found it hard to find activities to do with me and because he was a fan. That's the way my love for the game was forged. Today I still associate it with closeness to my father.

Do you support a particular team?
In Mexico, the Necaxa team and in Spain, F.C. Barcelona, the city where my father was born.

What motivates you to write fiction that takes place within the context of football?
One of the most interesting things about football is the passion it arouses in people. I am neither an expert nor a historian of the sport. I played with the Pumas until "Juvenil AA", the class immediately before the first team. I have lots of friends who have played at the professional level, but I don't see myself as someone who belongs to that scene. I prefer being a witness, whose main interest is the craziness and the forms of behaviour that football awakens. Essentially, I'm a fan of the passion.

How do football and politics intersect in Mexico?
Football is the best-organised entertainment on the planet and the one that produces the most money. It's no surprise that politicians have wanted to take advantage of it. In Mexico every twelve years the World Cup coincides with our elections, and the results of our team, if positive, usually favour the governing party. The politicians visit the team and try to identify themselves with it. But that has its limits. Our football is so corrupt that the

politicians support it at a distance. There are governors, like the one in Chiapas and the one in Aguascalientes who during their campaigns promised to bring first division football to their areas, but then distanced themselves from the topic, because it could dirty them too much.

Did any writer of football fiction influence this story?
I'd like to think that it's close to the atmosphere of Onetti, whom I admire and who sold tickets at the Centenario Stadium in Montevideo, but he didn't write football stories.

Do you see any lingering reluctance to incorporating football or sport as a dominant theme or plot driver among your generation of authors?
No, the prejudice that football was for the masses and couldn't be a theme for narrative or for sociological reflection has already been shattered. Now we have the opposite exaggeration: it has become in vogue to explain life through football.

Is there a particular identity or style associated with football in Mexico?
Slowness, lateral passes, the temptation to defend after making a goal, the idea that it's better to give the ball to someone else than take care of things yourself and the inability to convert penalties.

For the past twenty years Mexico has participated in the Copa América as a special invitee. Do you think that the commemorative edition of the tournament, Copa América Centenario, in the United States in 2016 in which six CONCACAF teams will compete with the ten CONMEBOL teams is a viable model for the future of

football on the continent?

The Copa América and the Copa de Oro are very disappointing. The Centenary Copa América will be the fusion of those two disasters in a country without true football culture. There are usually a few good games in the Copa América, but the constants are the low quality of refereeing, the poor condition of the pitches and the slacking quality of the players, who perform much better for their European clubs.

How would you describe the impact in Latin America of Brazil having hosted the World Cup in 2014?

Among the ranks of the "small teams", there were some really interesting ones who had great games: Costa Rica, Chile and Colombia. On the other hand, the region's two "giants" didn't achieve their objectives. Brazil was humiliated by Germany, with a goal fest that was difficult to have foreseen for the home team, and Argentina achieved second place, but in their case, only the triumph and definitive crowning of Messi would have been satisfactory. On the political level, the corruption scandals and the squandering of resources set a bad precedent for the region. Unfortunately, these lessons aren't learned as they should be. It's the same with political errors as it is with sports errors. Logically, Scolari was fired as Brazil's coach, since he had the team playing against their own nature with a "Europeanised" style. The strange thing is that he was replaced by Dunga, who represents the exact same approach.

How do you view the recent developments in the scandal surrounding corruption in FIFA?

That was something we had been writing about for a long time. FIFA is a mafia that carries on business wildly and pretends to be a "non-profit". Its fiscal opacity is absolute and the control it wields is worthy of a tyrant. The world of sports has become an island of immunity that the democracies of the developed world depend on to conduct their dirty business. No one would believe that a European president could be in power for more than 20 years, but that's possible in FIFA, the International Olympic Committee and the World Boxing Council, with the complicity of politicians, CEOs and TV broadcasters all over the democratic and developed world.

Paraguay
JAVIER VIVEROS

Javier Viveros was born in Asunción, Paraguay in 1977. He is a computer engineer and a candidate for a Masters in Linguistics at the Universidad Nacional de Asunción. He has published the following volumes of short stories: *La luz marchita* (Jakembo, 2005), *Ingenierías del insomnio* (Jakembo, 2008), *Urbano, demasiado urbano* (Arandurã, 2009), *Manual de esgrima para elefantes* (Arandurã, 2013) and *Fantasmario* (2015). He is also the author of volumes of poetry: *Dulce y doliente ayer* (Jakembo, 2007), *En una baldosa* (Jakembo, 2008), *Mensajéamena* (Arandurã, 2009), *Panambi ku'i* (Tercermundo, 2009). Additionally, he wrote the scripts for *Pólvora y polvo* (comic), *El supremo manuscrito* (feature film), *Celularis* (theatre) and *Epopeya* (comic). Several of his works were included in international anthologies of contemporary narrative, such as *Neues Vom Fluss* (Germany), *Los chongos de Roa Bastos* (Argentina) and *Cuentos del Paraguay* (Cuba). He is a fan of Club Sportivo Luqueño. Viveros currently resides in Asunción. "Football Inc." (Fútbol S.A.) first appeared in Spanish in *Ingenierías del insomnio* (Jakembo, 2008).

Football Inc.
For BUBA (R.I.P.) and for my brother Milci.

I

On week days the coach had us running from seven in the morning, he would order them to run around the Luqueño pitch some twenty times, we moved like robots, they went around dragging and overcome with sleep, some of us were yawning and that yawn spread to almost the entire group of players, and to some of us members of the coaching staff as well.

Move it, only fourteen laps to go, the coach yelled at us. Come on, after ten more laps you'll be breathing again and stretching our muscles, he would tell them to spur them on. As I ran at the rear of the pack, I would watch my friends who were in front of me, seeing them mostly from a side angle, and he could see on all or most of our faces that two or three hours more of sleep were what they needed.

As we finished each lap, we shouted out the number, the number they had completed; "nine", we yelled, not too eagerly, and to motivate them more I started to run too, he started to run the few remaining laps with them to reach the set number, so we would finish the routine. But he did no more than three laps. I ran along with them and he moved rapidly, at the head of the line, a real example, this guy, I reached the head of the pack, but as he grew more and more tired, I was losing ground and he usually finished last, I did it mainly just to show solidarity, like in the military, it's not totally necessary but he does it, we players looked positively on that attitude in our coach, but the midfielder (Acosta) "I don't give a damn that he jogs with us" and Acevedo (right-forward) "it makes me mad that he runs with us."

From a distance the coach's sharp eye would watch us doing laps around the pitch, he usually would watch them closely to begin organising the team mentally, last Sunday I had some pain in my right thigh and I'm aware that the coach is watching how I move, maybe Aguilera won't be able to start on Sunday, what do you think, doctor? It's only Tuesday, coach, we'll just have to wait and see. I'm sure I can recover, that it's just a little pain. I see him try to move, I try to move as usual, as if there were no pain, I always want to play, I believe he'll recover, coach, yes, I think so too, time's the universal healer.

Mondays were days off, the players' day, some people say that day should be eliminated, because they use it to get drunk and they say we throw away a whole week of training, most of us just relax, others of us would go to the whore houses or go out for a night on the town, and they say I guzzle even their sister's cologne. We always started off Tuesdays running laps, I give them light exercise to warm up, so our muscles start to get ready for a tougher workout, so their muscles tone up and get ready. Then we would begin calisthenics, in groups of three, they would do jumps from side to side, he would make us do five jumps on each side, the one in the middle will work the hardest, then we would change positions, balance, they would perform the depth jumps, "the fish leap" he would order, we would bump our chests and then I would tell them to do roll-ups, they would do push-ups, get to it, boys, we worked our legs, they sweated with the sit-ups, "the airplane!" he would yell. Then, with the battle over, we would stretch and they would gasp for air.

Tuesdays and Wednesdays we would work hard with the trainer. Thursdays and Fridays they always had to run laps, they gave us lighter exercises, we have them work less time with physical training, we play football and they usually make us practise with some special training devices, they would run through an obstacle course, we'd go around some cones that look to us like buoys, I'll do some free kicks against a wooden barrier, we used to train them to take advantage of set pieces, we practise headers on the corner kicks taken by Acosta, "that bastard is the king of the free kick," he's got a strong right foot, so I always let him take them, I hit it hard with the inside of my shoe and with the instep.

The coach makes us practise tactical moves, I would get them together in front of my magnetic board and he would be moving coloured magnets around trying to explain to them his ideas for facing the rival team on Sunday, plays we'd reproduce on the turf when they face the enemy, you are going to strangle them on the right wing, because that's where they have their opening, yes sir, like you say (Arévalos is speaking), Abente, I want you to stick to this guy (and the magnet left the board and then he put it back) you recover the ball (as if it were that easy), make a short pass and you break loose from your defender to join the attack, and Abente "whatever you say, coach." I coveted the captain's armband, but I was careful not to say so, he plays well, but he doesn't have qualities of leadership, so that's why I don't make him captain.

Sometimes we went to the club's gym, I would do my routine of sit-ups, they lifted weights, we need a lot more weights, you're the president of the club, you should be able to do something about it, let's see, no hurry, we'll see, coach, leave it to me. On Saturdays we all got together in the installations of the club, Sportivo Luqueño has the infrastructure to comfortably (not really) accommodate more than one group of players (a lie), it was the night before the game and was usually a really boring day (true), you could see their boredom everywhere, Aranda was reading some magazines, *Vanitas,* I think, I'll read my

Caretas Magazine, other players were watching TV (*Cinecanal*), we missed having alcohol, listening to music (*cumbia villera*) that was coming from outside the stadium gave them a kind of envy of freedom, but the time passed, slowly like in the minutes remaining to score a victory, but it passed.

Sundays were game days. As with everything else in life, sometimes we won and sometimes they lose. On the occasions when we lost, the public booed me, we fans sang songs against that coldheart, in the press we harassed him for my lack of skill in managing the team, for his deficient planning, for our chaotic and lacklustre game. Some seasons we had more wins than losses and ended up among the top five teams and they were heroes, they never won the championship, these players are just money-grubbers, we do what we can, I need a creative attacking midfielder. In other seasons the number of defeats was greater than the number of victories and we scored lots of ties and ended up near the bottom and I lose my job as coach, it's gone, I'm gone; gentlemen: I'd like to introduce your new coach. They received a prize (cash) for every game they won, for every draw they paid half as much and they just had to suck it up for the losses. But in spite of the irregularity of our performance in the league, we would never be relegated to the second division, Arturo, it looks like the Luqueño team is going to hold onto its status one more time, at times they end up in the middle of the standings and other times near the bottom, but we hold onto our place in the first division. So went the life of the team, such was its cyclical routine, until all of a sudden everything changed.

II

Key word: management. The topic had become fashionable on the continent. The Avellaneda Racing Club became managed and won the Argentine championship. Run a football team like a business enterprise. In Paraguay, Club Libertad became managed and won two local championships in a row and even played in the semifinals of the Copa Libertadores, losing out to the team that in the end would be the champion.

"*O Rei*" Sports, Pelé's company was managing several South American clubs and it was the luck of Sportivo Luqueño to be one of them. At first those of us on the team were suspicious, we were uncertain, wanted to see what would happen. But even beyond all the optimistic predictions the situation really turned out well, at least at first. We were paid at the end of every month, we got the prizes and bonuses with a punctuality previously unknown to us.

Lots of people say that Pelé was the best player in the world. My old man was one of them. To get his goat, I went along with those who claimed Maradona was the real king. "Pelé played when the defence had no idea what was happening. Whenever Maradona played the defenders were more on their toes, football had evolved, had become professional. Besides, Maradona played in Italy, where they kick a man to pieces." That's what I used to tell him and my old man would remind me – invariably – of stuff about more than a thousand goals and three world championships won. He would also tell me about a top-notch play carried out against the Uruguayan goalie Ladislao Mazurkiewicz and a great goal – after lifting the ball up over the Swedish defender's head – in some long ago final game in a world championship. I would listen to him, quietly. And then I would launch in with a fury telling him about the quip that the goal that Diego scored with his hand against England in Mexico '86 represented and then his second goal in the same game that was the real jewel, where from the midfield circle he dribbled the ball alone past half the Queen's team.

We would never reach any agreement on that subject. The

only thing that was certain and real was that Pelé's company was managing the club whose colours my colleagues and I were defending. He was our boss. We were now employees of a company, practically office workers (we clocked in and out, but didn't have to wear a tie). It was kind of strange being employed by the guy many considered to be the best player football had ever produced.

Pelé never showed up in the city of Luque. The company was headed by a man that he designated, a Brazilian by the name of Lucio Viega. He was, at the same time, president of the company and the coach of the club. He was a heavy-set fellow and no longer young, but he drove a flashy Porsche. It must be the only Porsche that drove through the potholes and it felt the brush of Luque's hills on its underside. Lucio Viega spoke a Portuguese that was only slightly infected by Spanish.

Little by little, changes began to show up in the company (in the club). The first change had to do with the image, a few women hired for each game would apply make-up to us before we went out on the pitch. "Aesthetics above all else," seemed to be the motto. Forget the jerseys over the shorts and the tight stockings. Everything had to be perfect; we had to show unblemished homogeneity.

Then came the rehearsed choreographies. The first one of us they indoctrinated was the starting centre-forward. Every time he made a goal he had to run up to the sign promoting one of our advertisers. He had to go – as soon as he had made the goal – and hug the poster, but being careful not to cover up the letters, so the camera could catch the whole thing. That goal would then make its way around all the sports pages on the continent, and the sponsor's ad would get continental coverage, and if the goal was really great, it was a sure bet that the news reports around the planet would cover it.

That was just the beginning. After that, each player was given his own routine. I was second central defender, and almost never made goals. But just in case I managed to scrape up a ball that dropped down from a bad clearance or was able to make contact on a corner kick, my mission was to run in front of the camera, press my thumb and index finger together and pass them in front of my mouth, just the way the star in a commercial of one of our sponsors, a toothpaste company, did. There was no limit to the kinds of celebrations we were to perform. And most of them were for publicity. Nothing like the old-time moves. Forget snorting the white line of the penalty box the way Fowler did. No more athletic jumps with fist in the air or rocking the baby like Bebeto. Climbing the wall to celebrate with the fans or wearing a mask were history.

Everything, absolutely everything, was planned. The idea was to make the team a spectacle. It was all scripted by them. We had group choreographies. In one of them, if the goal resulted in a 2-2 draw with the visiting team, we had to get in a single file line and hurl ourselves all together into the centre circle at the same time. Some of the celebrations were frankly outrageous. If we scored first as the visiting team, we had to rush over to the bench, put on capes and act out a scene where the guy who made the goal dresses up like a prince and chats with the man who set up the play, the latter dressed as a grave-digger with a shovel. If somebody made a third goal of his *hat-trick*, all eleven of us had to join the guys on the bench and applaud the fans. If one of the guys scored an Olympic goal, a goal made directly from a corner kick, we were to all get together in the rival team's box and organise a little Olympic winner's lap.

At home games we had to perform our individual or group choreographies in front of the sponsor's poster. On the road, since we couldn't be certain there would be posters of our sponsors, the solution was to get in front of the camera and make some gesture that would remind viewers of one of our sponsor's commercials.

Even the fans had joined the program. The company had organised a meeting with the leaders of the *barra brava*. And they came to an agreement (thanks to free passes and lots of alcohol). As a result, every Sunday, there were personalised chants to spur each player on. It was great hearing half the stadium chanting your name, celebrating your magical right foot or gladiator's dedication or calling for you to be named to the national team. And it inspired a weird feeling, knowing that the ones who were singing our praises now were the ones that on other occasions had insulted us for our poor results, the same ones who at one time or another came into our locker room with not very friendly intentions, the same ones who shattered the windshields of our cars and let the air out of our tyres. But that's the way it was. You get used to anything.

All of a sudden we all started to have nicknames or special symbols. I was "The Shield". They called another teammate "The White Elephant"; he always figures that was because he was a defensive barricade, a wall in front of the goalie. There were animals in abundance. The owner of the right wing was "Eel Acevedo". They called Acosta, the attacking midfielder, "The Laurelty Dragon". Another one was "Feline Aranda".

Journalists had been bought to do the commentaries. My old man always recorded the games for me, and when I saw them I could confirm that the reporters repeated our nicknames religiously. Besides that, the sports commentators began to see qualities in us that we didn't know we had. As bad as he was in the aerial game, in the eyes of the journalists my partner in the defence began to be an impregnable bastion, an anti-aircraft battery that Saddam would have liked to have instead of his

SAM surface-to-air missiles.

Aranda, who was a lefty and had his right leg only for the sake of symmetry, was described as the ambidextrous player par excellence by the sports press in Paraguay, "a player with ample development of both cerebral hemispheres who is a difference maker with both legs and has exquisite control of the ball." The public gives too much credit to the words that come from a loudspeaker or are splashed in ink.

III

"Good afternoon, ladies and gentlemen, Radio Catorce de Marzo's loyal listeners. We're here in Mbusu Stadium ready to begin the broadcast of the game between Sportivo Luqueño and Deportivo Mbusu in this penultimate round of the Spring Championship. The atmosphere is like one big party, Beatricio."

"A very good afternoon to you, Arturo, and to the illustrious audience who, through your broadcast always accompany us by means of the Hertzian waves transmitted through the ether. Yes indeed, a lively atmosphere. My intuition tells me that this is going to be one great game, given the ranking of both teams. I imagine the Deportivo Mbusu players will charge out like rabid pit bulls to take on their rivals from nearby Luque."

"We're all set for an exciting contest. The referee is tossing the coin. The local team's captain wins the toss, and he chooses the goal where his goalie is already standing. We're about to start, folks."

(...)

"The Deportivo Mbusu players are on the offensive. Leite kicks the ball, and his pass cuts like a knife in the backs of Luque's defence, Caldera moves in for a shot on goal, a defender trips him from behind, and that's a penalty, Beatricio, a penalty for Deportivo."

"That's right, Arturo. The hard-pressed Luqueño defence dozed off for a second, the pass had a surgeon's precision, the player intruded into the box, they closed on him and in a flash Caldera was down."

"Leite prepares to shoot. The referee verbally warns several Luqueño players who were trying to invade the box. The referee blows his whistle and... the goalie stops the shot. Leite pulls up his stockings and stomps the grass at the penalty spot, Beatricio."

The offender has been pardoned. Leite has missed a perfect opportunity. Even if the shot by the Deportivo player was off, you have to recognise the merit of the goalie, who guessed the ball's direction and stopped it cleanly. This goalie has been showing a high level of performance for some time, and his use of Occam's Razor and when I say Occam I'm not referring to the German O. Kahn, the goalie Oliver Kahn, but to the razor of the Franciscan Friar, William of Occam, the one that allows him to slice through things and always choose the simplest solution, take the easiest way out, without complicating the situation nor multiplying problems. It's exactly what this amazing goalie has done here.

(...)

"We're nearing the end of this first fifteen minutes of the first half with the score at 0-0, Acosta. 'The Laurelty dragon' is moving into the goal area, he's the driver, the real motor of the Luqueño team, he speeds up, puts it into fifth gear, Núñez runs up to block him, Acosta puts on the brakes, taps the ball forward to himself and the rival player kicks him down low and then bowls him over like being run down by a truck. Foul for Luqueño, Beatricio."

"We know 'The Laurelty dragon' is a football player who devours the pitch, an all-terrain machine with the dedication of a Spartan soldier. We also know that he's a player with a precise hermeneutics, one who keeps the rhythm and whose accurate reading of the game is one of the high points of this team. And at this point the Deportivo player had to resort to a really strong challenge, a violent action that deserves not just a yellow card, but more like an orange one."

"The Luqueño player, wearing the shirt with the number ten on it, is getting ready to take the free kick. The ball's in the box, Andrade heads it on where it finds 'Cobra' Alvarenga unmarked, and he takes a weak shot right into the goalie's hands. A gift, Beatricio."

"A great play by the Luqueño team, a drop-pass set piece by the book, but 'Cobra' Alvarenga didn't get it done, the Luqueño player's shot was lukewarm, neither Platonic nor Aristotelian, really poor on his part, neither concave nor convex, not to the centre nor a shot to the crossbar, a gift for the gatekeeper. A very alert goalie who stopped the ball securely, giving no chance for second shots, not punching it out toward the corner, he gripped it till that sphere was no more than a soft hum between his gloves, Arturo."

(...)

"Acosta put the team on his shoulders, with his instep he sends a lobbed cross to his teammate, Arévalos, who stops it with his chest. Arévalos is talented and can shoot with either foot, he swings past the eighteen-yard line through the area, feints a pass and switches direction so fast his defender falls down nearly breaking his own ankle trying to stay with him, he shoots with the other foot as if he were throwing the ball with his hand, placing it out of the goalie's reach. Goooooaaal! Gooooooaaal! Luque. Luque. Luque. Goooooal for Sportivo Luqueño."

"A magnificent goal for the Luqueño team. They set it up perfectly, first with 'The Laurelty dragon' and his white glove that puts the ball on the little medal his teammate Arévalos wears on his chest, and the latter who works his magic, sets up a beautiful play and takes a shot that was slow like Balzac, but one that goes past the line of no return and turns into the goal that breaks the draw in favour of the team from the city of Luque."

"But what's this, Beatricio? What's with the royal costumes they're using to celebrate? They're putting on a scene from the theatre. And what's Arévalos got in his hand? It looks like a skull like the ones medical students have. This is the beauty and the insanity of football. Deportivo Mbusu 0; Sportivo Luqueño 1!"

(…)

"We're halfway through the first period, the players from the home team are moving, they're controlling possession and advancing toward the opposing team's goal. Núñez contemplates the offensive horizon, getting a pass off in the middle of a forest of defending legs, Noguera controls the ball, does a give-and-go with a teammate, turns, nutmeg, what a play! Threatening a goal… ball out of bounds, Beatricio."

"Deportivo Mbusu was really close to tying the game. Noguera went into the goal area, received the give-and-go pass from his teammate, nutmegged the central defender and turned on a dime in front of the goalie, breaking through the defensive wall but finishing as if he had a pirate's leg, made of wood, and his shot misses just to the right of the post. A real shame that this twenty-four carat shot didn't result in a goal. A play seemingly from another game."

(…)

"Deportivo Mbusu is making a substitution. Leite leaves the pitch in the middle of a generalised booing, and Otazú, a young player from the reserves, takes his place. What difference can this change make for the team, Beatricio?"

"That's still an almost algebraic unknown. It's the second time that Otazú has had the honour of entering the pitch during a first division game, because the last game, a draw as the visiting team, was his debut. We could see there that he has promise. He's a young player, but has great technique and is fierce, especially when facing defenders where he shows some devilish dribble action capable of driving them crazy. The public hisses at Leite for his poor performance, and he heads directly for the showers. We don't know if he's mad about the substitution, about the result of the play, about the reaction of the public or about all the above."

(...)

"It's looking like the game's fallen into a well. The forwards are absorbed by the defenders' marking. Deportivo Mbusu is advancing. Otazú has the ball, he dribbles, he has it tied up, hitched to him, it's as if it's sewn to his left shoe. He gets to the box, shoots, the ball bounces off a Luqueño defender, a Deportivo player takes the rebound, shoots again, the goalie clears to the centre, Otazú takes the rebound and puts it in with real power. Goooaaal! Did I just say goal? A *won-der-ful gooo-al* from distance! Otazú ties the game. Deportivo 1, Luqueño 1."

"The reaction of the Deportivo team is worth noting. They suddenly shook themselves out of the status quo haze, following Otazú's rhythm, the player who just entered, the kid with the dirty face who in spite of his inexperience didn't let the pressure of the moment weigh him down, yes, ladies and gentlemen, he left the opposition scattered all over the pitch, and at his rhythm they shook off that tiresome haze that surrounded them, looked for the goal and after a series of rebounds Otazú took the ball and, finished with class, as the gods do, with an unstoppable shot from outside the box."

(...)

"It's the final minute, to maintain the score the Luqueños are forming a bird cage in the middle of the pitch, they're putting the game on ice. And the referee declares the end of the first half of the contest. The players head for the locker rooms to listen to their coaches' speeches. The Luqueño team has dominated during most of the game, playing like they were in their own stadium, in Feliciano Cáceres."

"That's just it; I see a very bad situation for the Mbusu team. They give the ball away, they're over there hanging from the crossbar, they're slow, they pass the ball with no enthusiasm, their lights are out. The players look tired, it's like they only have one lung like Mostaza Merlo. Except for the goal that produced the draw they've done absolutely nothing. It's not even a team, more like a shadow, to put it more graphically, I would say they're like a bunch of disconnected spirits. At this rate and with this temporary tie, Arturo, the Luqueños will remain among the top class of football in Paraguay."

IV

In football terms it wasn't going very well for us. But it seemed like the results didn't matter, at least not within the walls of the clubhouse. We always collected our pay at the end of the month and the company spent a lot on publicity.

I'd been able to buy a Nissan Terrano for myself, and I started to go out with one of the models that stood out the most. A lot of the other members of the team began to go out with models too. The married guys didn't go out with them; they just rented them by the night.

Several players had to resign and received their corresponding severance pay, "because they didn't fulfil the aesthetic standard set by the company." They started to bring in some foreign players. Most of them were players who had shone in another era, but were over the hill now. Our club turned into a veritable cemetery of elephants, where the greats came to put their sports careers to rest. For them to bring in good players was something new for us, the usual thing was that they would sell off the first person who raised his head a half-inch above the rest; they'd sell him fast to the highest bidder. That was the norm, because the president of the club himself was the owner of the rights of many players and there were businessmen-vultures watching every practice.

The newcomers were old players, but had great technique and experience. One of them was a lefty, a classic number ten, Reconto, a Uruguayan player who at another time had been one of the best on the planet. He had a truly enviable control of the ball and a wickedly accurate head shot. With the army of foreigners captained by Reconto, plus the legion of local players, our team began to win games.

We'd made the Luqueño sports fans fall in love with us again. The merchandising was overwhelming. They were selling yellow and blue pens, mugs, compasses, tee-shirts, backpacks, key rings with photos of the players, thermometers. They even sold bonsais stamped with the team's insignia. But the romance didn't last long; within two months the flood of foreigners had taken off as quickly as they had arrived. They'd only been contracted for sixty days. The only ones left on the team were a few Brazilian players.

It seems that FIFA had seen a video of several of our goal celebrations and put out their Circular No. 579 where they ordered referees to prohibit such group hoopla. "Choreographed celebrations that result in an excessive loss of time are not permitted," stated the published document. So we had to learn new individual celebrations to replace the group ones.

On weekdays we often saw managers from other first-division clubs in the office of our coach Lucas. Sometimes they even had their briefcases in their hands. They would be shut away for an hour talking (negotiating) and then they'd leave, and I couldn't help but see the scornful smile on the face of the visiting manager when he saw our training, a mocking smile as if saying "come on, trot along, boys, keep on training, it's all in vain because we've already fixed the result of the game."

That would piss me off and I would start to run like crazy, stirring up a certain fervour for battle in some of my teammates. Some, on the other hand, raised their index finger and rotated it around their right ear, indicating my limited mental health.

V
Live Transmission on Deportivo Mbusu's web page:

www.deportivombusu.com.py/online.php

The second half is about to begin. This one-one draw doesn't help us at all. We have faith that we can score more goals, our team is good enough and there's more than enough time for it. The fans urge us on frenetically.

46': The second half begins.

47': In an unfortunate play, the Luqueño team takes the ball, Acosta scores the goal that puts them ahead. To celebrate a little in front of the camera Acosta makes the *USpeak* cell phone company's well-known "thumb salute." The Luqueño team is now leading 2 to 1. But there's still a lot of ground to cover; this is just the beginning.

48': Otazú failed to take advantage of an opportunity after a great individual play, assisted by Núñez.

50': Our players are putting pressure on every sector of the pitch. The Luqueño players are trapped and are sending the ball in all directions. The ball is burning their boots.

51': Acosta is fouled by a push from Otazú. Free kick for the visitors.

52': A dipping shot by Acosta that grazes the crossbar.
55': The goalie sends it out and in three passes we are at the rival team's box. Mendoza shoots from along the end line.

57': Mendoza is on fire. He dances all alone through the entire defence and ends up shooting over the crossbar. Luqueño is saved.

59': Otazú takes off rapidly along the right-side lane, he enters the box, a defender knocks him down and the referee says nothing. Otazú stays on the ground demanding a penalty. The referee is working against us.

62': A childish foul by Núñez in midfield and up comes Luqueño in counter-attack with Acosta who takes the ball down the middle, shoots from some sixty feet out and we're saved: the ball passes very close to the right post.

65': Luqueño makes a change.
Incoming: Jorge Aranda.
Outgoing: Reinaldo Arévalos.

66': Arévalos comes out saying things to his coach and throws him his overshirt.

67': We put two crosses into the box, but the visiting team's goalie was on top of them.

68': Our coach makes a change.
Incoming: Antonio Rodríguez.
Outgoing: Roberto Núñez.

69': Yellow card for Acosta, for a foul on Rodríguez.

71': Aranda galloped into the box but our centre-back timed it well to apply the *offside* trap.

73': The nervousness of both teams is beginning to show. But more in the case of the Luqueños who are throwing wild tackles and elbow jabs. The referee? Like he's wearing dark sunglasses.

75': A mistake by the visitors' centre-back, and Fante recovers the ball, he gets to the box, is about to shoot when Aguilera appears opportunely to steal the ball and send it out of bounds.

76': Luqueño makes a change.
Incoming: Joao Acevedo
Outgoing: Tadrio Aquilera

77': Fante feints and scores a beautiful chip goal over the goalie's head but he had received the ball in an offside position, half a step behind the last Luqueño defender. We'll have to see the replay, because apparently we're playing against more than eleven men.

78': Yellow card for Acevedo, for calling for an imaginary foul.

80': The visiting team are mounting a counter-attack, three-on-three, Acosta has the ball, he takes off right down the middle, he wants to set up Aranda, and fortunately blows the pass.

81': The Luqueño centre laid it on with a really nasty tackle on Fante. Acosta kicks the ball outside for them to chase down. The referee doesn't even give the offender a verbal warning. These judges' behaviour is shameful.

82': Fante is being attended to off the pitch.

84': Fante is back on the pitch. Otazú returns the courtesy to the Luqueño team. The stadium applauds our team's *fair play*.

86': Yellow card for Aranda for going for a 50-50 ball with excessive force.

87': Their striker entered our box, Rodríguez marked him and the Luqueño player took a dive. The referee should give him a yellow card for faking the foul.

89': The referee signals two minutes of stoppage time, we'll go until the 92nd minute. Otazú fakes a dribble and is hit with a tremendous slide tackle by the Luqueño player who ends up seeing a red card, so now we're eleven against ten on the pitch. Although maybe it's too late to react; there's no time left.

90': Even so, our guys make an effort with the ever-in-motion Otazú who takes on the defence, resisting their marking, he spins and passes it to Fante who shoots and the ball is contained immediately by their goalie.

92': It's all over. Yet another defeat for the locals. Our men gave their all on the pitch, but there was no way, nothing you can do against the referee. The players shake hands in the middle of the pitch and we're signing off too. We close our transmission, not without first thanking you for joining us. Good night and until the next time.

VI

Radio "14th of March". Interview with Bernardo Acosta, the star player who wears the number 10 jersey for the Sportivo Luqueño team, "the man of the match".

I'm here because they chose me as the man of the match. Yeah, it was a really tough game. But thanks to God and the Virgin we were able to win with a goal straight out of the locker room. We hardly touched the ball in the second half and with all the confidence that our coach put in me I was able to hit a right-footed rocket shot, I kicked it hard and took the Deportivo defence by surprise. We knew it was going to be a complicated game because they have good players and are always strong playing on their home field, but we had our strengths too and luckily for us they weren't able to even the score after my goal and as visitors we leave very happy with our three points.

VII

I thought I could understand how the mind of our coach, Lucio Viega, worked. He was just the employee of a powerful enterprise, he had his MBA and had completed the coach's course, and the combination of those two degrees made him automatically an acceptable candidate to work for *"O Rei"* Sports. He was a solitary type, who acted and moved about as if he were on enemy terrain, seemed to distrust everything and everyone. Whenever he gave orders there was a hint of insecurity in his voice. I had already sketched his psychological profile. He was a person acclimated to defeats, used to shipwrecks, someone who always bet on the losing horses and for him his current state of job and financial success was a rare occurrence. He figured it was a trick of fate, a deception, a castle of sand that the wind or some clown would kick over at any time.

Once I ran into him at a karaoke. He was drinking and probably drunk, at least you would think so seeing the number of bottles on his lonely table. I saw him from a distance at first, without his noticing my presence. He asked for the microphone and sang *Un día de domingo* with the saddest voice and the most French-like Portuguese I had ever heard in my life. When he finished, I went over to speak to him.

"How's it going, coach?"

He shook my hand and we talked for a while. I always liked psychology, during my studies for my almost completed high school degree it was the subject that I came to dislike the least. After my conversation with the coach I realised he was conspiring against himself, unconsciously he was sabotaging himself and that explained his repeated failures. And I could also come to the conclusion that this was a respite and nothing more, the repeated defeats were giving him a breather, or he was giving himself a breather now. But that was going to change soon, that's what I sensed that night.

As for me, I was getting tired of being a piece of merchandise and losing with such regularity. We had accumulated seven defeats, two victories and five ties. At that rate we were going to end up at the bottom in the standings. The matches were almost always fixed, because the strategy the coach gave us was at times frankly a losing one. Sometimes, when we happened to be playing against lesser teams, the tactic was we'd come out like we were going to crush them. It was apparent that our games were for sale and the big teams could buy them, but not the smaller clubs. One day I decided to stir up my teammates, we got together and I told them my ideas. The team we were going to face was one that was demolishing their opponents in the local tournament games, they had won numerous Paraguayan championships. They roared like a Formula One racer motor in home contests but on the international level they turned into milquetoast. The name of the team was Real Lizard and they were suffering from a kind of stage fright or maybe a form of misunderstood patriotism (they only played well in Paraguay) or, on the other hand, maybe it was just an inferiority complex, staring at the knees of foreign teams and seeing them as if they were giants.

The strategy our coach outlined consisted of having six men on defence and four midfielders. It was a clear defensive strategy and playing to lose. I spoke with the guys the night of the meeting before the game. I felt like another person was speaking with my voice. I talked to them about sports glory, about triumph, about effort, about all the hope our city was placing on us, like a pot of gold at the end of the rainbow.

Saturday arrived, we played the game against the Lizard team. We stuffed their net full. João scored a magnificent goal. The ball curved twice like it had a life of its own and ended up not in the corner of the net, to tell the truth, it went in at about the goalie's waist level and with the power it was carrying as it passed, it knocked down a towel that was hanging from the net. That was the goal that opened up the scoring. We forgot about the tactical plan and went for the lead. With a corner shot our centre defender took advantage of the situation and finished magnificently. And the final blow was a penalty. The player who took it was about to run toward the camera to celebrate his goal with the choreography we had learned, but two of us grabbed him by his shirt and we walked with him to the middle of the field. The coach was furious, insulting us in a nearly incomprehensible Portuguese, gesticulating like an epileptic. He made the permitted three substitutions, but even with that we continued dominating the game and ended up winning.

The whole team was sanctioned. Economically, of course. Since I had been the leader of the rebellion, I was fired by the club; they showed me the memo that came from Río de Janeiro, signed and sealed by Pelé. They didn't give me any severance pay, but now I own my own player's rights. Although it's true I'm a little over the hill now, I can still sign up for another team. Maybe I'll even score a goal. If I manage to score that goal, I'll hug the teammate nearest to me after yelling my heart out and dedicating it to the fans.

Interview with Javier Viveros

What role did football play in your youth?
It always played a recreational role. I've played with my friends and I've gone to the stadiums. Even now I play with my colleagues from work. As a player I've always been mid-to-low skilled player. I mainly played on small 5-on-5 fields; I played the butcher defender in my youth – when I could still run like Eolo – and lately I play more of a cherry-picking forward: I'm in constant dialogue with the rival goalie, in the hope that the ball will come to me, so that I can try to ruffle the net.

Do you support a particular team?
Of course. The Sportivo Luqueño of Paraguay, which is the club of the city of Luque, where I lived my first two decades. We've never won an international tournament – and a total of only about three local tournaments – but, fortunately, enthusiasm is not something you measure by bronze pieces behind dirty glass in a showcase :).

I sympathise with Barcelona in Spain too. And it's important that I've done so since before the so-called Guardiola Era; I've been a follower ever since the rudder was in the hands of Charly Rexach.

Which is more important to you as a fan, a good result or a good game?
I opt for a good game, because for me football has to do with the aesthetic. I prefer a game full of beautiful plays even if it ends up with a thrashing. That's the philosophy of the tennis player, Fabrice Santoro, but applied to football. The French guy was a talented player, full of magic and subtle plays that drove

the public wild and, nevertheless, he has the record of being the player with the largest number of losses on the professional circuit.

What motivates you to write fiction that takes place within a Paraguayan context?

Tolstoy's famous statement: "paint your village and you'll paint the whole world." For the story to be credible without a whole lot of effort it's advisable to take elements from the reality closest to one. Of course, that doesn't mean you can't narrate something outside your own country. In fact, I've published a book called *Manual de esgrima para elefantes*, stories that take place in Africa. But I lived on that continent for three years, so I was also close to the themes I dealt with in that work.

Could you comment on the use of Guaraní in your writing?

Guaraní is one of the official languages of Paraguay, a large portion of the population speak it. I like it a lot; it's a language with great expressive power. I've written three books in which Guaraní is a protagonist and it always appears in my prose in some way, when not directly, then it appears hidden behind Spanish, holding it up with its syntax or nourishing it through lexical lending.

How do football and politics intersect in Paraguay?

Well, in this country politics always tried to be on the side of football, because that's the way to earn the sympathy of the masses. The dictator Stroessner's faithful supporters used to call him "the country's first sportsman" and everyone knew he was a fan of Club Libertad. Libertad means freedom. A paradox, right?

As it happens, Horacio Cartes was president of Club

Libertad. He put up the money and the club won several local tourneys and even did well in the Copa Libertadores. That's how he secured his image as a winner, and currently he's our country's president... It's the application of the Latin *panem et circenses*.

What is your opinion about the recent developments in the scandal surrounding corruption in FIFA?
It didn't surprise me too much. It was something we all knew was going on, but that no one could prove... until the FBI got involved. That CONMEBOL and FIFA have that level of scoundrels is damaging to football, very damaging. The bad apples need to be removed from the basket, and urgently.

Do you see any connection between the creative process and the way in which someone plays football or behaves as a fan?
At least in my case there isn't any. When I write I'm Apollonian; pure reason, I have to have the text perfectly worked out in my head before I sit down to give it shape at my computer. And when I play football or am a fan, I'm more moved by the Dionysian, infected with a warlike fervour, taken away by a passion that knows no limits.

Did any writer of football fiction influence this story?
Yes. In fiction and in football. The mixing of voices in the first part of the story is a direct legacy of *Los cachorros* by Vargas Llosa. And in its structure there's influence of *Los detectives Salvajes* by Bolaño, who wrote a masterly text with a football theme: the story titled "Buba", which is in his book *Putas asesinas*. The dedication of my story to Buba (R.I.P.) is not gratuitous.

Do you see any lingering reluctance to incorporating football or sport as a dominant theme or plot driver among your generation of authors?

There is some resistance. Many writers still consider it a kind of sub-literature, a lesser literature. Although there are fewer of those writers in my generation; my generation recognises football's character as a global epidemic.

What is the place of football fiction in the literature of your country?

As far as I know, none. Except for the story *El crack* by Augusto Roa Bastos, I haven't heard of any other example of the genre. For the book *Punta Karaja* that I edited with my friend, the Cerro Porteño supporter, Juan Heilbon, we had to ask some of the authors we knew to write football stories; in the end the book had 11 stories by 11 different authors and we distributed it later on the web in PDF format.

Is there a particular identity or style associated with football in Paraguay?

Yes, our football is characterised as committed, hard-fought and good defence. Along the lines of Uruguay but with fewer fouls and with two world titles less.

What is your evaluation of the Paraguayan national team's performance in the 2015 Copa América?

The team left me pleasantly surprised, ending up among the four best teams when few had faith in them. Even if Argentina put a tennis-like score of 6-1 on them in the semifinals, at least we were left with the conviction that the World Cup in Russia isn't so far out of reach for the team.

What does the Paraguayan team need in order to have World Cup hopes in the future?

Just smart managers who hand over the team's rudder to truly qualified professionals. Good players we've always had and there are more all the time. It's a shame that capable managers aren't directly proportional in number. With Paraguay's terrible campaign in the qualifying rounds a run of four World Cup participations in a row came to an end. But we'll come back. And I hope it'll be to cheer goals by the red and white in the country of the much-loved Dostoyevsky.

Peru
SERGIO GALARZA

Sergio Galarza was born in Lima on August 3, 1976. He is the author of the following volumes of short stories: *Matacabros* (Asma, 1996), *El infierno es un buen lugar* (Asma, 1997), *Todas las mujeres son galgos* (Lecturamoral, 1999), *La soledad de los aviones* (Estruendomudo, 2005), and *Algunas formas de decir adiós* (Algaida, 2014), which won the XI Premio Iberoamericano de Relatos Cortos de Cádiz. He also wrote the collection of *crónicas Los Rolling Stones in Perú* (Periférica, 2007). His novel *Paseador de perros* (Candaya, 2009) resulted in his recognition as the Nuevo Talento Fnac (New Talent Fnac). A second novel was *JFK* (Candaya, 2012). Galarza Puente studied law but never practised the profession. He has worked in a university, was a news editor for a television station as well as culture editor for a magazine. He is a fan of Atlético Madrid, and lives in the Legazpi district of that city, with its red and black spirit, and plays football several times a week. An earlier version of "Where the Spiders Nest" (Donde anidan las arañas) first appeared in Spanish in *Selección peruana, 1990-2005* (Estruendomudo, 2005).

Where the Spiders Nest

My father never taught me to play football. He was an athlete, well built, as they say, dark complexion, played handball and rode his bicycle to the store to buy cigarettes. On weekend outings to his company's club in Chosica we did take in a few games together. He liked to be goalie, but every time I try to evoke a memory in which the ball rolled from his feet to mine any place else, the neighbourhood park or in front of our house, nothing comes to mind. All I see is my own image, sitting at the school door after the daily training session, waiting for someone to remember to pick me up, as it gets darker and all the guys on the team have already gone home.

Before I got on the school team, I would get out of class at three in the afternoon, but with all the distractions on the way to the bus stop, like letting the air out of the tyres of the collective shuttle vans, throwing stones at cars from the overpass of the Vía Expresa and at the transvestites who would wait for their clientele at the intersection of the Paseo de la República and Javier Prado, and checking out the porno magazines (especially *Macho*, a Spanish magazine with stories that guaranteed an erection), I would get home at four-thirty. Then I would eat alone, because my grandmother would have her lunch punctually at noon, Mom would eat whenever her work schedule allowed, and my father would scarf down a bite at the office. I would eat fast, and without changing my clothes or catching what was on TV, I'd grab the ball and would train in the inner patio, practicing self-passes against the wall, dribbles against imaginary rivals who fell down behind me and saving goals right on the goal line. My position has always been centre-forward. Whenever I heard one of my parents open the entrance gate I would hide the ball behind some plants and climb the stairs taking off my kit.

Once I was in my room, I would pick up any notebook that I had left on the floor and with my gaze fixed on some of the many battles lost by our army, on the strange mathematical hieroglyphics that I had never managed to figure out on my own, or on St. Augustine's maxims, always with the same result after a few minutes: my right index finger in my nose and then the snot on my tongue.

My parents knew my attitude was pure pretence, but they weren't saying anything because my grades in school were still not as bad as they would be later. I was passing exams thanks to my ability to escape that third watchful eye that teachers boast of having. They were afraid I'd join "the neighbourhood loafers", the phrase my parents used to refer to the kids and the not really kids anymore who lived from one corner to corner, from store to store, poorly dressed, with their tee-shirt draped over their shoulders or hanging out of the back pocket of their torn pants, spitting every other minute as if they were trying to expel their problems and sorrows, annoying the neighbours by ringing door bells just for the heck of it and kicking a ball around in the park, until nightfall and hunger sent them home. I didn't consider them loafers. They were free. And that's what I wanted to be.

During dinner I would beg my parents to let me go out on the street when school let out. No way. Their answer remained firm and negative every night. I could have disobeyed, but it was risky leaving grandma alone. Several times, when we were at home, she had forgotten to turn off the gas or had left the front door of the house unlocked. That old lady was a danger and I was at the end of my fuckin' patience with her. As revenge, I would interrupt her in her room as she was losing herself in the romantic labyrinths of her soap operas. I would turn down the volume on the TV, claiming that it was too loud and I couldn't study. I would put the dog on her bed, something she hated. I would ring the doorbell, forcing her to get up to see who it was. It was cruel, until Grandma fell down the stairs going to open the door for the ghost invented by her grandson. My grandmother was stretched out in front of the door like a pile of bones. I was so terrified that I vomited, had nightmares and carried a weight on my conscience that left me agonising in bed for a couple of days.

In one of my recurring nightmares during my agony a ball of bones with my grandma's face rolled down the stairs and when I opened the door we both let out a silent scream that woke me up in a cold sweat.

The good part: because of the accident they hired a nurse to take care of Grandma. It was time to loaf a little.

Autumn. The last days. The sun sets earlier. At five in the afternoon the streets in our neighbourhood would be pervaded by a special aroma, like warm bread with a soft drink. The wind blows and the kids run around laughing nervously at the barking of dogs. There I am, standing on a corner. Some girls, their hair wet, pass by me; I act as if they were invisible when they glance my way. The only thing that interests me is loafing. Where could those lazy asses be? I ask myself. The fuckers. If my father had heard me talk like that, he would have punched me in the mouth. So let him do it, I'll knock the shit out of him. I laugh to myself and walk toward the park. The aroma of the street envelops me, I feel like I just took a shower, I feel like kicking something. I find them in the middle of a game, buried in the excitement of every play, insulting each other. I think that if my father had seen them, he would have knocked their teeth down their throats. This time I don't laugh and I walk away.

A week goes by, at the end of which I find myself once again kicking a ball around in the patio of my house. It's not the same. The courtyard smells like a trunk of clothes. I go out to the street and look on the corners. To the park! Before it's too late. The sky is covered with threads of orange. I get there in time. I see that the loafers need another player to begin their game. I pretend to ignore them until they call me over. But I don't know how to play goalie, I tell them. You're on defence then. For how many goals? Until it gets dark.

Autumn comes to an end. Winter is an incredible hassle, I can just imagine how exciting summer will be in the neighbourhood. The whistles start as soon as I get home from school. It's our call of the wild. We're the grey kids who decorate the corners of our neighbourhood, the park warriors, the loafers who munch on bread and drink free sodas at Cuervo's store. He's an old man who always touches the girls' hands when he gives them change. The winter is cruel, worse than those referees who won't give even a minute of extra time. It drizzles and nobody likes to play on a wet field. The street smells like the patio of my house. So when the winter comes to an end, life returns to the park. The corners are once again the cement islands of the grey boys. And the aroma of loafing takes over the neighbourhood.

At the end of the year, there's a tryout at school for the new season. At first we're fifty – some kids dreaming of wearing the yellow school jersey. After two weeks of training comes the first cut. No more dreams of glory for the ones cut, just silently crying themselves to sleep that night. At the age of eleven the greatest disappointment a kid can experience is being left off the school team, I have no doubt of that, I've never felt an angst like that, that empty feeling in the belly that crushes even the strongest, the anticipated suffering of failure that leaves your soul battered like being thrashed in a game.

Being left off a football team is the only grief possible for a kid until the parties start up and the girls make kebabs of our hearts.

Every ball that lands at my feet is like a blessing and I look up to find the coach. I always see him talking with somebody's father. It doesn't matter, I advance toward the opponents' goal, I make passes and try really hard to help my current team win. The next week there's another cut. Now we're down to thirty and the team needs eighteen players instead of twenty-two. According to the coach, the school can't afford more kits than that. I practise hard. Final exams are drawing near along with the final cut. My father never comes to watch the practices and is always late to pick me up, because if he leaves work any earlier, he'll be fired, or so says Mom. Grandma is fed up with the nurse who doesn't leave her side for a single second as if they had instructed her to be her shadow. I don't see the park loafers anymore. And when the coach decides on the eighteen lucky guys, sweat has turned into my second skin and I dream football, football and nothing but football. How can I ever forget that moment when I heard my name! I'm on the team and my father can delay picking me up for as long as he wants that afternoon. I could care less about the final exams now. Did they ever really matter? I've just touched heaven and while angels may need wings to reach heaven, all I need to get there is jersey number sixteen.

A month after the team had been selected, the coach told us that our first game would be in a couple weeks. Some positions, it can't be denied, had been filled long before the ninety minutes began. You could appreciate the talent of some of my teammates from how they tied their boots to how they wiped off their sweat. The holders of other positions, among them that of defensive midfielder, or stopper, however you want to call it, a key position on the team and in my life, were open to question; their talent could be limited to the brand of boots they wore and the ability of their parents to clap the coach on the back and cover him with kisses at the end of each practice. This kind of preference earned the hard way by parents became notorious during the friendly games the team played in preparation for the season. And what a preparation it was! I would have preferred a million times kicking the ball against the wall in the patio of my house rather than putting on that jersey and sitting around with my mouth shut not soaking it with sweat. Rage alone is one of the worst sensations I endured during my football days. If I could have at least licked off the sweat of defeat dripping down my face.

The rest of the future reserve players, eleven year olds, like me, with an extra large-sized naiveté, didn't seem to share my concerns and kept on practicing hard. I did too. I mean, I would practise as hard or harder than anybody else, not because I was naive, but rather guided by that desire and that blind faith that I have in making goals at the last minute. Several times I ended up stretched out on the side of the field, exhausted, feeling like I was sinking into the turf and imagining the priest-director of the school praying for my release from this world at the same time he's taking off my number ten jersey and putting it on himself.

When the moment of truth arrived, my father took me to my first official game. It happened to be a home game on our school's field, which influenced the other fathers to expose us and themselves to ridicule. The opening ceremony had been the day before, but they prepared a special ceremony that delayed the beginning of the game for half an hour. Each member of the team was introduced, topped off by a choreography performed by the mothers, a kind of childish round dance around the team. Here a clarification of vital importance: my mom stayed at home that Sunday morning. If she had participated, I don't doubt that I would have hung up my boots then and there. Seeing her wave streamers around wouldn't have offended my dignity as her son, not even hearing her intone cheers, but the choreography turned out to be as pathetic as a sports idol on the threshold of retirement dragging his legs across the field, a pitiful spectacle that emblazoned itself in my store of undesirable memories due to the powerlessness that grows on the reserve players' bench when you see your team's inadequacy.

The final score is also etched in my memory: a four to nothing that made half the team cry because in the final minute we missed a penalty. If we had converted it, the score would have been four to one. The difference was clear to the player charged with taking the shot, who fell to his knees on the ground and burst out crying! Then the rest of the players were infected with the crying and ran to their parents as soon as they heard the final whistle. Without a game plan and with a weak spirit, a team guided by a coach who only knew how to shout "Come on, guys!", not even the greatest of divine forces could have helped us. I have to emphasise that at no moment did I feel part of that group of losers. They were so different from the loafers in my neighbourhood; warriors on potholed streets who I decided to join again, to forget the crushing losses that eliminated us from the championship.

My father told me I hadn't fought hard enough for a place on the team. His words were like those tiny pebbles that get in your boots; you think you can endure them and keep on running on the field, but they bug you so much that the only solution is to stop and take off the boots. That was his judgment when I announced that I was distancing myself from the team, disillusioned with official football. I didn't understand and never will why the neighbourhood loafers played like hell every afternoon, what drove them to live with skinned knees and elbows, how could an afternoon pick-up game, as insignificant as a moment of silence for the death of an equipment manager, unleash such passion translated into colliding, spitting and cursing. While my teammates were only worrying about the latest model boots, imposing their elegance on every imaginable bad play, on every fall, on every complaint and curse for the goals being scored on us.

I began to miss practices. It was summer and morning laziness kept me wrapped in the bed sheets. The heat kept me asleep until lunchtime and digestion put me to sleep again until a machine-gun blast of whistles invaded the neighbourhood. Those summer games in parks and on the streets were unforgettable, kicking the ball over the cars that interrupted the game, even using the trees as walls to kick the ball against. Also unforgettable was the night I reflected on whether I should hang onto jersey number sixteen. Nobody at home knew about my cutting practices; I had told them not to bother to pick me up and not to say anything, I'd be the one to let the coach know of my decision to stop playing, so my father was surprised one day, when he took advantage of his lunch hour from work to go see me practise.

At dinnertime he asked me how I was doing on the team, whether I saw any possibility of playing soon, or if I had finally given up. The tone of his final words, mother's turning her eyes away, the atmosphere of excessive politeness floating over our plates when I refused to eat my green beans, engulfed me until I managed to clear away the smoke that hid the orchestra seats from the balcony. Adults and the songs they sing to make kids confess were beginning to sound out of tune. I got up from the table without excusing myself. They didn't say anything to me.

Grandmother and her soaps were occupying the TV. I sought refuge in my new collection of adventure stories. All those books presented kingdoms, pirates, heroic animals. Those authors had never been pumped up with excitement by a ball, their spirits had never been crushed by disappointment seeing their goalie about to be defeated, they only knew about unrequited love, struggles against nature, and dumb things like that which at that moment were no good at all to me. I slept badly for a couple nights. I had underestimated my parents; I have to recognise the subtlety of their behaviour. Their statements of support followed by the sentence of failure, something like "We hope they'll give you the chance to show that you know how to play and play better than those spoiled brats, too bad you're quitting," achieved their objective.

My return to the team was received with indifference, as if I'd never been on the pitch or on the bench with the reserve players. The reaction was in part favourable to me. There were already enough pressures around me. Mom's smiling and silent attentions and my father's casual hints about practice at dinner every night would bring a couple of goddammits to the tip of my tongue. I can imagine the disaster that those goddammits would have unleashed at the table. Dad's hand would hurt, although not as much as Mom's. Just remembering the stinging in my cheeks produced by those hands on rare and well-deserved occasions, made me bite my lips and keep my mouth shut. I learned to know myself and discovered that anger made me stronger. Of course outside my house I let it rip.

Another season arrived. Why mention the first game and the line-up. We'll get straight to the point. Without knowing how, we got to the last game of our group with the possibility of qualifying for the next round. The coach was pacing the locker room biting his lips and rubbing his head. The responsibility resting on his shoulders was far greater than his aspirations. It's a virus that's displayed on the frozen faces and trembling legs of his spoiled brats. We eternal reserve players have not yet been infected by the virus; the chance for that is still far off. So we think, we're sure that we're immune. We could bet our mothers and we'd lose them. The coach just gave me my entry card. Go warm up with the group, he tells me. There are three sick players, vomiting in the showers, and one of them occupies the position of defensive midfielder. I can barely tie my boots, it's the lack of practice. Time to jump onto the field. My father is in the stands. He's developed the habit of accompanying me to every game. The first play catches me cold, with no time to react. And like a heavenly dispatch, the ball comes to me on the rebound. I launch a fierce counter-attack that's bungled by the forwards. The game's rhythm is exhausting. No rival player has been able to penetrate my marking since that first play. We get to the final minute of the first period. Another dispatch from heaven. I look for someone to pass it to. Take it, I tell myself, the virus is going to get you if you don't. I head for the goal passing by rivals with speed and I take a shot. Goal. My dad's in the stands. My sweat is a nectar of the gods to me.

Up to here, nothing but the truth. Or lies, however you want to take it. What happened later? We lost. The coach congratulated the team at half-time and said we had to hold on to the lead. The three players who had been sick in the locker room returned. I didn't ask for explanations for my substitution. How much did we lose by? I don't want to remember. My father took me home before the game ended. All during lunch he never tired of talking about my goal.

The next week I formally quit the team. Later I played on other teams and when I was fifteen my parents retired me from official tournaments because of my terrible grades in school. Now I'm over twenty and I play on Sundays from time to time, if my hangover permits and there are enough people for a six-on-six game. I play with strangers. No longer on park fields these days. The loafers are still there, like spectators of the neighbourhood's new generations. Their reflections sleeping in the grass are not going to wake up one of these days. Each time I see them I go back in time, my father is late picking me up from practice, a responsibility too big for his aspirations is still weighing on the coach, my dad in the stands, and all those football things.

Interview with Sergio Galarza

What role did football play in your youth?

I've been playing football since I was a kid, for me it's something that's always been there, as much a part of me as my own skin. I believe that my personality, the construction of my persona, can be seen in the steps I passed through as a football player. When I was a teenager, I was part of my school team and even though I was a reserve player I almost always used to play in the second half, but I didn't have enough discipline to aspire to a place on the first team. It should be said that we were a very weak team, so if I had made a little more effort, I would have made it. After leaving school I stopped playing for a few years, but I took it up again, joining a team of former students and it's there that I've recently really started playing again. This coincides with my beginnings as a writer; I became a centre-back in charge of recovering balls and strengthening my leg. Before, I was a weak player in every sense. My first books are raging stories of adolescents, with that same strong leg. After I turned twenty-nine, when I moved to Madrid, I believe I started to play better, with higher criteria at the moment of kicking passes. I think my writing has matured in the same way. I demand more of myself than I used to, searching for the right word, but maintaining that intensity that I want to transmit.

Do you support a particular team?

In Peru I started out as a fan of San Agustín, a team that was associated with my high school and that became national champion in its first year in the first division. Then I went to Alianza Lima in 1987 when the Fokker tragedy occurred and the whole team died. You feel it when a team needs you, and that's what happened to me with Alianza. I put up with being mocked for almost twenty years until we became champions. I'm still an Alianza fan, but I'm no longer wrapped up in Peruvian football. It's slow, bad and its structure is corrupt from the bottom up. It's a shame we aren't qualifying for the World Cup and that a lot of good players who are playing on foreign teams no longer feel like fighting for the Peruvian team and only want to be selected to be able to do their own thing, something they're not allowed to do in their own clubs.

In Spain I'm for Atlético de Madrid. I live near the stadium and go when I can and some day I want to do the rounds dressed in the red and white. I tell my reasons for being a fan of the Atlético in my first novel. I used the protagonist to speak of this passion that never ends.

Which is more important to you as a fan, a good result or a good game?

One likes to win, and a few years ago I would have taken all the possible points without caring how my team was playing, but nowadays I can't stand bad games. I get mad when I see one of those multimillionaire players miss a pass, a goal, when they have poor control of the ball on those fields that are like incredible carpets.

What motivates you to write fiction that takes place within a Peruvian context?

My last books take place in Spain, but I'm writing stories again that are based on my adolescence and school experience in Lima. They're stories that seemed pretty normal to me because I lived them every day, but I started to realise that that violent universe I grew up in deserves to be narrated; it's not common for a priest to give money to the students who go up to his bedroom, or to beat up a classmate until the kid decides not to come to school any more, and for your childhood friends to self-destruct is painful when you look back and see that you didn't do anything to prevent it.

How do football and politics intersect in Peru?

Informality reigns in both areas. There's no long-range plan, that's the big problem in Peru, we keep on living in the short term, which means a huge lack of solidarity. And while in football we keep on believing in the stars who'll take us to the World Cup, in politics there's the figure of the *caudillo*. We need to pay more attention to the team. What I don't see is a political handling of football. Politicians have tried to climb aboard the train of the few important victories that we've had, but the people have rejected them, they're not welcome, incredible, it's a space that looks easy enough to conquer to be manipulated, but I don't remember anyone that has managed to do it, except some mayor who later fell from grace.

How do you view the recent developments in the scandal surrounding corruption in FIFA?

Like all important global businesses, this one had to be corrupt, no question about it. But it's interesting to see that it has been the North Americans who have taken action and not on behalf of transparency in football, but rather it's business that interests them. What we need are players like Sócrates or Caszely, who rebel against the bosses and put things in their place, or who at least make the fans see that football has turned into a circus.

Do you see any connection between the creative process and the way in which someone plays football or behaves as a fan?

To me there's a big connection. I've explained it before. As I've calmed down as a player, saving my strength because I'm no longer twenty years old to be running around the field, my creative process has come to resemble the day before the game, concentration. When I was twenty, what I wanted was to finish off a story, at times without much thought for the road to be travelled, I didn't value the word as I do now, I could sacrifice a sentence, leave it just as it had come out because it worked instead of thinking about the tone, the rhythm, the sonority, the feeling that prose with rough patches could inspire in the reader. As a fan in that period I wanted to win at any cost. Today I still want championships, but no longer at any price.

Did any writer of football fiction influence this story?
No, but there is a story I read a lot in that period: "Hombre de punta" by Jorge Asís, and I still like his book that contains that story, *La lección del maestro*. I believe it's a great story. Since then I haven't read anything like it that excited me in that way, not even *High Fidelity* by Nick Hornby, a novel that I've given as gifts several times. I owe myself a football book.

Do you see any lingering reluctance to incorporating football or sport as a dominant theme or plot driver among your generation of authors?
I don't believe that it's resistance, but rather inability, which in this case, I connect with the lack of writers who are players. If you're going to write about football you have to have played sometime in your life. In general I'm one of those people who trust more in first-hand experience, particularly with topics like sports, war and family. Whoever writes a book about footbal, necessarily must know the smell of a locker room, must understand what are known as the codes of football and that

they're all nonsense, must know what it's like to experience defeat in sports for months on end, of course, that is if it's going to be a book about the game itself. Books that revolve around football without going onto the pitch are of no interest to me, that's what the press and nonfiction are for.

What is the place of football fiction in the literature of your country?

At first glance it doesn't occupy a big space, but there are several writers, among them the most representative, like Vargas Llosa, Bryce Echenique and Julio Ramón Ribeyro, who have devoted memorable texts to it. Jorge Eslava, a friend, writer and fantastic goalie, headed up the anthology *Bien Jugado* that brought together several of these texts. Besides, in Peru there are several writers who play football, both fiction writers and poets. Publishers even organise competitions, something unheard of in Spain, where the writers are more formal.

Is there a particular identity or style associated with football in Peru?

When I was a child I used to hear that our *juego bonito* was admired, that after Brazil we had the best touch on the continent, but that was a legend like the one that said that Peru's national anthem was given second place after "The Marseillaise" in I don't remember what contest. I doubt that we have a style, we're weak at scoring and it seems to me that Peru gives up pretty quickly when playing as a visitor. I still don't understand the difference in playing at home and as a visitor. If a player has his head together, playing as a visitor becomes just an anecdote.

How would you describe the impact in Latin America of Brazil having hosted the World Cup in 2014?

I don't know what impact the World Cup of football can have in South America where football is a drug. With or without the World Cup, the people keep on having breakfast, eating lunch and dining with football. The politicians keep on taking advantage of the sport when it's convenient, and life, as I know it, on every level is held up with its daily dose of corruption.

Has Peru's recent success at the Copa América created hope for future World Cup qualification?

Peruvians who are fans always believe that we'll make it to a World Cup. This success is relative, because while it's true that I saw a team that had more order and pressed its rivals more, the tournament was mediocre in general. I have no idea which players from this team will reach the qualifying rounds, and I don't know if Guerrero, Farfán and Lobatón will get there at an age that will allow them to go on helping the younger players. In any case, if the qualifying rounds were right now, I believe that, yes, we would qualify. But since that's not the case, I imagine that the other teams will have time to recover and it's probable that there'll be another disappointment and that everything will remain the same. Peruvian football is poorly structured, the work of the clubs in the lower divisions is lamentable, the kids are lost because they don't get a solid training, they want to be footballers to get women and stand out in their neighbourhoods, not because they enjoy competing against powerful teams or they want to play in more competitive leagues. If Peru makes it to the World Cup, no one will dare question the structure of which I'm speaking and if we don't make it, it will just be discussed all over again without really dealing with the problem. In this sense, I don't have hope for change.

Uruguay
CARLOS ABIN

Carlos Abin was born in La Paz, Uruguay on February 28, 1947. He is a lawyer and notary, who has been an associate of the legal firm Grupo Asesor del General Liber Seregni since 1983. He has written two collections of short stories, *Colgado del travesaño* (Alfaguara, 2006) and *L'ultimo rigore* (Sentieri Meridiani, 2012), and the novel *El olor de santidad* (Banda Oriental, 2012, Onetti Prize). He is also the author of a nonfiction book, *El alca: Un camino hacia la anexión: propuesta de alternativas para América Latina* (Plataforma Interamericana de Derechos Humanos, 2003). He was Uruguay's ambassador to Italy from 2005 to 2009. As a journalist he has contributed to the *Semanario Brecha* and the *Revista del Sur*, as well as to international publications. He is a fan of Peñarol. An earlier version of "The Final Penalty" (El último penal) first appeared in Spanish in *Colgado del travesaño* (Alfaguara, 2006).

The Final Penalty

Sitting around one of the three Formica tables in "El pajarito" – a combination grocery store and bar – two older men were keeping each other company in silence. Lost in their own thoughts they seemed to be oblivious to the commotion of the other customers, each one submerged in the depths of the glass he had in front of him. From time to time one of them, bald, his grey beard somewhat neglected, would make a brief comment to which the other, very thin, with large child-like eyes, responded with an imperceptible nod. Then he would fall silent, waiting for his companion to return to the idea. The bearded man took the initiative, without a doubt. His friend just waited. Their glasses were untouched. The thin man had been served a draft beer, which he would glance at when the intervals between the other man's comments became too long. Anyone might say that an entire world was going by between the sides of that glass, in which the ice was melting uselessly. The bearded man had ordered a whiskey, but he wasn't drinking either. He would pick up the glass by its top, with four fingers, give it a half turn and set it down on the table again. The rings of moisture formed a complex figure on the Formica. They looked at each other. The thin man waited a moment and smiled timidly; the bearded man leaned forward, extended his right arm and gave him an affectionate pat on the shoulder, while he shook his head in a gesture that seemed to say, "I can't believe it". Then he took a pack of Nevadas out of his shirt pocket and, without offering one to the thin man, lit the cigarette. He laid the cheap lighter on the table and made a sudden movement, as if to clear the smoke away. The lighter fell to the floor and Manuel, who was passing by carrying a bag containing orders, bent over and picked it up, laying it on the table next to the glass of whiskey. The bearded man stared at him for a moment, surprised, and then smiled kindly: "Thanks, kid."

In the doorway of the grocery store, his hands on the doorframe, Mr Villaseca was observing the scene. He moved to one side to let Manuel leave, and remarked to him as he passed, "Do you know who the guy with the lighter is?" "Yeah," replied the boy, "it's Mochila's lawyer friend. Today's Friday and they'll spend the whole morning there, waiting for their ice to melt."

Villaseca shot a rapid glance at the table, confirmed that everything was the same, looked at Manuel again and asked, "But do you know the story of those two fellows?"

"He wants to talk," thought Manuel. Villaseca was a good man, but he couldn't help his condition: he was a teacher, he had to ask questions. In the store, outside the classroom, Manuel felt more self-assured: "I've heard a few things. I think they played football together or something like that. I heard that the lawyer, when he was young, was a phenomenon. My father is the one who knows all about it."

Villaseca shook his head in the negative: "Back then, your father hadn't arrived in this town yet. I played with them, I can tell you the whole story." And softening his expression, he added, "I'm a teacher thanks to the lawyer's grandfather."

Manuel put the bag down on the floor. It had never occurred to him that at some point, in the remote past, Villaseca had not been a teacher. And even less that he had played football. He began to see him in a different light, his eyes emitting a sparkle of curiosity, enough so that the teacher returned to the task at hand. It was clear he felt like talking and now he had grabbed his attention.

"This story begins more than forty years ago. The lawyer's grandfather had a house built on the new street, in front of the

Socavón cliff, facing the sea, you know where it is? The lawyer's nickname is Lalo, he was probably about ten back then. He would spend all summer with the old man and would help him out. They had a bricklayer, don Pietro, kind of short and bent over, who was a real demon. The old man and Lalo worked with him. The three of them built the house. Sometimes Juan González would come for a few days, but as soon as he earned a few pesos, he would disappear until hunger forced him to return. Whenever Juan returned, he stood out front across the street. He couldn't bring himself to come over. He would clap his hands and stand there waiting. Nothing happened. Just the sounds of work. He would clap again, and again, nothing. On the third or fourth try the grandfather's voice would be heard: "Don Juan González from the shores of the Pando, if you've come to work, then come on over; if not, go to hell." That's the way the first summer went, they would be working from December to March. My old man would come to make a little money, to help out in some way, he was pretty good with wood and would lend a hand with the scaffolding, and later with the doors and windows. The Italian, who was the soul of honesty, counted the nails he gave him and then counted the ones my father returned to him. Sitting on a pile of bricks, I idled the day away, keeping them company. Every once in a while the Italian would pass his rough hand over my head and say in his broken accent: '*Look at Lalo, kid, look how he work.*'"

"Lalo would bring bricks, carry buckets of mortar, push along bags of Portland cement because they were too heavy for him to lift. He shovelled sand. Always serious, never complaining. At times it was clear that he was dead tired, but he never said anything. Devoted to his grandfather, they understood each other without words. Sometimes the old man would call to him and say: 'Run along to the beach and have a swim. Don't go in too deep. When you hear the sound of the soup ladle hitting the pan, come on back for lunch.' Whenever my father let me, I went with him. After a while we'd hear the old man beating on a work bucket with a spoon: that was the signal, the barbecue was ready and we had to get back."

Villaseca took off his glasses and began to clean them mechanically with his blue tie, the only one he was known to wear. He put them back on carefully, verifying that the world around him was still the same, he squeezed the end of his nose between his thumb and index finger while he squinted his eyes to better concentrate on his memories, then pulled up a chair, sat down somewhat ceremoniously, and announced: "Now we get to the part about football."

"In front of the house there was a large vacant lot, between the street and the beach. That summer several kids from the nearby cottages got together and formed a team. There were the three Pérez Brito kids, and with their cousins they were six or seven, and then there was fat Luis Alberto, who lived at the naval base behind the field; his father was the Captain in charge of the base. And there were two or three more from around there. They formed a team and named it 'La Victoria'. You've probably never heard of 'the headless woman', but the name of the team came from there. Where the old street ended, just before the steps, beside the Pérez Brito house, there was a statue, a reproduction of Winged Victory of Samothrace, a woman with wings and no head, that the people in the resort colloquially called 'the headless woman'. It was there for years, until one day it disappeared during a storm, carried off by the sea – or the wind, as some believe – she must have had those big white plaster wings for something. The sailors from the base, who like good military men twiddled their thumbs most of the time, cut some eucalyptus branches and made goals.

They marked midfield – by eye – and the end lines. For the sides it wasn't necessary: on one side the pitch ended where the grass ended, in other words at the street; on the other side was the Socavón, a gully full of weeds, foxtails, bamboo and black acacias. At the bottom was a trickle of questionable water that flowed out to the sea. The kids were kicking a ball around a couple of days to test the field; the sailors would butt in and give them advice. Lalo stood on the porch of his house and watched them. Since they didn't invite him to play, he stayed there, never saying a word. And it went on like that for a period of time. It was already the beginning of February, and one day out of the blue La Victoria found an opponent. The news spread like wildfire: Sunday at four in the afternoon the first game would be played, against a team from Sarandí, the resort's poorest section. The Captain showed up on the field, walked all over it and offered some advice. The sailors cut the grass and firmed up the goals. An uncle of the Pérez Brito boys bought some blue jerseys in the market and the kids practised all day Saturday with the team in place. Lalo continued watching from his house. Sometimes he picked up a book – his grandfather was always buying him books, the ones with yellow covers from the 'Robin Hood series'. He would sit in a deck chair and read, while the rest were playing ball. He would look up once in a while and watch the game. I was quite a bit younger and was nearby because my old man was the gardener for all the cottages, and I would wave to him and he would make a gesture letting me know that he recognised me. He never tried to approach us. He would watch us a few minutes and then go back to his book."

"On Sunday, a little before the game, people – the players' parents and the neighbours – started to arrive. My old man struck up a conversation with Lalo's grandfather. They pulled out some chairs and sat down in the yard: it was the best place, front row seats, right next to the field. Later, the opposing team showed up; they didn't have jerseys like ours, but their size was pretty impressive. The captain, 'Susurro', had a voice that was strangely deep and sonorous. He came onto the pitch and without any ceremony ordered the goalie to take his position in the box that faced the back of the naval base. There were eleven of them, while there were only ten on the La Victoria team. When the Captain got there, Lalo's grandfather invited him to join them in his yard; he called to Maneiro – one of the oldest sailors – handed him a whistle and told him: 'You're the referee.' Maneiro, who was dressed in white like all the sailors, went to the middle of the pitch and blew the whistle. The teams took their positions on the field, the Sarandí team following Susurro's order, and ours following the directions of Juan Francisco, the oldest of the Pérez Brito boys. That's when the Captain jumped up: 'This team is missing a player' and he called Juan Francisco. 'We don't have any more players, sir, we couldn't get anyone else.' The Captain glanced around, as if he were looking for a candidate, and saw Lalo sitting there, a distracted look on his face. 'Don't you want to play, Lalo?' he asked him. "How about it? We need a player.' Lalo said that he did, stood up and walked over toward the field. Somebody gave him a jersey, he put it on – it was too big – so he tucked a good part of it into his shorts and looked around for a position. Juan Francisco stopped him: 'You'll play left-midfield' – it was an easy position, one of those positions made for guys who didn't know how to play. Lalo took his position on the field, and Maneiro gave the order to move."

"The game was pretty even. The guys from Sarandí were big and strong, but ours were more skilled. The ball came and went and, except for a shot from distance by Juan Francisco that zoomed by a post, there wasn't much for the goalies to worry about. I think they were all a little nervous. Lalo didn't touch the ball once. Nobody knew him, no one passed him the ball and, on top of that, the game seemed to be stuck more on the other side of the field. Until the moment arrived. A deflection landed at the feet of Sarandí's right-forward, and the kid put his head down and took off down the line full speed ahead. It looked like he was going to sail right past Lalo, but Lalo cleanly nabbed the ball and kept it while the other guy went flying down the pitch past him. 'Pass it, idiot! Over here, over here!' Three or four of our teammates yelled at Lalo, in a hurry before the other team recovered the ball. Lalo stared at the field, and right then and there I realised that he knew how to play better than all the others together. He took off toward the goal, dodged one player, then another, and stopped – everyone was still yelling at him, 'Pass it, pass it!' but he, as if he didn't hear them, aimed for the goal, dodged two or three more and went in, ball and all. *Golazo*, a great goal! It was the La Victoria's first, and everybody was astounded. Lalo didn't celebrate it, went back to his position when the Sarandí team was already moving out of midfield. We won twelve to nil; Lalo scored nine goals and they named him club president. The female cousins – they all had lots of cousins, both male and female – had bought a notebook and wrote in it the names of all the players. At the top of the list was Lalo. Beside his name it said 'President, 9 goals'. Juan Francisco had scored two with fierce shots, and Matías, the youngest of the Pérez Brito boys, scored the other one. Lalo scored a tremendous pile of goals for himself, dribbling through almost the entire opposing team. He ran with the ball tied to his foot, his head always held high, with total control of the situation. One after the other, the opponents tried to take the ball from him and each time he invented a new move, a twist, a step, an unfathomable feint and pulled away from them. He knew how to avoid being kicked. Now nobody asked him for the ball, they left him to it. But Matías, who couldn't have been more than seven or eight years old, ran beside him, accompanying him. After dodging the goalie, Lalo saw him coming and gave the ball a little kick: 'Do it, Mati' he yelled and the kid kicked it with all he had. From that day on Matías became Lalo's devoted sidekick."

Villaseca sighed deeply, as if overcome by his memories. He took out another cigarette, lit it and took a long drag. Manuel had sat down on the sidewalk, on top of a stump of concrete, the remains of the base of some billboard, and gazed at him entranced. At the table the two men were now talking animatedly. The bearded man lifted the glass to his lips, barely wetting them, the thin guy was gesturing with restraint, excited by the conversation. It was clear that he was giving his companion a respectful deference, but in any case, an aura of solid comradeship enveloped the two friends.

"Look at them, Manuel," said Villaseca, pointing at them without letting go of his cigarette. "The best part is still to come."

"I would tag along with my old man and help him with the yards. I went to all the games, but almost never played. Whenever they needed a player, it was always Lalo – who by now had a lot of authority on the field – who would call me over: 'Come on, Peludo, we need players; you go up in front, you're fast.' His grandfather would chat with my old man, he had read a lot, knew about plants and weather. He would ask a lot of questions, and my father, with his cap in his hand, would answer deliberately. One morning, while they were talking, dad was drinking fresh water – the old man had appeared suddenly with a bottle and two glasses – I realised that they were talking about me. I was returning with the tarp rolled up under my arm – I had gone off to throw dead leaves and weeds into the gully – and I noticed that they quit talking and stood looking at me. 'So how's the gardener's helper doing in school?' the old man asked. 'Well, very well,' my father answered. 'He doesn't miss a day, applies himself and always does his homework. He'll go on to the next grade without a hitch.' 'This boy has to study. They should all study,' stated the grandfather and scratched his cheek with his index finger – a sign that he was thinking about something, or so Lalo had told me. 'So what would you like to study when you finish high school? You need to be thinking about it already in order to make a good choice,' he told me, looking me straight in the eye. 'I want to be a history teacher,' I answered, without lowering my eyes. I still don't know where that answer, which fixed my destiny forever, came from. 'An excellent idea!' the old man answered enthusiastically. 'I can see that you're a boy who thinks and knows what he wants. An excellent idea!' And on that still cool summer morning, I, with a dirty tarp under my arm, wearing a ragged straw hat, my green workpants, my shoes full of holes, my back to the field, took a deep breath and in the presence of my father and that imposing old man assumed the commitment of becoming a history teacher. So, kid, you see how life is."

"The games continued, once or twice a week. The team was fantastic, I never saw them lose or even tie. They were winning on their own pitch and when they were visitors – sometimes not too easily. Lalo made the difference. It was really hard to get the ball away from him, and he almost always scored at least one goal. He was good-looking. They hit him a lot – especially on team's fields, far from the protection of the sailors – but he put up with it and never complained. I never saw him shout or writhe in pain. He never got mad about being kicked. He just got up and went on, sometimes limping for a while. They started to mark him with two and three defenders, and that's when another player, faster and more of a team player, showed up. Dribbling is beautiful but it slows the game down. Lalo was a pretty fast runner, but his mental speed was incredible. He would figure out the play before he got the ball and would pass it on with a single touch. Sometimes, before he made the pass, he would yell to you, 'Peludo, pass it fast to El Cuchí.' And you knew there was no way to go wrong, he would make you look at the teammate he had indicated and he had said 'fast' which meant 'as soon as you get it, pass it on to so and so.' He was never wrong, if your pass was on the mark, the ball was already halfway to a goal.

"Sarandí had constructed their own field, so they could play as the home team and with the illusion that that way they would beat us. They never even managed to draw even with us. We would go there with a certain amount of fear. There were some parents who could no longer stand the continuous humiliation of their sons and did whatever they could to have them win at any cost. Of course, Lalo was the principal object of their hatred, 'that skinny son of a bitch that always shits on us,' as I heard the notary Bossi, the angriest of the offended parents, say. Several summers went by that way. La Victoria became the obsession of the Sarandís. Somebody had the bright idea of challenging us to play on the beach. 'Playing on the sand is something else, we'll get them.' We accepted the challenge and arranged a day and time. It was January and the heat was terrible. When we got to the agreed upon location, they were already there and had set up the goals. They had picked the pitch and so we had to move to the other side. When the teams took the field, we saw that the notary Bossi and Raúl Sosa's father – the one we called 'Dick Tracy' because he had a broken nose like the comic book character – were on the field. They had put two grown men on the team! Juan Francisco and Luis Alberto started to protest, but were ignored. 'Are you scared?' Bossi, who was always an idiot, mocked. We couldn't back down, so we decided to go ahead and play. Just when we are about to get started, Bossi points to Lalo and shouts to the whole team: 'Today this guy's not going to get a single goal, right?' and he glared at him with murder in his eyes. Lalo was unperturbed. I started the play and passed the ball to him. Then he did something I'd never seen before and never saw again. He took the ball and headed straight, vertically, for the opponents' goal. Bossi headed out to tackle him and got stuck in the sand. He didn't even touch him. Lalo kept on advancing, dodging opponents like they were wooden monkeys. Dick Tracy, who was around six foot five and pretty fat, was waiting for him. Bossi was yelling, 'Kill him, Rubén! Kill him!' Lalo headed straight into that wall and they crashed into each other. I can't explain how he did it, but the big guy ended up stretched out on the sand, and couldn't get up. Many years later I read that judo was a martial art whose secret consisted in using the rival's weight against him. Lalo did something like that instinctively. He crashed into a guy who weighed three times more than he did and was almost a foot taller, and the other guy fell dead on the ground. He kept on going straight as an arrow toward the opponents' goal and scored the first goal: not one of the opposing players had even touched the ball, and the score was already one to nil. Bossi was hoarse from so much ranting, his face was purple and his breathing was ragged, we thought he was going to have a heart attack. Lalo left the pitch and went into the sea. He dived in and swam for a while, oblivious to the game. But the Sarandí team was shattered. That unbelievable goal disarmed them; they couldn't touch the ball. Besides Bossi was beginning to tire, they carried a beat-up Dick Tracy off the field, and a little while later we scored another goal, a head shot by Luis Alberto off a corner kick. After a long swim in the ocean, Lalo came back onto the field. It was as if he were bored, he didn't attempt a single dribble. Whenever he got the ball, he passed it and stayed in place, looking around. That was my day of glory, I made two goals and earned a place on the team. Lalo – who knew I could run like a rabbit – made two long passes to me and twice left me standing alone in front of the goalie. Luckily, I didn't fail."

Villaseca wiped the lenses of his glasses with his tie again, his nearsighted gaze lost in the distance. Manuel was impressed, he would never have imagined him "eating up the ground" as the football announcers put it, fast as a deer, to receive an exact pass and meet the goalie "face to face".

"The team's fame was spreading all along the coast. Its unbeaten record over several years started to become a popular legend in the resort and town, and new challenges began appearing: two games – home and away – against some boys from San Luis, the team of a Salesian school from Pando, another resort club. We won all the games and the legend grew. Lalo's game had matured, he didn't hog the ball as much, those impossible goals in which he dribbled through half the opposing team were rare. But he was still uncontrollable. He had developed a surprising view of the game. He was playing, but he was also thinking. He would detect the opponents' weaknesses and invent the means to exploit them. The best team we faced was the Salesian team from Pando. In the game on their turf at the end of the first half we were losing two to nil. It was a disaster! That had never happened to us before. The team was well organised, had been playing together for a long time and, besides, were a real team. When the second half was about to begin, Lalo said 'I'm going to midfield', which seemed crazy to us. We needed three goals to win – nobody even considered the possibility of a tie – and just at that moment the highest scoring player decides to play midfield. Mati tried to point that out to him, but Lalo answered him: 'We're losing because they have the ball. We have to get it ourselves and hold on to it. We can't mess up passes or dribble; they run a lot and defend well. They're good, the best we've played against.' And he was right. From midfield he was able to get a better handle on the game, we recovered the ball, kept it as much as possible, and defended better. Lalo made fearsome passes, we disarmed their defence. Soon the score was 2 to 2, and they were really nervous. The game was very tough right up to the end, but we refused to allow a tie. With very little time left there was a free kick at an angle. Lalo asked to take it himself and sent the whole team forward. The opposing players formed a perfect wall, and Lalo messed up; the shot went directly at the wall and the ball deflected toward the middle. It was then that fat Luis Alberto, who always played defence because of his build, foresaw the possibility of the goal of his life. The ball rose and he, who was just arriving inside the box, took off like a racehorse and taking advantage of his height put in an unstoppable header. Three to two. We had won our most difficult game, and the big guy had a heroic tale to tell his grandchildren. Every once in a while I see him in the supermarket and wave to him from a distance, patting my forehead twice. He gives me a big smile, happy as a lark and still enjoying that goal, the most important one in the entire history of La Victoria."

"And now we get to Mochila's story. He was living with his mother, in La Estación and already as a child was doing odd jobs in the resort during the season. They were very poor. His mother was a cleaning lady, his father had disappeared years before and they were surviving as best they could. He loved football and was a good back, in spite of his small size. He had strength, determination and speed. He didn't shy away from tackles and, besides, he was very good at jumping. He played on the Estación Flores team, a club made up of people from the town and the nearby small farms, most of them as poor as he was. Football was life on Sunday afternoons in the fall and winter, while in the summer, those who could, picked up a job in the resort. They depended on the rich who summered there to pull together a few pesos to help them through the winter, which were always harsh for those people. I'm one of them myself."

"Mochila had seen a lot of La Victoria's games in which I hardly participated. He would greet me, raising his eyebrows, as if he hardly recognised me, and would stand far off with an attitude of 'This doesn't interest me much'. I believe his innermost desire was to see us lose. Many times, when we were ahead by two or three goals, he would quietly fade away; he didn't want to see another win by the rich kids with their recently laundered jerseys, their new ball in perfect condition, their well cared-for pitch and their parents cheering them on and celebrating their deeds. The social barriers were so strong, that it never occurred to anyone that the resort kids could face the poor boys from La Estación. The fact is they had different seasons. La Victoria only existed during the summer, precisely when the Estación players were working for the rich people who spent their summer at the seaside. I don't know where the challenge came from, but during the last week of February in '61 a game was arranged. Only one, there was no time for a rematch. It was agreed that we'd play on our pitch and the opponent – based on age and size – was the team from Estación, Mochila's team. In general they were older than us, but we had faith in ourselves. Their team was pretty experienced – they played from March to November in the regional championships

– and they always finished near the top. We were better trained, had played eight or nine games that season, and this would be the last one of the summer."

Villaseca uselessly cleaned his glasses again with his tie, put them back on and directed his gaze at table three, probably trying to sharpen his memory by contemplating that day's two protagonists. Oblivious to his scrutiny, the two men had fallen back into their shared silence, concentrating on the untouched contents of the glasses in front of them.

"I'm not going to keep you in suspense, kid. We won four to nil; Lalo made all four goals, all penalty kicks. Just look how things turn out. The game started at six in the evening, and there were many more people than usual. To begin with, all the sailors were there. Many of them lived in La Estación or had relatives there – the kids from the town who followed the La Estación team during the season, some family members and, of course, all our team's parents, siblings and an infinite number of cousins. It was a strange spectacle: the sailors – dressed in white – behind the goal that faced the back of the naval base, La Victoria's fans crowded into Lalo's grandfather's yard, most of them standing since there weren't enough chairs, deck chairs and even benches stolen from neighbouring cottages. And behind the other goal, all the Estación fans – very different in their clothes, general shabbiness and behaviour. There for the first time I understood the distance that separated us from those people who could give themselves the luxury of vacationing in the summer. But I was on 'the other team' and had to play. Don't think for a minute that I didn't experience a certain amount of apprehension, of remorse. I saw my Aunt Shirley among the Estación fans and waved at her. She smiled at me, returning my greeting, and I immediately felt like a traitor. But the game was already beginning. I played miserably, didn't make a single good kick. The game was pretty scrappy, a lot of back and forth in the midfield. Their fitness and spacing were killing us, we were bearing up and hitting back as best we could. But there was Lalo. He received the ball pretty far up the pitch and set out for the goal, 'vertical', as he would say and usually did. When he was advancing with that determination we saw a goal on the horizon, usually they couldn't stop him. And so it was, until he got to the box. Mochila met him and Lalo neutralised him with two fakes and went to the right. Mochila hit him from behind: penalty. Naturally Lalo took it and put it in the net. This situation repeated itself more or less the same at the beginning of the second half. Another penalty kick and two to nil. Except that Mochila's foul was a lot more violent – you could see that he was building up anger – and much higher. He kicked him out of meanness a little below the knee. El Rulo, one of the youngest sailors, came onto the pitch and shouted at him: 'Don't be a wise guy, Milton. Ease off the kid.' Mochila shrugged his shoulders while the other sailors pulled El Rulo back behind the goal. Some fifteen or twenty minutes later, about the middle of the second period, Lalo and Mochila faced each other again. Lalo was coming up fast, the ball tied to his foot, with his eye on the goal; Mochila – who had already paid for his mistake twice – faced him ready for anything. He struck him in the same place, the same leg, and for the first time in all those years I heard Lalo cry out. He fell to the ground, sat up quickly and began to rub the injured leg. We ran over to him, we thought he had broken it. Rulo went up to Mochila and gave him a couple of shoves, and right away a brawl started. As always happened, some guys wanted to fight and others tried to separate them, you never know anyone's intentions in that kind of brawl. Some punches were thrown, but I can't be sure of anything because I was kneeling beside Lalo, staring with consternation at the outline of Mochila's boot on his right leg. 'I'm fine, I'm fine,' Lalo kept repeating and started to stand up. Juan Francisco gave him support from behind and he was finally on his feet. He stomped heavily two or three times and then, as if nothing had happened, went to look for the ball. Maneiro blew the whistle like a crazy man and tried to clear the field. Finally everything got back to normal and Lalo could take the penalty kick. Three to nil and Rulo's shout 'that one was for your sister, Mochila' resounded in the silence that followed the celebration of the goal."

"Lalo was injured, a goose egg swelling where he had been hit, he couldn't run very well and limped on that leg. But three goals is a big difference; and they were done for, they no longer tried to use their physical superiority against us; I think they realised that one more foul would unleash a disaster. Lalo moved to the right, playing close to the sideline, almost at a standstill. You could see that his leg was hurting. He would receive the ball once in a while and would limit himself to passing it back without too much effort. He even failed to trap a couple of passes that ended up going under his foot. I saw how every once in a while he would rub the swelling, or press his index finger across the edge of the bone, which was by now completely deformed. He kept on limping. When he lost the second pass, he lost his patience. The fact is that the next pass that he received – a deflection because nobody would pass to him any more so as not to endanger him – he caught in the instep of the injured leg, went to the end of the pitch and started to run as best he could, parallel to the end line. He entered the box and, when Mochila came out to meet him – unsteady, of course – he nutmegged him, left the pitch to avoid him, returned with a dance step and went directly toward the goal. It was too much. Mochila, blind with rage, took him down again and also pushed him from behind. The grass was wet in that area, and Lalo slipped and the push propelled him into an acacia thicket that was almost directly behind the goal. A few days earlier the sailors had trimmed the branches that were threatening to overhang the field, and as fate would have it, a branch that had been left with a sharp point after the pruning, jabbed him in the middle of the goose egg that had formed on his leg. He didn't cry out, he didn't say anything, but he got up biting his tongue; he now had a hole, round as a peso, and blood was flowing from the wound. He crossed the pitch toward the house, Juan Francisco wrapped an arm under Lalo's arms and held him up as he walked. We ran over while behind us all hell was breaking loose. His buddies couldn't control Rulo, who punched Mochila in the face, shouting all the while 'you son of a bitch, I'm gonna kill you, you son of a thousand bitches.' Some men from among the Estación fans ran over to separate them, and I heard Fat Barreix, uncle of the Pérez Brito boys, tell the Captain: 'Arrest that piece of shit, please; arrest him, don't you see he almost killed Lalo. It's a case of assault and battery, you've got to arrest him.' Meanwhile Lalo's father came over with a first aid kit, cleaned his wound, and applied some kind of medicine – maybe it was alcohol, I don't know. Lalo almost passed out, his eyes rolled halfway up in his head, but his dad squeezed his earlobes and he came to. 'Bandage me up, Dad, ' he said, his voice weak. His father nodded in agreement and finished the treatment. Then he applied a bandage, slowly and carefully while the whole team watched the scene. One young cousin, a girl, was crying and a hell of a racket could be heard. The Captain crossed the street and walked onto the field. He grabbed Rulo by one arm, 'Well done, kid,' he told him and patted him on the back. Then, directing himself to one of the veteran sailors who happened to be nearby, added, 'Manso, this guy is under arrest; take him away,' and then went back to his place in the improvised stands."

"Lalo, his injuries now treated and bandaged, stood up as though he were going back onto the field. He leaned on Matías' shoulder and said, 'I've got to take the penalty.' His mother looked at him, fear in her eyes and almost crying, she started to say, 'Lalo, Lalo, come over here.' His father stopped her: 'Let him be, honey, if he wants to go back out, then let him.'"

"He went back onto the pitch dragging his leg and looked for the ball. He placed it on the penalty spot and waited there for things to settle down, since by then and after the Captain had come onto the field, things had subsided considerably. Juan Francisco came up: 'Let me, Lalo, I'll kick it. You're not gonna be able to, can't you see your leg's really fucked up.' Lalo, without looking at him, replied: 'The penalty kick is mine, the foul was on me, and I'm going to take it with my left foot.' When Mochila saw that his enemy, in spite of everything, was going to take the penalty kick, he told the goalie: 'Move aside, I'll stop it.' So Lalo and Mochila faced each other yet again, the former with a hole in his right leg, that he could hardly move, the latter with an eye that was starting to swell and bruises on his forehead. There was a deadly silence. Maneiro blew the whistle, and Lalo moved forward limping with pain; he got to the ball and took a furious kick with his left foot, a look of rage in his eyes I had never seen before. It was a goal. Mochila ended up on the ground, I think he was crying. He was crying out of his own anger, the anger of impotence, of poverty, of his mother, the maid, of shame. That was the last game. The next summer the team fell apart. Several of the boys had grown up and were interested in other things. Some didn't even come with their parents for the summer. They went to a friend's house, or went camping somewhere. Lalo kept on coming in

January or February for two or three years, then came exams and I think he had a girlfriend in Montevideo. And, as far as I know, he abandoned football completely, he wanted to be a lawyer. He went to the university and I almost never saw him until years later when he showed up in the middle of winter with a group of friends, some of them older. They stayed for a few days, always shut up in the house; Lalo only went out to buy firewood or food. One day I ran into him in the grocery store, he acted very strange, and barely said hello, as if he didn't trust me."

"I kept on studying. Lalo's grandfather gave my dad money to pay my bus fare, as well as for my books. That way I managed to finish high school and went to Montevideo to study to be a history teacher. I lived in a boarding house with some other guys, but once a month I went to visit the old man at his home. By then he was pretty sick, but he was always glad to see me, always very serious and addressing me with respect. I think he got a lot of pleasure seeing me advance in my career. He never talked about Lalo. One time, when I brought up the topic, don Ciriaco said: 'He's around and about. Going to be a lawyer.' I never ran into him at his grandfather's house, nor could I get anything more than some vague statement out of the old man about his grandson. The old man stopped going to the resort, his poor health made it impossible. One Sunday in the winter – I think it was in '69 – I dropped by, as I did every month, and found the house closed up. It was strange, because the old man almost never went out. I went around the neighbourhood asking about him, and got the sad news that he had died a couple of weeks earlier. His wife – Lalo's grandmother – had gone to visit her family in Argentina, she was from Tandil. I broke down crying right there on the street. Later I took a bus and went to Estación Flores to tell my father. We mourned the old man a lot; he was a stern man, dry in his conversation, but honourable. I tell you again that I owe my career to him. He never stopped supporting me."

"A while later I heard that Lalo was involved in politics. His name would show up at times in the commentaries of the people from the FEUU (Federation of University Students), he had become a militant activist with them. I believe he even quit his studies for three or four years. I think I saw him more than once from a distance in some student demonstration. One day – I know all this from the comments of friends and other colleagues – he disappeared, as if the earth swallowed him and for a long time I knew nothing more of him. Dad had stopped working as a gardener; he was pretty old, and the cottage was in terrible shape. I would go by there and it seemed like the grass was going to swallow it up. The same with the field. Nobody could have imagined that only a few years earlier that little corner of the world was full of people, there were some great games and an amazing, skinny football player."

"Mochila joined the military. His mother died of pneumonia during the winter of '66, killed by hunger, cold and weariness. La Chicha, his sister, left and was never heard from again. After her mother's burial, she didn't go home again. Some people say she was a prostitute in Tomás Gomensoro, a shitty town up in the region of Artigas, the country's far north; others say that she joined up with a smuggler and is living hidden away in Livramento. The two versions aren't really contradictory, but the fact is that Mochila was left alone and starving in a shack that was falling down. The military were getting powerful in this country back then and were recruiting men. A lot of poor people, with no jobs or even much desire to work, like Mochila, joined the army. He had housing, fresh meat and *mate*. With the little bit of salary that he earned he had enough to go out for a good time once in a while. Of course he had to swallow his pride, obey orders and keep his mouth shut. I lost track of him too. At first because he spent a lot of time in the guardhouse until they tamed him. Later, when things got rough, because he was in the barracks, always on a state of alert and there were no passes of any kind. It was a miracle their little shack didn't fall down."

"One afternoon, – Mochila was a corporal by then and the military were beginning to take over the country – troops surrounded a couple blocks in the La Unión neighbourhood in Montevideo. They were going from house to house looking for subversives. They called it *Operación Rastrillo*. No one could leave the area that was surrounded. The soldiers went into every house, they were demanding identification, in some cases they were even going through wardrobes; if they found something, they would arrest the suspects. Mochila, at the head of a small group – I don't know exactly what the right word is, battalion, operative unit or whatever – he bangs on a door and waits, his men behind him, guns in their hands and ready to fire. The door opens and a tall, thin guy with dark hair is opening it: it's Lalo. As if he were talking to his wife, he shouts inside: 'Teresa, you'll never guess who's here?' And right away – without leaving time for an answer – he adds: 'Milton, my cousin from Estación Flores' and then turning to Mochila: 'What are you doing around here, Milton?' and he hugs him, gun and all. 'Wait a second.' Mochila stiffens in surprise, he can't figure out how to react. By now he had recognised Lalo. Lalo returns with two bottles of mineral water, real cold, and says: 'Colonel, this is for the men, they must be dying with the heat.' Mochila takes the bottles, stares at him and smiles: 'Thanks, cousin, say hello to my aunt,' and then to the soldiers, 'nothing's going on here; it's my cousin Lalo's house.'

They say that half the leadership of the Movement was inside the house, pistols drawn. If Lalo's play had failed, there would have been a hell of a shoot-out. But they went away. Mochila and Lalo face to face once again, and this time it was a draw in which they both ended up winning. Without saying another word, right then and there they became friends forever.

The years passed. The dictatorship crushed us all — just imagine how hard it was to give history classes, when the history of this country is full of revolutions, uprisings and rebellion. We gradually turned inward, shutting ourselves off in our own shells, cooking in our own juices, getting closer and closer to some kind of insanity. You could breathe the fear and distrust. Many were imprisoned, tortured and disappeared. Many more left the country – some forever. Silence, pain, death and fear merged in a long winter that lasted more than a decade. Mochila couldn't stand it. They tried to force him to torture, to coerce him to be an accomplice. That was the method the military used to maintain unity among the troops and prevent desertions: the guilt, the shame, the degradation of the torturer who could survive only by breathing the same shit as his cohorts. They say that Mochila managed to deliver some blows when he first started. Later he witnessed electric prodding, water boarding and hangings; it was a way of preparing him for when his turn came. But the first time they put a prod in his hand and tried to force him to apply it to the nipples of a girl, an architecture student, he couldn't do it. He started to cry, threw the prod to hell and walked out. He never came back. They didn't pursue him and didn't go looking for him. He went back to the shack in Estación Flores and spent the next two or three years completely sloshed. He stole, ate sporadically and kept on drinking. I don't know how he survived. It was pitiful to see him, he was a human wreck: dirty, aged, almost always drunk and spouting off nonsense. He must have been on the threshold of insanity more than once."

"The military couldn't overcome their own failure; the indifference of a lot of people and the resistance and rebellion of others defeated them. They never succeeded in convincing anybody; they were invaders of their own country; and this ungovernable country ended up isolating them, throwing them out like a plague. Nothing was left standing; only the machismo of the kit, the refuge in the 'military family', the shreds of an apparent pride, pure hot air, just crowing, which amounts to nothing more than poorly disguised shame and fear of justice. In '84 we had elections and in March of '85 we began to rebuild our democracy."

"And that winter; I figure it must have been August of '85, Lalo shows up again. By then he had his law degree and even had a pretty run-down car. He came to my old man's house to see if he still had a key to his family's cottage. Dad hardly recognised him, he was already pretty old by then, that would have been the year he died. But he gave him the key and asked about his grandfather. 'He's fine,' Lalo lied, and gave me a hug: 'Peludo, can you give me a hand with the house?'"

"So for one weekend I was a gardener again. I was working with Lalo, cleaning up the yard, carting away branches, years of accumulated dead leaves, weasel nests and every imaginable kind of trash. We opened the cottage and aired it out and began to talk, catching up, remembering old times and slowly arriving at the present, reliving so many things that had gotten caught up in the wires of our lives."

"At a moment when we were taking a breather – we were already getting up in years, were completely out of shape and tired easily – the topic of Mochila came up. I told him what I knew, what I just told you. Lalo was dumbstruck: 'Is he still in that shack in la Estación?' he asked me. I nodded in the affirmative. 'Wait here for me for a moment, Peludo; I'm going over there and I'll be back before long.' He climbed into his car and rushed off. I kept on with the work; without really understanding what had gotten into him. Within an hour, an hour and a half, he showed up with Mochila in the car. Mochila was carrying a miserable little bag with four pieces of clothing, he was a bit drunk and completely down and out. With no signs of disgust, Lalo helped him out of the car and practically carried him into the house, Mochila leaning on his shoulder with Lalo's arm around his waist. He sat him down in the big easy chair in the living room and said to me: 'Peludo, heat up some water, a lot of water, Milton's going to take a bath.'"

"He kept him there in his house for three weeks. He fed him, brought him clothes, cut off the alcohol. Mochila, still half in a daze with the effects of a binge that had lasted years, let him have his way. Amazingly, he never ran off, never tried to get some wine or a little grappa. He was half dead, no heart for anything. He was little more than a vegetable, but he started to get better."

"Lalo stayed with him all the time. He talked and talked to him – I can't imagine what he could have told him. He only went out to buy food or something he needed for the house. When he felt sure that Mochila wouldn't run away, he called for El Chino Borro, the builder:

'Do you know Milton Barrios' house?'

'You mean Mochila?'

'Yeah, Mochila, Mr Milton Barrios. You know where he lives?'

'Yeah, sure, in a lousy shack, over in La Estación. It'll fall down with the first big wind...'

'O.K. I want you to calculate how much it would cost to tear it down and build a small house: cement blocks, windows, an iron door, tile floor, a bathroom and a kitchen.'"

"Borro was amazed: 'Did you buy that lot, sir?'

'No, Borro. I'm paying off an old debt to a friend. Please, figure it all out, get me the numbers and I'll talk to Bartesaghi at the stall and order everything you need. How long will it take you to finish the job?'

'Let me see...' Borro still couldn't digest the news. He rubbed his chin pensively: '... If it doesn't rain and the construction is simple, three or four weeks...'

'I need it to be no more than two. Put people to work right now tearing it down. You can have the boards and tin from the shack. Don't dilly-dally; I'm in a hurry.'"

"So he ordered him to build the house right then and there. He paid Borro and gradually paid off the bill for the building supplies. When the little house was ready, he got Mochila in his car and took him out there. The poor guy didn't know what to say, he had left a pigsty half stupefied and was now coming back clean, sober, well fed and clothed; and he found a fabulous new house! It was unbelievable."

"And ever since then, every Friday between December and March – which is when the lawyer comes back here – they meet in 'El Pajarito', table number three, order a drink – which they never imbibe – and spend two or three hours like this, exchanging a few ideas, one comment or another and that's it. The rest of the time is spent in pure silence; like in mass, like they were nursing their memories."

Manuel didn't know what to say. The men at table three were still there as always, without speaking, lost in the depths of their glasses. Villaseca picked up the bag of supplies and offered a general "Have a good day".

"Good day, Peludo. Come over here a moment, please." The lawyer leaned back in his chair and with a friendly gesture, beckoned to the teacher to come over. Speaking to Manuel, he requested, "You too, kid... come over here for a second, both of you..."

Villaseca and Manuel approached the table. The lawyer gestured for them to pull up two chairs. "Something to drink?"

"No, no, Lalo, thanks a lot," replied the teacher. Manuel was too impressed to even speak. He shook his head no and waited expectantly.

"Che, Peludo. What were you telling this kid? Don't tell me you're still spreading that legend of the extraordinary football player?"

"Lalo, it's an old and first-rate story, a story I'm very fond of. I told him the whole thing, the truth, as you well know... Mochila's my witness..." It was as if Villaseca had been caught committing some shameful mistake; he responded like someone justifying or explaining himself. Manuel began to suspect that the whole story was a tall tale. The lawyer didn't look like someone who had ever played football. So he wasn't surprised when he held up his right hand in front of the teacher as if saying: "Hold on, my friend." Then he explained: "Look, kid, Mr Villaseca's a fine fellow, self-sacrificing and studious. Many years ago my grandfather helped him out a little so he could finish his studies, and he's excessively grateful. That's why he tells that legend... The truth is I never played football. I had polio when I was twelve and it destroyed my leg. If I can walk fine now it's because they took me to São Paulo for surgery. I wouldn't be able to kick a ball even in my dreams... And you, Peludo, stop kidding around with those stories, what will people think?"

The teacher took a deep breath, resigned, looked at Manuel as if asking for forgiveness, said, "See you later," picked up his things and left without saying another word.

Manuel stayed glued to his chair not knowing what to do. Mochila was laughing. He held out his hand and patted Manuel on the head: "Chao, Manuel. Give my regards to your old man. You can beat it now."

He rushed out of the bar. On the street he looked back and spied the two friends, hoping he could catch some other piece of information. They were still as always, silent, navigating in the depths of their glasses, both of them with a gentle smile on their lips. The lawyer lit another cigarette and looked at Mochila, who put his head between his hands. It didn't seem to him that they uttered another word. He turned around and hurried off for his house. Three blocks later he passed the door of Mr Villaseca's house. "Peludo", as he now knew he was called, was standing in the doorway waiting for him.

"Manuel, I have to talk to you." The teacher had come off badly in the conversation in 'El Pajarito'. Manuel approached him, ready to hear an explanation; curiosity had gotten the better of him. Villaseca looked hurt. He invited him in. Manuel entered the house and without waiting for an invitation, sat down, alert to the teacher's words.

"Manuel, what happened today is really unpleasant for me. I mean to tell you that I didn't lie, that my story is the absolute truth. It's true that I have a debt of gratitude with the lawyer's family, especially his grandfather, Don Ciriaco. But I haven't deceived you; I didn't invent the story I told you. It's exactly how I lived it. Maybe I exaggerate a little in my judgments about Lalo as a football player, but what I'm telling you is nothing more than my memory, events that happened during my childhood, just as they impressed me back then. Lalo was truly a marvellous player, he would have been a great professional, a leader. But his family's entire story, beginning with Don Ciriaco himself, pushed him toward something else, toward books, politics, the intellectual life. That was stronger in him than sport. Football was just a game for him, something for kids, and at the end of the day he lost the desire to play; because he found better things to do, things he considered more important."

Manuel listened in silence not knowing what to believe. Villaseca must have seen his doubts because he went on justifying himself. "He denies everything, because none of that was essential to his life. What was important came later, and part of it is the way he rescued Mochila from poverty and from alcohol. For Lalo, the most important thing is to try to erase that past, not his, but Mochila's, Señor Milton Barrios, as he insists on calling him. He wants to avoid humiliations, bad memories, he wants to be sure that Mochila will end his days as a respectable person, his years of hunger, poverty and the loneliness he had to endure, all behind him. I don't know that he doesn't still feel guilty for the four penalty kicks he turned into goals the afternoon of the last game. It seems to me that when he kicked the last one, the one he shot with his left foot because his right leg was smashed, he had doubts. He had doubts when he saw that Mochila went into the goal, that he was making it a personal matter, I think he was about to kick it right into Mochila's hands to let him win at least once. And later, so I think, he must have thought often that that well-aimed shot, taken with more anger than quality, ended up ruining the life of the poor guy who couldn't admit that he, Lalo, was a superior player, but above all, his superiority as a rich kid."

With a mechanical gesture, Villaseca wiped his glasses again with his wrinkled tie, looked into the distance through a crack in the door, which had remained ajar, and added: "Mochila saved his life. That afternoon of the army search in La Unión, one wrong gesture from Corporal Barrios or the slightest desire for revenge, would have ended Lalo's life. Either he would have been arrested, or been caught in an exchange of gunfire. Mochila, with great class, sold the lie, played it with both balls together, went off with the bottles of mineral water and with the soldiers. That explains everything Lalo has done for him since then. That weekend that I came to help him clean up the house that had been abandoned for so many years, he told me something I've never been able to forget. We were in the front yard, Lalo had stopped and was looking toward the pitch – I believe he was replaying that final penalty – and he told me, his voice breaking, "You know, Peludo? I think that every unnecessary victory is, in some way, a crime" and he stooped down again to pull out the remaining weeds.

Interview with Carlos Abin

What role did football play in your youth?

I'm Uruguayan. That means that a few days after my birth one of my uncles showed up at home with a football ball as a gift. I don't remember it, but I imagine that even before I started to walk I had made contact with it, that friend that would accompany me and to which I'd always express my affection and my loyalty. Throughout my childhood and adolescence, football – played in the courtyard of my house, in the street, in the countryside, at school – occupied almost all my free time and was the main focus of my interest. I was a student at the Colegio Pío, with the Salesian Fathers. Class hours and recess – during which I played football and only football, without even imagining an alternative – took turns in a balanced way. Furthermore, the school had several football fields on its grounds that were famous all over the country. Saturday afternoons – no longer "bothered" by classes – and on Sundays, we would go back to the school to embrace our passion for football. Since I was a really good student I never missed a game because of low grades, although more than once I was on the edge of doing so because of some misconduct or other. During the second cycle of high school and in law school (I'm a lawyer and a notary) I kept on playing whenever I could, although I didn't manage to play in the University League. At the age of 22 I had to choose between devoting weekends to football or my girlfriend – who later became and still is, after 43 years, my wife. As you can deduce from that last sentence, she won, although with time, patience and a lot of affection, I managed to convert her into an addicted "fan," into a woman who enjoys, suffers and appreciates this marvellous sport.

Do you support a particular team?

I'm a fan of Peñarol, Uruguay's most glorious club, and one of the best in America and in the world. That's the way I feel, although I understand that others can think the same thing about their own club, and rightly so. It's clear that we're operating in a subjective area here, although – without a doubt in the case of Peñarol – there are many objective criteria that make that affirmation dangerously close to the truth. When my father reached his eightieth birthday, as his oldest son I was entrusted with the responsibility of saying a few words at the celebration. I thanked the "old man" for many things that were important in my life – on my behalf and on behalf of my siblings – and one of them was having taught me to love that club that was destined to glory. I'm also a fan of Uruguay's national team, as you can well imagine. Football is part of our culture and a decisive element of our identity.

What motivates you to write fiction that takes place within a Uruguayan context?

Ever since I learned to read I've felt the impulse to write. There's a moment in my childhood – I couldn't say exactly when it happened – when I began to look at some aspects of reality with "a writer's eye", that is, noticing gestures, looks, words and the way people talked. Later – during my adolescence – I surprised myself thinking about how to express this or that attitude, or how to reproduce a dialogue that I had witnessed or imagined: I was already on my way. The context was unavoidably that of my own country, its people, its customs, the places I frequented. Context is a basic component of the material base on which to anchor the flight of imagination. Even more: I'm sure that what I write can only have some possibility of reaching a certain universality if it's authentic. And a good part of authenticity for me is found in the fact that in my literature I can faithfully and honestly reveal the context in which I was born, educated, grew up, fell in love, and worked all my life. There's something else that literally ties me to the Uruguayan context: I write for my fellow citizens above all. When I do it, when I sit down at the keyboard and the monitor, without even proposing it to myself, I take a point of reference for that virtual dialogue that takes place between the writer and his potential readers. And that point of reference – which weighs on style and bears on many of the infinite number of decisions you have to make when you put your ideas down "in black and white" consists of my children, my friends, my neighbours... That dialogue is processed inside me and I feel it really powerfully; in some cases, I can even sense what they're going to feel when they read me. I can write stories located in a framework of other contexts, but mine is the decisive one, always – in one way or another – I either use it as a point of departure or I come back to it.

How do football and politics intersect in Uruguay?

Since football is so popular and inspires very powerful support and passions, the intersection – maybe it would be better to say the convergence – between football and politics is inevitable. Many political leaders tested their wings and became known first as managers of one of the principal teams; others used football as a gradual and non-traumatic way of exiting politics, while maintaining to a certain degree their position in the public sphere through sport. A few players, after retiring, have accepted the challenge of entering politics, although none of them have stood out in this activity. In any case, in Uruguay there's a limit, which I'm not aware has ever been crossed: politics never weighs in on sports scores. Maybe I'm showing my innocence by making this bald affirmation, but the fact is that I never knew nor have I heard of the opposite happening – or that anyone pretended that it did.

Do you see any connection between the creative process and the way in which someone plays football or behaves as a fan?
Writing, playing football and being a fan are three very different activities and it's reasonable to think that they provoke different attitudes even in the same person. Certainly each one has a definite personality, some biases in conduct, some ways of seeing things and of responding to the stimuli that come from the reality that predominates over others, at least as a tendency. Writing and playing football are activities that suppose an effort, a strong and constant commitment. In my case, I would say that to write – now that I'm writing – and to play football – when I used to play – my fundamental characteristic has been and still is determination: on the field, to win and never give up; in literature to pursue the planned objective until it's achieved. On the other hand, I live my condition as a fan from another perspective, since my attitude in this case isn't one of leading, but instead is passive. I'm very calm in the stadium, I see myself as a spectator – with no preconception of adding my encouragement–; in *la tertulia* with my friends, I see myself as being tolerant; I don't understand the fan who never misses a game, who at each one shouts until he loses his voice, who is even capable of violence because of football or who professes a certain kind of fundamentalism in support of the banner that creates passion in him and blinds him definitively.

Did any writer of football fiction influence this story?
No. I thought up this story from beginning to end, day after day for a week, while I was driving my car to work in the morning

and returning home at night. I put it together in my head, the idea was there, I really liked it and it didn't take any effort to get back to it, at will. When I had the whole story figured out and I would say had even put down whole paragraphs "in my head", one Saturday morning I sat down to write it and finished it that weekend. It was never corrected, in my judgment it didn't need to be.

Do you see any lingering reluctance to incorporating football or sport as a dominant theme or plot driver among your generation of authors?

No, not at all. In the last few years new narrative works related to football have begun to appear – and even an occasional poetic incursion. It's an activity of enormous social importance in the country and intense emotional impact that even constitutes a central element of national identity, of the image that we Uruguayans have of ourselves. I'm proud to have contributed in some way to the ascent of football into the pantheon of great topics in our national literature with the publication of my book of short stories *Colgado de la travesaño* almost ten years ago. Some additional developments are needed; a period of maturation and consolidation is necessary, but football and everything that surrounds it is already there, it already "took the pitch".

Is there a particular identity or style associated with football in Uruguay?

Yes, of course. Uruguayan football is characterised by the fact that in general it counts on a strong, solid defence, where tough but loyal players predominate; at midfield the creative players and the rougher ones alternate, the first feed the attack, the second work with the defence. Our forwards tend to be skilful or even very skilful, there are some who are light and fast; and others heavier and powerful. But the differential element in Uruguayan football is character: no one gives up until the end; the physical and psychological commitments are sometimes moving; the collective determination, really strong. This factor has allowed them to achieve some results that at first glance seem impossible or miraculous, that always make our teams fearsome rivals, capable of compensating for their technical weaknesses with the boundless determination to win.

How would you describe the impact in Latin America of Brazil having hosted the World Cup in 2014?
Having an event of the magnitude of a World Cup of football always has a considerable impact. Brazil was shaken to the foundation. Much more than the sport itself, the choice of the players who would make up the national team, the endless polemics over whether "So-and-So should be on the team or that What's-his-Name" doesn't have what it takes," the issues surrounding completing the work on the stadiums, the organisation and publicity, the disputes about reduced price tickets for some sectors of the population (senior citizens for example), all this captured the attention of the public and for months dominated the headlines in the press. The expectations of millions of fans in the region were notorious; no country on the subcontinent could escape the excitement caused by a World Cup being held so near by, not to mention those fortunate people, who would travel to Brazil in large contingents to enjoy the privilege of seeing the Cup live. The way I see it, the two occurrences that had the greatest repercussions from the point of view of football as a sport were the overwhelming victory of Germany over the host team – a score of historic dimensions and probably unrepeatable – and the fact that, for the first time, a European team won a World Cup on American soil.

How do you view the recent developments in the scandal surrounding corruption in FIFA?

For us FIFA's corruption is nothing new. The specialised press and the public in Uruguay have never trusted FIFA and were suspicious of their operations: tricks and shameful little advantages in certain draws, a tendency to benefit their "favourites", generally European teams, to the detriment of the competition, especially if they are from small countries with a low population and – as a consequence – of relatively little or at least less interest from the economic point of view; unequal criteria in matters of justice – as evidenced in the cases of Suárez and Jara, like so many others –, and an endless number of etceteras. FIFA has turned football into a business on a universal scale and consequently managed to have the logic and the criteria of *business* applied to the game, and as a result what is lost and distorted is the spirit of sportsmanship, healthy competition under fair conditions, and also justice with a single voice, balanced and serious.

We're delighting in our celebration of the arrest of a well-known, corrupt compatriot who devoted a good part of his time at the head of the Uruguayan Football Association and then in his capacity as head of CONMEBOL and a member of FIFA's project hierarchy to do damage to the sport, to the national team, and to Uruguayan football in general, while he padded his bank accounts and filled his pockets.

What is your opinion of the incidents of provocation involving the Uruguayan player, Luis Suárez, in the 2014 World Cup and the Chilean player, Gonzalo Jara, in the 2015 Copa América, and the subsequent bans sanctioned against them by FIFA?

This is a very well articulated question because in both cases

269

provocation was at the heart of the incidents. Suárez was provoked by Chiellini throughout the game. The Italian player constantly attacked the Uruguayan physically, committed an infinite number of fouls (which the referee refused to call), pushed him, antagonised him constantly, spit on him... in summary, made him the victim of innumerable small provocations, acting in that grey area that's usually between what is proper conduct and what is illegal. Suárez' bite was a reaction – uncontrolled, perhaps very primal – in the face of persisting harassment. It was also a reaction without any consequences: the physical injury to Chiellini was very slight (little more than a mark on the skin of his shoulder); his honour and his dignity were unharmed, and he couldn't even prevent Suárez from remaining on the field nor keeping Uruguay from winning the game with an absolutely legitimate goal by Diego Godín. The episode in Santiago, Chile is another matter: Gonzalo Jara coldly, treacherously and with premeditation gave Cavani an obscene, aggressive and degrading greeting and then ostentatiously pretended that the player he attacked had struck him, a non-existent blow. A provocation followed by deception to produce the desired effect: the expulsion of the Uruguayan player. The referee, whose action was clearly biased in favour of the local team, had no doubts took advantage of the situation, "bought into" the deception of the despicable Chilean player and made the ejection. One wonders what would have happened if the decision had been impartial, and instead of ejecting the affected player, he had sent the provoker-deceiver to the showers. There were 30 minutes left to play. Chile was winning 1-0 and dominated possession of the ball, but Uruguay – as is well known – has a fast and lethal counter-attack. Cavani is a world-class goal scorer, and had it been the Celeste playing with an extra player, the story would certainly have been different.

FIFA suspended Gonzalo Jara for 3 games and then lowered the sanction to 2. On the other hand, they punished Suárez with 9 games, forced him to withdraw from the World Cup and prohibited him from staying with his teammates. The lack of balance and impartiality which was apparent in some calls – always in favour of the home team – strikes me as a joke when compared with the lack of balance and sense of justice of FIFA's disciplinary authorities. It's clear that Jara's unsportsmanlike and lowly attitude cannot be compared to the inopportune bite of a player who was provoked throughout an entire match. But, who would risk a cent today putting a bet on the morality of FIFA? Let's not ask the elm tree to give us pears...

Venezuela
MIGUEL HIDALGO PRINCE

Miguel Hidalgo Prince was born on January 26, 1984 in Caracas. He earned a degree in Humanities from the University of Venezuela. In 2009 he received special mention in the VI Concurso Nacional de Cuentos de Sacven (VI National Short Story Competition of Sacven). He published his first book in 2012, a collection of short stories, *Todas las batallas perdidas* (Bid & co). In the same year he once again received a special mention in the Premio de Cuento para Autores Jóvenes (Short Story Prize for Young Authors), a competition organised by the Policlínica Metropolitana since 2008. He is currently working on his second collection of stories. He is a fan of Barcelona in the Spanish League and of the Caracas Football Club in the national league, as well as of the Deportivo Táchira team. He resides in Caracas. "Losers' Afternoon" (Tarde de perdedores) appeared first in Spanish in *Todas las batallas perdidas* (Bid & co, 2012).

Losers' Afternoon

Our kits had cost a fortune and were a beautiful baby-chick yellow. We were eliminated from the tournament after the second game of the first round. The first game was against the School of Medicine. They took us for a bitter ride at seven to nil. The second game was even worse for us, and we were defeated by the Veterinary School team. Twelve goals scored against us and a round nil for our side. As a consolation prize, and so they could finish placing the teams that would end up qualifying for the next round, we were given a third opportunity. Our definitive executioners would be the Employees, the team made up by security guards, doormen, and the janitorial staff of the university.

I played defence because I didn't know how to move the ball and because I was the fattest guy on the team. Raúl and Matías were wingers who made the crosses and set up the plays. But both of them were right-footed and they had to take turns on the left, our weak spot. Raúl was the school's small-time drug dealer, and to this day I've never known anyone who knows more about drugs than he did. Matías was a pain in the neck, but had an unbeatable sense for sports. Goyo was the forward and our captain. He stood out in practices, but at the moment of truth he messed things up all by himself. So far in the current season he hadn't finished anything on his own. The closest he came to scoring was in the game against the School of Medicine. He smashed the ball against the crossbar and the rebound ended up favouring the opposing team that took advantage of our slip-up and scored their third goal. Most of the fault can be attributed to Goyo himself for playing on his own and never passing the ball. Our goalie was Enrique, the guy with the most experience.

He could stop the shots, but when he lost his temper because of our mistakes, he would start to play badly and that's when the barrage of goals would begin. And there was also Beto, our only option for a substitute from the bench. He had all the necessary attitude, but unfortunately had been born three months early so his legs never really developed as they supposedly should have. Even though he knew he wasn't going to play, he would show up on the field, kits on and ready. His girlfriend was always with him, the only person who cheered for us. In short, that was the team.

We were ready to hand victory to the Employees by forfeit. But since we had already lost everything and had nothing to gain, we opted for death on the field. Besides, our kits still looked new and we wanted to show them off.

It was an afternoon in January with whimsical weather. Once in a while the clouds would clear and the ground of the pitch would become an atomic reflector. We got there one by one, while the Employees' team had formed a circle in the middle of the pitch and were doing calisthenics.

We sat down on the ground once we were all there and somebody uttered a few supposedly encouraging words. Something about having fun and playing our game. Think about the team and all that stuff. That kind of speech.

Goyo, the referee and the other captain tossed a coin into the air. The kick-off went to the Employees, but we got to choose the side of the field. Everybody took their positions and in twenty seconds of the opening whistle they'd already scored the first goal. A hard and cold bucket of water. They sewed up Matías and Raúl with a string of three passes, then dropped a cross on me, and their striker, an old guy who looked like he might be Ecuadorian, had no pity on Enrique. An early goal lowers any team's spirit. For us it was a routine thing. I stared at the toes of my Adidas Samba Milleniums in resignation. There's still thirty-nine minutes and forty seconds of torture to go, I thought.

The second goal came in the fourth minute. I committed a foul at the edge of the box against one of the security guards. The guys on their bench called him Torito. He played with his head down and attacked anything that crossed his path. But he couldn't get past me, so I stepped on him, and as if that were not enough, I knocked him down with all my force. They gave me a yellow card, but it was worth it. Torito himself took the free kick. With a left-footed kick he drilled Raúl, who was standing in the wall with Goyo. The rebound created an opening on the right. Matías didn't get to the ball and when one of the employees took a bicycle kick, he ended up looking ridiculous there in the penalty area. Enrique didn't even see the shot. The ball once again was in the back of our net.

The third goal was on a header in the twelfth minute. A toss by their goalie and our miserable communication allowed Torito to get through our line of defence and finish with a diving header with more luck than intention, adding to his personal stats. He celebrated by doing handsprings in the middle of the field.

The fourth goal was scored by the Ecuadorian at about one minute fifteen. He came dancing from midfield and left Raúl and Matías behind. He did a give-and-go with one of his teammates, who centred the ball to his left foot. He found me in front of him, but nutmegged me and collected the ball with his right foot. It was a little bit in front of him and he had to fight for it with Enrique, who had ran out of the box to intercept it. The Ecuadorian lifted the ball over his head with class and finished with a back heel just to show off. Enrique pounded the ground with his doubled up fists.

The fifth goal occurred around one minute twenty. There was a double change in the Employees' line-up, so there were fresh players on the field. Beto shouted to Goyo that the team needed a substitution. Goyo shook his head and told him to wait till the second half. Enrique sent the ball into the pitch with his hand, but he did it so badly that it landed right at a rival's feet. Goyo was alone at the Employees' penalty spot, yelling for them to pass it to him, but the ball never came. Raúl and Matías didn't have time to come back and so I was alone against three. They passed the ball around, playing with me, and then shot at Enrique who grazed the ball with a finger, but it was moving with too much malice and power. There was nothing he could do.

The whistle blew ending the first period. For the first time in my life, time seemed to me to be a merciful phenomenon. Disillusioned, we walked back to our bench. Goyo was furious. Enrique apologised for his mistake, but made a point of adding that the rest of us were not doing so well. Raúl complained that Torito had injured him. I was about to suffer respiratory arrest and dropped face down on the ground. Goyo started to lay out strategies. With the point of a stick he traced the outline of a pitch in the dusty film that covered the ground. He drew arrows and triangulations. He plotted out two plays that according to him were foolproof. They all ended with him scoring the goal. Enrique said that wasn't worth a damn. Matías declared that he had a broken rib. I couldn't get out a single word and squatted to catch my breath. Raúl searched through his bag and took out a big thermos of water followed by a bag full of a sand-coloured powder. Guys, he said. Enrique and Goyo were delivering insults to each other at the same time. Guys, Raúl repeated, showing us what he had in each hand. We all shut up. Goyo erased his dirt pitch with the sole of his shoe and said, what the hell is that, dude? An electric smile spread across Raúl's face. He had the expression of a person who was trying to convince a bunch of nonbelievers. This is our team spirit, he said. He unscrewed the top of the thermos and dumped the powder into the water. He closed the thermos again and shook it up like a baby's bottle. He was laughing while he was doing it, which made him look deranged. There, he said and opened the thermos again. He took two big swigs and licked his lips. Then he passed the bottle to Matías. This is going to cure you, he told him. Matías stared at the thermos unconvinced. Then he looked at us and then back at Raúl. It's now or never, said Raúl. Are you a loser or a winner? Matías wiped his mouth with his jersey and took a big mouthful. He savoured it for a few seconds and then swallowed. Then he took another even bigger mouthful. O.K. O.K. Pass it around, said Raúl. Goyo took two swallows and said it tasted a little like chalk. Then he passed the thermos to me. I must admit that as soon as I tasted the water, my lips, tongue and throat went numb. I took a second sip and handed the thermos to Enrique. I don't need this shit, he said. I shrugged and was about to drink the little that remained, but Beto grabbed the thermos and raised it to his lips. His girlfriend pinched him to get him to leave her a few drops. That's the way I like it, team, said Raúl. This is going to lift our spirits, you'll see. We'll make history. This is our afternoon. Another day you have to try *salvia divinorum* ×10. In a pipe, with a catalytic lighter, said Raúl. That's paradise, team. This is just a tiny bit. It'll be a little while before it takes effect, he added.

Not much is clear to me, but just as Raúl had said, a few minutes after the drink, we still didn't feel anything. We started to do stretches to avoid cramping and that's when everything got intense. We were invaded by an extraordinary sense of comfort and our legs started to respond to a superior force, as if they were governed by themselves alone and didn't need the rest of our bodies.

We changed sides on the field.

Now the sun was inclining its rays toward our hemisphere. In the background, at what seemed like an enormous distance, the horizon was orange. Each of our rivals had a different, shining aura. The Ecuadorian, for example, was projecting blue shadows from his shoulders and had an indecipherable magnetism. Torito was being metamorphosed into a hairy, white minotaur and exhaled smoke through his nose with every breath. One of our opponents was covered with sparkling, iridescent scales. Another, the defender, was a formless shadow. All you could see were his eyes burning like two flaming holes. The goalie was a wall, a nuke wide and impenetrable. He seemed to have elastic and gymnastic qualities. I recalled Yashin, the black spider of the Soviet Union, when the Soviet Union existed.

The whistle blew.

The waves kept getting bigger until they were woven in our heads like a magical web of bellflowers. Then came a period of silence. Harmonious, gentle.

I remember seeing a bunch of identical and translucent Matíases, one following in the footsteps of another at an inhuman speed all over the pitch and without any special direction. It was a Matías who was leaving a wake of thousands of Matíases, and each one of them was a replica of the Matías who passed a millionth of a second before. Until they knocked him down and all the Matíases came together in the Matías who was face down, twisting in ecstasy on the ground.

At some point I saw Raúl petrified in one corner of the field. I imagined him as a marble statue, who strangely could see through me and was telling me to pass the ball to him without needing to move his lips. But I didn't have the ball.

I know that Beto was telling us something from the bench and that his voice was projecting intensely, clearly and sharply like the song of a whale. His girlfriend was laughing. She had the expression of someone dying laughing, but we couldn't hear her.

I remember that I shot a ball that was pearly white, brittle like an eggshell, and exploded into a thousand pieces in thousands of different colours and that everything was illuminated by cosmic sparks.

I saw Enrique hurl himself at a loose ball, secure it against his chest with his arms and then throw it toward the middle of the pitch as if it were a hand grenade. He shouted something that broke into thousands of echoes until it became a single, reverberating sound. He was waving his arm from one side to the other. He could have been waving goodbye or saying hello. The yellow of his jersey glittered in the sunlight and radiated a hypnotising energy.

The ball continued falling from a great height when I saw Goyo make an amazing leap, fly through the air, turn on his own axis in slow motion, line up his hip with the ball that was spinning in a kind of orbit, over everything. I saw Goyo kick the ball with tremendous force, with the catapult effect that you get only when you're in full flight. A world-class bicycle kick. Unrepeatable. Unforgettable. I saw the ball falling into our goal, between Enrique's legs, and he didn't have the least idea of what was happening.

Goyo eagerly celebrated the goal. He pulled off his jersey and waved it with one hand while he was running around the field, although I don't know if his way of moving could be called precisely running. I think that besides Enrique, I was the only one who realised that it was an own-goal. Everybody, including Beto and his girlfriend, who, euphoric, had gotten up from the bench, were celebrating the goal and following Goyo.

At that point everything came to a halt. The weather suddenly got worse and the sky was covered by lead-coloured clouds. It brought a downpour that frightened the other team, as well as the coaches and the few persons remaining in the stands watching our magnificent defeat. We were the only ones who stayed. Enrique kept on raving, but now nothing he was saying made any sense and nobody was paying any attention to him. Beto began kissing his girlfriend on her cheeks and forehead. His eyes were bugged out and he was licking her face all over. She was laughing, or seemed to be laughing, while at the same time performing a kind of tribal dance. Matías, Raúl, Goyo and I joined hands and we made a circle around them. We circled around them and watched them for hours. They were kissing each other passionately and with abandon. Now that I think about it, it was an unsurpassable moment. One of those that happens in the sports world only once every so often. The world and all it was made of immediately acquired a different hue, a tremendous quality, almost divine. Beto's girlfriend took off her tee-shirt and then the rest of us followed suit, all except Goyo, who ever since his big stellar play already looked like an Indian. I wanted to explain that small detail of the own-goal to my teammates, but things were going so well that I decided to leave it until later. Enrique left. To cry or to curse, it made no difference. The universe was smiling on us. Every drop was an event. A superior act. The water was purifying us and giving us back the sensation of being blessed. From one moment to the next it stopped raining and a huge star appeared on high giving us goosebumps with its fingers of light. We felt the heat penetrating every pore of our skin and lighting up something inside, a kind of torch of life-giving and devastating fire. We looked up, offering our faces to the sun. There was something miraculous in the air, something we had never noticed before. Everything was clearer, easier, lighter. Beto and his girlfriend had their chins locked together in a kiss worthy of the movies. I lost all sense of time and space.

I can't speak for the others, but after that everything went blank for me.

I came to and was sitting in a grass-covered field. I was barefoot. The rest of the team was around me. All except Goyo, who was standing, stretching his arms, were lying on their backs, gazing in wonder at the sky, at the leaves on the trees, at their own hands. I didn't know how I had gotten there. At a certain moment I had a revelation that later on lost any meaning.

The trip faded. The afternoon did too.

That game never started up again. It was suspended and the score was left as it was before it started to rain. The teams went on classifying for the next rounds and won their medals and trophies. The Metallurgy team was crowned champion, that's all I know. After that infamous day, we were never the same again. We didn't improve our game, but it's not that we got worse either. We never signed up for another tournament, but we kept on practising and playing pick-up games every week. Sometimes, when we're in the mood, we decide to put on the baby-chick yellow kits.

Interview with Miguel Hidalgo Prince

What role did football play in your youth?

When I was a child, I saw football as a strange and sacred rite, an activity of gladiators that could only be performed well by Europeans and Brazilians. Having been born in a country more inclined to baseball than to football caused me a certain amount of confusion: at the age of nine, being the worst pitcher on the baseball team of what used to be called the Instituto Nacional de Capacitación y Educación (INCE), super-bored by the "national sport", my dreams were a long way from making it to the Big Leagues. Maybe they weren't on the football field either, I'm still not very clear on that, but I do know that I was much more drawn to kicking balls and making goals that would go down in the annals of history than I was to batting homeruns or striking out adversaries. For me football was a real spectacle. Baseball struck me as slow, monotonous and complicated. The excitement of football was reborn every four years, with every World Cup competition. The first World Cup I remember was Italy 1990, that infected me with a fever for collecting cards to fill my Panini album and initiated me in the ritual of watching games on TV. By 1994 I was living football as never before. I was interested in the lives of the players, their eccentricities, their whims. For example: Why did Bebeto celebrate his goals as if he were rocking a baby? Why did Davis, one of the black players from Holland, wear glasses like a skydiver? In 1994 I began to think seriously about sadness, failure and frustration when I saw Roberto Baggio miss the crucial penalty shot against Brazil. Images like that leave a mark on anybody. That year I read a magazine that summarised the history of all the World Cup competitions. Thanks to the wordy biographies and reviews written by some enthusiastic sports reporter whose name I've forgotten, in my mind I saw Yashin, Cruyff, Kempes, Platini and Garrincha play. Never live, just inside my head, as if they were myths or the invention of a comic book author. Purely fuel to fire thousands of stories, possible only in the imagination. For me football was like fiction. By the time I was a teenager and then during my university days, like many in Venezuela, I would satisfy my desire for making goals like Zidane with futsal or indoor football. In fact my story arose from the time I was part of the indoor football team of the Humanities department of the Central University of Venezuela. We were a group of semi-sedentary readers and would-be writers, devotees of alcohol and other "odds-and-ends". A disconcerted, disillusioned team without much talent or style, who accumulated more grief than glory, but who persisted game after game in search of some kind of honour for our baby-chick yellow uniform, our school colour. Football was always there. It was the point of reference when we tried some spectacular dribble, a give-and-go, a tricky pass, a shot at the goal. Indoor football was the fastest and easiest way to do something that resembled regular football, a sport reserved for the great, the chosen ones.

Do you support a particular team?

For reasons that are based more on sentiment than on any true commitment as a fan, I support Barcelona in the Spanish League and the Caracas Football Club, my city's team, in the national league. The Deportivo Táchira, classic rival of Caracas, inspires a certain morbid curiosity in me, above all because of their wild supporters, who are usually unruly and staunch defenders of their team's colours.

Which is more important to you as a fan, a good result or a good game?

Anybody can think that the goal is all-important, and maybe they're not wrong. Maybe that's not subject to debate. But I get enormous satisfaction from anticipating that ecstasy that you feel when the ball crosses the rivals' goal line. I like frenetic games where both teams bombard each other with shots to the point of angst. Then it's not so much a question of whether one team racks up so many goals, but the fight, the distance travelled.

How do you view the recent developments in the scandal surrounding corruption in FIFA?

I'm not surprised. Wherever there's money, there's vice. And as if that were not enough, there's a Venezuelan implicated. That puts a stain on the ball and even more on our country.

How do football and politics intersect in Venezuela?

I think that in Venezuela politics and football can be confused in the feelings aroused by our national team, the Vinotinto, whose primary patron is the government, although it also depends on powerful private enterprises. I believe that the Vinotinto, with all its defects, brings together a genuine national spirit, over and above the interests and the canned ideologies that abound here. It is, if you will, a true political act of reconciliation and of coming together with your fellow citizens: everyone joined in a single end, with their faith devoted to a national sentiment, which some detractors might say can be superficial, and that too is understandable. Even people who don't believe in the team or in football have something to say about it. That's already a point of contact for various opinions on sports, social issues or politics.

What is the current state of affairs in Venezuelan politics?
I'll give you a simple answer to such a complex question: in Venezuela everything is backward. This country is taking a nosedive from the political, economic and social point of view. It's a field of factional struggles and serious structural failures. To draw a comparison with football, we could say that the government is the corrupt referee biased for a single team: he turns a blind eye or pulls out the red card, depending on whatever is convenient. Does this scenario look to you like fair play, a clean game, a good example of what the sport is?

Do you see any connection between the creative process and the way in which someone plays football or behaves as a fan?
Playing with passion and testing strategies, writing with a warm heart and correcting with cold reason. I suspect that something of that, shall we say, balanced method can function perfectly well both when you're on the football field or facing a blank page. The page is also like a football field, with its rules, its margins, its mysteries and its clear objectives.

Did any writer of football fiction influence this story?
I often re-read the story "El silbido" ("The Whistle") by Juan Villoro, which has inspired me for this story and others. I also revisit the short story "Buba" by Roberto Bolaño from time to time. Likewise some stories by Massiani, Soriano and Fontanarrosa, which are always charged with humour, something that I value. The stories by Villoro and Bolaño also have a lot of humour, to be fair. I believe that's what interests me. Irony, creativity and the humour in sports fiction.

Do you see any lingering reluctance to incorporating football or sport as a dominant theme or plot driver among your generation of authors?

I don't believe that that's the case, at least not as a conscious act. More than a persistent resistance, it's a matter of different interests. We could say the same about the incorporation of other sports or of ballet or of taxidermy, for example.

What is the place of football fiction in the literature of your country?

A lot has been written about football in my country. Including fiction. There are, if my memory doesn't fail me, at least two serious chronologies about football in Venezuela, as well as a work written by Manuel Llorens, who also writes fiction, titled *Terapia para el emperador* (Therapy for the Emperor), which reflects on his work as a psychologist with the Venezuelan national football team. I couldn't properly speak about football fiction in our literary tradition, because I'd be sure to say something foolish. I remember with great affection the story "El Llanero Solitario tiene la cabeza pelada como un cepillo de dientes" (The Lone Ranger has his Hair Cut Like a Toothbrush), by Francisco Massiani, who was an amateur player, as far as I know. I also remember a more contemporary story related to football and which also pays homage to Massiani. "La malla contraria" (The Rival Net), by Rodrigo Blanco Calderón is one of my favourite stories from *Una larga fila de hombres* (A Long Line of Men), his first book. Regarding the role played by that category of fiction, the truth is I don't have an answer. Perhaps the same role played by baseball fiction, teen fiction, detective fiction, erotic fiction, etc. It's one more vision directed at our collective identity, which is not uniform, but rather quite the opposite. Football is strange. Venezuelans are strange too.

Perhaps football fiction is one component of our multicoloured literary or collective identity.

Is there a particular identity or style associated with football in Venezuela?

I'm afraid my response is going to seem a little cynical. I believe that our game's identity is one of growth. We're still a little bit in diapers. While it's true that football in Venezuela is getting better (we can see that in the fact that our players are drawing the attention of European and Asian teams), we still have a long way to go. That's something that can't be accomplished overnight. Our football's aesthetic is still undefined; it's in development. Venezuelan football, for now, is lacking its own voice. Those characteristics by which one can identify the *toque criollo* and say "that's Venezuelan football" are still being formed. The good part is that our football is also invested with a hopeful attitude, a positive outlook, the attitude of good winners and, what the hell, good losers too.

How would you describe the impact in Latin America of Brazil having hosted the World Cup in 2014?

I believe that it had an important media impact, above all because of the prior events related with the protests for social changes in the host country. In regard to sports, I don't know. I suppose it was a bit disappointing that a team in the region didn't win the Cup.

What does the Venezuelan team need in order to have World Cup hopes in the future?

I think they need more time to better define their game. They have the players, the support, and devoted fans with their faith placed in a future for football full of glory. Starting with the youth is important. It's necessary to start developing players at a very young age. That way they can try other strategies than just the long ball game, which I think our team abuses. It's necessary to learn how to play with ball control, to cross midfield with passes and shots. There's no advantage to desperation. Shortcuts result in negligence. Hard work is also a talent and it has to be exercised. Like a profession. Just like writing.

Credits